BE NOT AFRAID

K.R. MORRISON

Copyright © 2022 K.R. Morrison
Cover by Fantasia Cover Designs
All Rights Reserved.
Publisher: Tenebris ad Lucem

"If you stand before the power of Hell
and Death is at your side
Know that I am with you
through it all."

For God did not make Death, he takes no pleasure in destroying the living.

To exist -- for this he created all things; the creatures of the world have health in them, in them is no fatal poison, and Hades has no power over the world: for uprightness is immortal.

16 But the godless call for Death with deed and word, counting him friend, they wear themselves out for him; with him they make a pact, worthy as they are to belong to him.

(Wisdom 1: 13-16)

CHAPTER 1

With a groan, Lydia pushed back from the computer and rubbed her eyes. It seemed as if she'd been staring at the screen for hours. She looked at her watch.

Six o'clock! Where had the time gone? More importantly, where had the people gone? No phones rang, no one passed by. It seemed she was all alone in the huge room, if not the building.

She peeked out from her cubicle. The guy who used the last cube in this row was gone, which surprised her. She'd never seen his office empty; he was there in the mornings when she got in and was usually still working away when she scooted out in the evening, five minutes to the tick after her shift was up.

Tonight was different, though. Lydia had been given a new assignment, and this morning she thought she would have it sewn up at quitting time. However, it seemed that an amount had gotten input into the wrong place somewhere in the accounting process, causing a daylong hunt for the offending number. At this point, it was still hiding among the credits and debits.

When she reached an imbalance at the end once again, she sighed, muttered, "One more time around the park, James," and went back to the beginning. Ten minutes into the project again, Lydia decided she'd better take a break. *Okay,* she thought to herself, *better step back for a bit. Maybe the answer will hit me after I do something else.*

She got up, stretched, and picked up her tea. Absentmindedly, her mind on the accounting problem, she took a sip and realized her drink had gone cold. Worse, she had left the teabag in the cup! Making a face, she spit the cold, bitter brew back in with the rest. *Guess this means a trip to the break room for more hot water,* she thought to herself. She reasoned that the short walk would help restore her energy, and maybe she could wake up enough to figure out where that errant number was hiding.

Lydia smiled to herself. At least this accounting error could be considered the toughest problem in her life right now, which she considered a blessing. She glanced at the picture of her family in its silver frame on her desk: Steve, her wonderful husband of 25 years;

Pat, their son and the eldest, heading into his third year at the local community college; and Trudy, her dear daughter and best friend, who had recently graduated from high school and was enrolled in the university downstate. Lydia was fortunate that the kids could visit almost every weekend. Their smiling, laughing faces bolstered her spirits as she thought of how blessed she truly was.

Ah, but tonight she would be alone at home, something she always had mixed feelings about. Steve was on an extended business trip to Taiwan, so Lydia was in no hurry to get home. Getting this project done was more interesting than going home to a cold house, a quick-heat meal, and endless games of Solitaire.

Lydia walked out of her cube, noting her favorite Scripture she had pinned to the wall just today: 'I can do all things in Christ who strengthens me.' She sighed and offered up a small prayer: "OK, Lord, strengthen my ability to get this project done before I fall asleep on my keyboard."

Her heels clicked loudly on the bare floor as she walked down the lonely hallway towards the intersection that led to the break room. The building was downright eerie at night without the company of other employees and the noise of business being carried out. Usually, she had to be very careful going around corners so as not to bump into other people who were in a mad dash going the other way. Fortunately, the hallways were equipped with mirrors at the corners so that accidents could be avoided. Lydia had heard of several incidents where people had actually gotten broken bones and concussions from collisions with co-workers, a result of not looking in the mirrors before careening into the hallways.

No problem tonight, of course. In the break room, after emptying her cup and rinsing it, Lydia refilled it with hot water and started back. Just as she stepped back in the hall, she decided to take her time and go back through another section of the building, just to see if anyone else was still slaving away. Then she'd go past the security office to make sure someone would be available to escort her to her car.

Normally she would have scoffed at the idea of being helped out to the parking lot once the sun went down, but there had been stories in the news recently about the local animal population—deer, raccoons, dogs, cats—being found with their throats torn out; the general consensus was that wolves had found their way out of the high hills ringing the valley and were preying on the local fauna. Just to be on the safe side, people were warned not to travel alone at night, not even out to their cars in a public parking lot.

Ned, the shift superintendant, was indeed in his office, eyes glued to his small TV and his mouth full of cheeseburger. "Good to see you're still here, Ned. I'll be needing you soon. Armed escort and all that."

The affable security guard waved a beefy hand and swallowed. "My pleasure, ma'am. One of the few benefits of this job!"

Lydia smiled, thanked Ned, and continued back to her office. He was such a flirt! She was at the age where she welcomed such silliness, as long as it didn't go beyond mere words. She passed by a row of large windows. Outside were the trails and gardens she knew so well, but she could see nothing but her own reflection due to the darkness outside. It was beautiful during the day, with the sunshine filtering through the leaves and the small birds and squirrels that lived in the woods surrounding the building.

It didn't seem so nice now. She felt so exposed! Who knows what night creatures were out there, staring in? The feeling made her nervous, and she hurried past the row of windows, not daring to look out. *Now I know how a goldfish feels,* she thought to herself.

The emptiness of the cubicles was no less unnerving. The room she was passing through was huge, with a rabbits' warren of little cube-offices. Lydia entertained herself with the mental image of a maze, with doughnuts in one corner of the room, and employees having to find their way through the alleyways to get to them. She laughed, thinking further that, if there was beer instead of doughnuts, most of these people would probably scale the upholstered walls and walk across the tops of them for it!

Okay, she thought, *I'm getting a little punchy. Maybe I should just go home and leave off trying to figure out that accounting mess until tomorrow.* The thought of beer had gotten her thirsty for more than just this rapidly cooling water in her tea mug. Two frosty bottles awaited her at home...Lost in thought, she turned a corner—and ran right into someone! A young man, not much older than her son.

"Whoa—sorry! I wasn't expecting anyone here! It's so empty, I thought I was here alone!"

He smiled down at her. "Quite alright, madam. I was not being careful either. Are you all right?

"Um, yeah thanks."

Madam? That was different.

He was about six feet tall, and very good-looking. He was impeccably dressed in a business suit, which looked like it had been tailor-made for him. His brown, curly hair was the same color as his eyes...which seemed to draw her in like a magnet. She suddenly felt odd, as if all of her thoughts were being swept into oblivion...

She broke off eye contact, rather embarrassed for having been staring so stupidly at him. *Why did that happen?* she thought. It made no sense, given her state of marital happiness, but there was something about him...

Lydia hastily turned toward a window and looked out, so that he wouldn't see how flustered she was. "Wow, dark out there,' she laughed, a little nervously. "These winter nights start early. Well, at least the stars are out!"

She broke off. All she could see in the window was her own reflection and the walls of the cubicles behind her! *How rude!* she thought to herself. He'd just up and left without so much as a good-bye! Well, fine, she had work to do anyway.

Lydia turned from the window to continue back to her office, and there he was again, standing in the same place! "Oh!" Lydia exclaimed, surprised. "I thought you'd left!"

"No, I...saw a computer still on and went to shut it off. I apologize for seeming rude."

"Oh..well..no problem. I didn't think..." Rude? She'd just thought that herself. How did he come up with the same idea? Odd coincidence!

She laughed. "Well, guess I'd better be getting back to my cube. Nice meeting you...um...?" She looked questioningly at him.

"Vlad."

"Ah. Vlad." *Interesting name.* Lydia thought that if she was a guy whose parents had named her Vlad, she would have sued them. *Geez, what a name to give a kid!*

"G'night. See you around," she said to him.

He smiled. "I'm sure of it."

Oops, outta here. It's getting a little weird. "Uh, yeah."

She hurried on, but thought she would take a quick glance up in one of the many mirrors for one last look. After all, he was really easy on the eyes.

Gone. Again. *Phoo.*

Lydia glanced down the hall behind her, and stopped in her tracks. Vlad was still standing in the same place! She flicked her eyes up to the corner mirror above where they had been conversing.

HE WAS NOT IN THE MIRROR!

Yet there he stood, watching her! Puzzled and a little alarmed, she gave a weak wave as she started to turn in at her own area. Vlad looked up at the mirror for a brief instant, then directly at Lydia. He smiled and slowly turned to walk away, his eyes on her until he disappeared from view.

Lydia's heart hammered in her throat. No reflection in either the window or the mirror? She could believe what he had said about stepping away to check on a computer, but what about the mirror?

Maybe the mirror was on a funny angle, Lydia thought. *Yes, that must be it.* She held onto that reasoning like a drowning person holding a scrap of driftwood. "I must be more tired than I thought," she muttered. "Okay, change of plan. Time to leave. Go home and let the error find its own self out in that computer program!"

The night was getting way too weird.

She ducked into her cube, after quickly looking around to make sure she was alone. Oh Lord, she suddenly did not want to be alone! Oh, for the companionship of even the obnoxious old letch who occupied the cube across from her! Suddenly he seemed the most harmless of people! At least she'd know who, or *what*, she was dealing with! The memory of that young stranger staring at her and smiling as he walked off; she imagined sharks looked just like that before striking their prey.

"Oh, good grief! I must be imagining things! This is what happens when I spend ten hours in a lonely cube swearing...oops, I mean *staring* at a computer screen." *Outta here. Beer. Sleep. Safe, warm house, with drapes drawn, keeping the shadows outside...*

Lydia called security in order to arrange escort to her car. Ned's voice on the other end was a blessing tenfold.

"Oh, I wouldn't miss a chance to walk you anywhere in the world, young lady!"

Lydia laughed, relief flooding her as she heard his familiar, cheerful voice. "I might take you up on that, Ned!"

"Really?"

"Well, if Steve can come along."

"Rats!" Ned pretended to be disappointed, but then he cheered up. "Sure. Okay, bring him along. We have to have someone around to fetch us drinks and carry our stuff!"

"So true! See you in ten!"

"I'll be there in nine!"

With a sigh of relief, Lydia hung up the phone and sat at the keyboard. Now to save her files and power down, lock the drawers, and get the heck outta Dodge! As she clicked icons and saved documents, she suddenly felt a cold breeze on the back of her neck, as if someone had opened a freezer door behind her. Lydia's short hair stood on end, and her arms erupted in goose bumps.

"Stupid heating system," she muttered to herself. Why couldn't it figure out which season they were in? What was with the sudden air-conditioning, and at this time of night?

She felt a sudden sharp pricking at the base of her neck, like tiny needles. "What the...?"

Slapping at the irritation, she went back to her work. Something, however, was strangely...wrong. She looked at the hand she'd slapped her neck with, and almost shrieked!

Her fingers had blood on them! Lydia felt gingerly at the spot she had just slapped, and drew back fresh blood once again. *Mosquitoes?*

Her mind, no longer happy at all, started putting two and two together, but she had to continue to force the answer to come up with zero, because of the outrageousness of what the sum wanted to be.

Cold air, neck bleeding, animals dying with torn throats, stranger in building WITH NO REFLECTION. *OH GOD OH GOD OH GOD NED GET HERE NOW!!!!*

Lydia gathered her things, and, without shutting off her desk light or putting anything away, turned to dash out and into the night, Ned or no Ned.

She turned, and stopped abruptly, her heart in her throat. *Oh God, help me...*

Vlad was standing right in her doorway, leaning on the wall, that same smile on his face. She gave a small squeak of surprise, as her whole body tensed and her throat went dry. Her heart hammered in her chest. What was he doing here? How did he find her? That cold breeze, the blood from her neck...

Animals with torn throats...

No reflection...

No!! No way!! This wasn't real! Such things didn't happen, did they? Were the old folktales true? How?

He was talking to her. She tried to focus, to take control of the panic that threatened to overwhelm her. "Are you alright?" he asked, looking concerned. "You look a little pale."

Lydia swallowed hard. "Um, yeah...just...tired. Really tired. I'm just leaving. 'Bye." She tried to brush past him without touching him. The thoughts she had had ever since she encountered him in the hall were wracking her with nausea, and her body trembled with fear.

Vlad put a hand on her shoulder, and she stiffened, her breath coming in short, quick gasps. *Oh Lord, keep me safe!!*

"You're bleeding, just here." He touched a fingertip to her neck and brought fresh blood back on it. Lydia hunched her shoulders, trying to get away from his closeness.

He looked intently at his finger. Lydia tried to use this moment to resume her escape, but how to get out the door without him following? She broke out in a cold sweat, fear and despair urging her on.

"Yes, I know," she rasped. "I...um...scratched an itch too hard. Happens sometimes."

Just then, her cell phone rang. She pulled it from her pocket; it was Steve! *Oh thank goodness!* He was calling to say he'd gotten home, she hoped.

"Steve!" Lydia was almost crying.

"Hi, babe. Hey, I'm stuck in New York. They had to cancel my flight, which worked out, because the boss is sending me to Austria tomorrow morning for a month."

"Oh..." Lydia felt her life disappear, as Vlad looked on with a smile on his lips.

"Sorry, babe. Oops...gotta go. They're picking me up for dinner."

"Um, okay...Love you!!!" She had never meant it so much as now. Would she ever see him again? She was deathly afraid of whatever this person was in front of her.

"Love you, too. Bye!" With a click, he was gone.

Lydia felt a dark chasm open up in front of her. As she tried once again to get out of her office, she was startled to realize that Vlad was looking at her chest.

He reached out and grabbed the crucifix around her neck. "You actually believe in this...symbol?" he asked her. There was a slight sneer on his otherwise pleasantly smiling face.

Lydia felt suddenly like she was in a place, spiritually, that she knew well. "This is not merely a symbol. Jesus is my life. With His help, I would never deny him."

"You believe in that life-after-death mentality?"

"Yes, of course. God willing, I'll spend eternity with Him. Nothing else is more important."

Vlad looked at her through narrowed eyes. "Ah. Have you ever considered never having to ever leave this earth...to live with family and friends here forever?"

The sirens in Lydia's head went off again. *Where was he going with this?* "No, absolutely not! This earth, this universe, will pass away. It isn't permanent."

He gave a short, derisive laugh. "Doesn't feel that way to me." He smiled again at Lydia, giving her face a long look.

"Hmmm...a challenge. This should be interesting."

"What...what do you mean?" Lydia stammered.

Okay, she told herself in a rush of thought, *calm down, don't act stupid, don't alarm him or let on you're down to your last nerve and about to scream and run....*

Vlad looked again at the tip of his bloodied finger, and, watching Lydia's face, slowly put it into his mouth. His eyes got huge, and she felt herself being drawn in again, drowning in his hypnotic stare...

And then the lights went out.

CHAPTER 2

Oh, God help me! Lydia pushed past Vlad and streaked down the corridor to the exit. *Where is Ned?* She got to the door and stopped short, panic all but overtaking her. Vlad had gotten to the door ahead of her!

Lydia's mind raced. *I have to get out of here! He can't find out where I live, or what car I drive, or...How can I get past him?*

"Let me walk you to your car," Vlad was saying. "A woman alone in a dark parking lot is a very, shall we say, appealing target."

Lydia shook her head. "Security ought to be along (*NED WHERE ARE YOU!!!*) any minute. I can wait. You go on ahead."

"Nonsense. It would be my pleasure to see you safely to your car."

That's what I'm afraid of, Lydia thought. Very few options presented themselves to her as she tried to think of ways to get away without him following. Running back into the dark building would be insane, since he seemed to have no problem following her, and, indeed, seemed to know somehow where she was going before she got there. So, since Ned was obviously busy trying to figure out the power outage, the only thing she could think of was to pretend to go to the correct car, wait until Vlad went away, and then go to her own vehicle.

He opened the office door for her, and she had no choice but to walk out. He stuck right by her side, which meant no running into the night screaming her head off. *So much for Option Three.*

Lydia looked up at the night sky. Stars blazed in the frosty night air. She recalled, as a child, how she imagined God was just on the other side of those stars, and it always comforted her to think of Him that way, looking down at her as she looked up at the sky.

Vlad interrupted her thoughts. "The night is beautiful, isn't it?"

Lydia jumped, but tried to regain whatever composure she had left. "Um...yeah," she stammered. "I love the stars, and the moon, but the night can be scary, and I need to get home. I'm fine from here...that's my car just over there." She pointed to a co-worker's car, parked on the lot overnight while he was on a business trip.

Oh, leave now, leave, leave, LEAVE!

Lydia swallowed hard. He was not going anywhere! Her throat was dry from the panic that was ready to overtake her again. Option Two was not working. She started praying again. *Lord, I am powerless. If this...man?...is a danger, I need Your protection. I feel dread and panic; help me know Your peace.*

Vlad was staring at her, his face half in shadow. "You are so quiet. May I know your thoughts?"

"Oh, it's nothing. I...I just really need a drink. I never did have my tea, and I'm really thirsty."

"Ah. As am I."

Something about how he said that made her turn to look at him with alarm.

Those eyes! She turned away again, looking at the ground. The moon shone full, casting shadows everywhere in the unlit parking lot. She could see her own shadow on the pavement...and it was alone...

Lydia stiffened in alarm. Her pulse hammered at her throat, and she glanced once again at Vlad's face.

His eyes seemed to be glowing red, and once again she felt powerless to resist him. Thoughts swirled in her head; life, friends, family. She could see eternity in his eyes. Maybe she was wrong...maybe this was okay...

Suddenly there was a gentle, but overpowering Voice in her head.

"Fight him, Lydia! For the sake of your own soul, and for love of your Lord God, fight him!"

With a violent shake of her head, Lydia broke eye contact with Vlad, and, without another moment's thought, began running. Fortunately, she was close to the edge of the greenway surrounding the office complex. She crashed through the trees, never looking back to see if he was in pursuit, and hid behind a particularly large oak. Tall grasses and thorny brambles tore her skin where it was exposed, but she found it a small sacrifice in exchange for getting away from—she could barely come to terms with the word—a vampire.

Breathing heavily, she peeked out from behind the trunk to see if she could see Vlad searching for her. Her plan was to sneak back via the back parking lot, which wasn't too far from where she stood. She thought it would be easy enough, since it was so dark...

"But the dark is not an issue for me." His voice came from behind her!

OhGodohnononoohGod!

She screamed and tried to bolt, but he laid his hand on her shoulder and spun her around, pinning her to the tree.

"Look at me, Lydia!" he commanded.

She squeezed her eyes shut, kicking and clawing at him, but he had immense strength, and she found herself practically helpless. He put his lips to her ear and whispered, "Do you really believe your Christ will rescue you? Well, where is he? I see no one but you and me here. No angels, no chariots of fire, no avenging heavenly horde. All that praying...what a waste."

His words shocked her into opening her eyes. His breath smelled of blood, and unknown centuries of deaths, and hatred. In his eyes could be read the passage of eons. As Lydia struggled again to break away, he smiled broadly, triumphantly.

This was not the smile she first looked on when she first encountered him. Moonlight glinted on sharp, inch-long fangs.

Lydia screamed again. "Oh no, please! Lord God rescue me! Oh God! No! NO!!"

Vlad laughed, and then spat, "Forget your God! You are mine!" He struck like a cobra, his fangs driving deeply and painfully into Lydia's throat, and her blood flowed freely into his maw from her punctured jugular vein. Her scream became a gurgle, as her heartbeat slowed almost to a stop, and her body went limp as she lost consciousness.

Above the two figures, in the night sky, a single star flared red for just a moment, and then all was still.

CHAPTER 3

Lydia woke, feeling blankets over her and a pillow under her head. Lying there with her eyes closed, she almost laughed aloud in relief. She had dreamed the whole thing! She took a mental inventory of herself, making an intense effort not to allow the dream's details to enter her mind. Her throat felt sore, but that was all.

I must be coming down with a cold, she thought. *Sheesh, what a nightmare! Well, best get going. I suppose I should have a look at the time.*

She opened her eyes. And sat bolt upright, looking wildly around at where she found herself.

Where was she? In a bedroom, yes, but certainly not her own! Instead of her modern, low-budget, comfortable bed and furniture, she was in an old-fashioned four-poster bed, surrounded by dark, seemingly ancient bedroom pieces; bureaus with ornate carvings, shelves full of musty books, and a washstand with a mirror over it. The mirror was draped with a sheet. There was a single, dim lamp glowing on a table beside the bed.

Her bright, sunny windows with her homemade curtains were gone. In their place was a single window with heavy, dusty drapes that looked like they hadn't been taken down and cleaned in ages. The floor was of a lighter wood than the furniture, bare of any rugs.

Lydia stepped cautiously out of the bed; her throat was so dry that her need to find water overcame her fear. The sight of the pitcher and the bowl on the washstand gave her hope that she might find refreshment there. She was so weak as she tottered across the floor that she almost fell.

Something else was odd. She stopped, looked down at herself, and stared in complete disbelief. Instead of her jeans and sweatshirt, she was now dressed in a long, white, silky nightgown!

Rushing to the washstand, barely able to fight her rising terror, she threw the sheet off the mirror and stared in fright at herself. There she was, her short brown hair, blue eyes, and the ever-present freckles she knew so well. But beyond that, everything else was horribly wrong! Her throat was bruised and purpled, the skin puckered around two holes. They had not healed over, and threatened to leak blood with every move.

Lydia raised her hand to her neck, revulsion and panic rising in her like the ocean's tide. She started to shake, as her muscles tensed and a scream traveled rapidly up from the pit of her fear-frozen stomach.

Fighting the urge to lose all control, she ran to the window to try the latch. She pushed open the drapes, choking at the dust that flew around. Rusted shut!

She had to get out! Going out through the bedroom door meant going through a strange house in what she could now see was the dead of night, so that option was not one she wished to pursue.

Lydia looked out the window at a cloudless night over a great sea of blackness. She couldn't tell what was out there—trees, marshes, water, or who knows what—but she knew she would rather crash down and die on whatever was below her than to face whatever awaited her within these walls.

Picking up a heavy ceramic vase from a table near the window, she hurled it at the glass with all her strength. The vase shattered against the thick, unmoving pane, leaving the window without even a scratch.

In a frenzy, Lydia pushed, tugged, scratched, lunged, and beat at the window until she was exhausted. She sat in a nearby chair, trying to get a grip on the terror that was trying to take possession of her.

"Okay, think, Lydia!" she told herself. "Just calm down and think of a plan. Granted, I have no idea where I am or how I got here, or why. I don't even want to think about what happened yesterday. I'll sort that out once I'm out of here. Right now, I just have to get away from this place and to somewhere safe. Lord, help me make the right decisions to get back to my family and my life!"

It seemed the only thing she could do was to creep out of the bedroom and find the fastest way out on silent and, she suddenly remembered, bare feet. Although Lydia figured it was futile, she searched the drawers and small closet to see if, by any chance, her own clothes were in the room. No luck, which wasn't a real surprise.

She turned to the door, her heart pounding, hoping against hope that it would open silently, or that, that...being...would be gone, or both. Lydia put her hand on the knob and turned it, oh so slowly, listening for footsteps on the other side of the door. She was shaking again, and in a cold sweat she eased the door silently open, first a crack, then an inch; enough to look out.

The area outside of the doorway looked clear. She flung the door open the rest of the way, preparing for a full-speed dash to the stairs.

He was right there! It was as if he'd been there waiting for her to try and make a move such as this.

Lydia screeched and slammed the door. Locking it, she ran to the window and hammered at the latch.

"OpenopenopenohGodohGodpleaseopen!"

"It's good to see you up and so full of energy," came Vlad's voice, right in her ear. She whirled around to find him inches from her. He came even closer, backing her up against the window. Lydia avoided his gaze and tried to make herself as small as possible, scrunching her shoulders up to her chin and pushing him with her hands, trying to keep him from getting any closer.

She suddenly remembered the crucifix around her neck. *Oh, salvation!*

She felt for the chain. It was gone!

Vlad gave a low, deep laugh. "Are you looking for this?" he asked.

Lydia gasped. He was holding her necklace by the chain, the crucifix shining in the lamplight. Her fear was replaced by anger, and she swiped at the cross. "How dare you, you...MONSTER! Give that back, and let me out of here!"

He just laughed again, a sound that made Lydia's heart freeze in her chest.

"I think not. It gets in the way." He pocketed it and then turned intense, angry eyes on Lydia.

"You will not need it anyway. I have decided that you will belong to me, and there is no power that can change that. Look, you are even dressed in your bridal best!" He indicated the nightgown, and Lydia tried to cover herself from his gaze.

She shook her head, not only to answer an emphatic "NO!" but also to break that stare that threatened to overtake her senses again. "No! That will not happen! God won't let it happen! I am, and always will be, His alone!"

Vlad sighed, as if Lydia was a little girl who couldn't learn her school lessons. "You do not seem to understand, Lydia. You are now cursed."

Lydia's eyes widened in alarm.

"Your soul is forfeit. I have taken you from your precious Lord, and he will not want you back. You are a filthy rag in his eyes."

All of Lydia's being revolted in anger at his words, and she gathered the force from within her to push him away and run to the other side of the room, where she tried in vain to get the door open. "'The Lord is my light and my salvation!'" she shouted. "'Whom shall I fear? Of whom should I be afraid?'"

Vlad sneered. "Throwing worn-out Scripture at me isn't going to change anything! I brought you here to be my bride, and you should be grateful!"

"Grateful? For what? Why should I be grateful? Besides," she ended lamely, "I'm already married." At least she *hoped* her family was still alive...

Vlad looked at her for a long, cold moment. At last he spoke. "I was going to kill you like all the rest. Make a full meal out of you and leave you where you lay. You have no idea how tired I was of hunting and killing animals when it was human blood I craved." He looked thoughtful. Then he muttered, seemingly to himself, "Far too long..."

He leered as he approached her slowly, taking his time, knowing she had no escape. He passed his eyes up and down her body.

Lydia gasped and shrank back, horrified. What was he about to do now?

Vlad's gaze hardened. "You don't have to worry about your precious 'virtue.' That is not what I am interested in. Although it could be an interesting...diversion..."

As he came closer, Lydia backed up until she was once again pressed against a wall. Something he said earlier suddenly hit her. She trembled violently, understanding finally dawning on her.

"Yes, Lydia," Vlad whispered, reading her mind, "For far too long, I have walked this earth alone. I have finally decided to choose someone to be my companion through the ages, and it is you."

At this, Lydia crumpled to the floor, sobbing. The horror of his words, and the certainty of having to spend her nights doing the same evil work he did, and had done to her, was more than she could bear. She wailed a desperate prayer, "Out of the depths I cry to You, O Lord! Lord, hear my voice! O let your ears be attentive to my voice in supplication!"

With a roar, Vlad was over her, pulling her up by the arm and dragging her over to the mirror. "I tell you, I have already claimed you! Look!" He pointed to her reflection in the mirror.

At first, Lydia couldn't detect anything but her own reflection being held at an awkward angle by an unseen force. Then she realized what she was seeing, and her blood ran cold.

She could see the furniture through her reflection! "No! Oh, dear God, no!"

She broke free from Vlad's grasp and lunged at the mirror, in the wild hope that maybe she was hallucinating. But, no. She was somewhat diaphanous, and getting more and more transparent by the minute. Without really wanting to, but seemingly powerless to fight her morbid curiosity, she ran the tip of her tongue over her teeth.

Oh Lord, this can't be happening! Her incisors had sharpened, and were slightly longer than they had been just a few hours before.

Lydia wailed to the heavens as Vlad swept her up and deposited her on the bed. He slapped her, hard, across the face. "You will not say that Name again in my presence!"

Lydia whimpered in deep despair as Vlad bore down on her. Her breathing came in short, horrified gasps as he pushed her chin up. Her pulse pounded in her throat, and he seemed mesmerized by its movement. He murmured, "Just a couple of times more in my embrace, Lydia, and you are mine forever!"

Suddenly he was staring fully into her eyes. She fought him, kicking and screaming, but it was useless. She once again felt his bloodied, horrid breath on her face, saw the wide-open mouth with those terrible fangs. When he struck, her heartbeat slowed with the rapid loss of blood. She could feel him drawing it out of her veins, and the painful contraction within her as the blood left her limbs.

Lydia despaired as she felt her chance for eternal happiness being sucked away with her life fluids. She looked toward the window, and, as she faded into unconsciousness, whispered, "My God, my God, why have You abandoned me?"

Her last memory was of a Voice, still, warm, peaceful, in a place Vlad could not reach:

"I am here."

CHAPTER 4

Lydia woke alone. Judging from the light outside the window, it was either dusk or dawn. It was so hard to tell; being imprisoned in this room made the hours all run together, and she had not seen the sun since the last morning she'd walked into her office.

Whichever it was, dawn or dusk, the light was hurting her eyes. She felt she needed to get away from it and retreat into the dark. Her throat was parched from lack of water, but, even though it had been hours since she'd eaten, she was surprised that she was not hungry.

With what little she knew, or guessed about vampires, Lydia figured that Vlad was asleep in some other room, or maybe out hunting more poor animals, depending on the actual time. She couldn't tell; her watch was gone, along with her cell phone and all of the rest of her belongings.

She sat on the bed and stared at the door for a long time, trying to build up enough courage to go and open it. What if he was waiting out in the hallway like before? It made her tremble just to think about it.

Finally, her needs won out. Hoping to escape the dim light in the room, and being overcome by thirst, she mastered her fear and walked to the door. It seemed to take a lifetime to cover that short distance, her heart pounding and her nerves on edge. The thought of that monster waiting to pounce on her turned her veins to ice.

Her stomach in knots, she put out a trembling hand and touched the doorknob. She drew it back, and considered running back to the bed to hide under the blankets. Or maybe, she thought, she could climb into one of the old wardrobes and hide in the corner for the rest of her life.

Lydia turned back and made the first few steps in what would surely be a panicked dash to the other side of the room. The light outside had gotten brighter, and she felt an all-consuming need to escape it. Pulling the drapes closed would probably have taken care of the burning sensation she felt, but she couldn't bear going anywhere near the light now streaming into the room. The first edge of the sun was peeking up over what Lydia could now see was a forest, and its rays felt like hot pokers wherever it touched her.

Once again, the only choice was to flee through the bedroom door and into whatever new terrors awaited within the darkness of the house. Returning to the door, she turned the knob and opened it just enough to see out. Fearing an attack, Lydia looked quickly about, and, seeing no one, left the room, closing the door on the now-unbearable heat and light.

She crept down the hallway, noticing that her eyesight was immeasurably better in the dark than it used to be. There were a couple of doors to her left, and a railing that overlooked the first floor on her right. Heart racing, she moved slowly towards the stairs at the end of the hall, jumping at every sound.

Lydia could hardly believe her luck when she reached the top of the stairs without incident. She made her way down, peering fearfully into every shadow, expecting at any moment for Vlad to step out of one of them and grab her.

She noticed that all of the furniture was covered in sheets and coated with years of dust. As she wandered around, trying to find a means of escape, she saw that the floor did not show any sign of footprints through the thick layer of gray that covered it. If Vlad used the front door, he must not be leaving any marks. Just like he didn't throw a shadow or reflect an image in glass.

She could tell that the house was once very grand, but the neglect was very apparent. Cobwebs hung thickly from chandeliers, and the shrouded furniture gave mute testimony to a better time.

A thought stopped her in her tracks. Footprints! Maybe Vlad didn't leave any, but she sure was! It would be very apparent that she had gotten out. Would he hunt her down? Very likely. She had to get away as fast as possible. Hopefully there would be a town or a village nearby. The brief look she had had at the forest through the bedroom window was enough to let her know that she had no idea where she was.

The front door was now just ahead of her. She was only a few feet from freedom! She felt like laughing; the problem of the footprints now seemed inconsequential. She could be long gone by the time Vlad found out, especially now that it was...

Daylight!

The light hit her through the small windows on the door. It was so hot! She couldn't fathom it. Why was it like this? It felt like the middle of summer in the desert. Wasn't it still winter? Or had she been stuck here so long that it was now August? If so, that summer sun burning through the glass windows of the front door was being intensified like a magnifying glass on her skin.

She stepped out of the light, and stood beside the door. It was a huge, wooden, ornate structure, and it looked like it could withstand a siege. There were carvings on it; she was a little uneasy when she saw what they were. Some, like wolves and gargoyles, she could make out easily, but the others looked like some sort of Celtic runes.

Okay, she told herself, *no time to play 'Guess the Architecture.' Who knows how much time I have before...it...wakes up.* Hoping the door would even open, Lydia turned the knob and pulled. It opened easily, silently, something that she barely had time to be surprised about before the full force of the light hit her like a thousand knives. She howled in pain and shrank back.

At the same time, a mass of cold air hit her from behind, and a hand clamped down on her shoulder. Another hand slammed the door closed, and Vlad whirled her to face him. She screamed in fear and frustration as he picked her up bodily and marched back through the house.

He did not drag her back up to the bedroom this time. "It is clear that I will have to keep a closer eye on you," he growled as he opened a door under the stairs.

Lydia stopped struggling long enough to realize that he was taking her down to a lower floor. The damp, musty smell of a basement hit her nose. This made her struggle and scream even harder, but his strength was fueled by the anger and evil that owned him, and his hold on her was like a vise.

They got to the bottom of the steps, and he dropped her to her feet. Immediately she ran back up the stairs to the open door. Vlad waved his arm, and the door shut and locked itself before she was halfway up. She turned back on him, gasping in short breaths, frightened out of her wits.

He sighed. "I tire of this, Lydia. Understand this: I know where you are and what you are doing at all times. You have interrupted my rest, and have almost done damage to both of us."

Lydia's anger finally overcame her fear, and she exploded. She raced down the steps at him. "What do I care? It would have been great to see you damaged, or destroyed! If I'd known you were there, I would have done what I could to put you directly in the sun's path!"

"It would have destroyed you as well."

Lydia stalked away. "Good! I wish it had! I'd rather be a pile of dust than to be stuck here with you! Why didn't you just kill me when you had the chance?"

He advanced on her with a rapidity and intensity that made her run. Even though she knew she couldn't get away, it was the instinct born of survival at any cost that caused her to at least make the attempt. As she ran, she looked for some type of sanctuary, no matter how tenuous.

There was a lot of furniture stored in this room. She ran between chairs, over small tables, and through stacks of shelving, Vlad in controlled, deliberate pursuit. She finally ran out of anywhere to run. In an act of desperation, she tried to squeeze between the basement wall and the back of an old dusty china cabinet.

Vlad was right at her side, pulling her out and pressing her against the wall. His gaze was hard and angry. Lydia shut her eyes tight and turned her head away, trying to blot out the truth of his presence. Her fingernails dug into the palms of her hands, which were cold and clammy.

His grip on her lessened, but the press of his body against hers kept her pinned to the wall. Expecting the sharp pain of his fangs on her bruised throat, Lydia tensed her muscles and waited, eyes still closed, barely breathing.

The attack did not come.

Vlad leaned over and whispered in her ear, "As I said before, I could have killed you, but once I had a taste of your blood, I knew I wanted more, and that would not happen if you were dead, now would it?"

Lydia shuddered. Repulsed, she whimpered and tried to squeeze out from under the press of his body. She opened her eyes to see him gazing intently at her throat. He put a finger on her pulsing jugular vein, impervious to her attempts to get away from him. He caressed the vein almost lovingly, if such a creature could love.

Lydia's stomach roiled, and she tried to shrink back from his touch. Her body tensed again, and a cold sweat broke out all over her body as her bile rose. She shook uncontrollably as he continued to stroke her bruised, torn neck. She whimpered again, and a small prayer escaped her.

"God help me!" She held her breath, alarmed, and waited for him to strike her.

He just gave a small smile and shook his head. "No, that won't happen. Your soul is mine."

Lydia sobbed uncontrollably, then shrieked as he picked her up, carried her to an old dusty couch, and laid her on it. Holding her shoulders down, he bent down and fanged her throat again, but not with the hunger he had displayed before.

He murmured to himself as Lydia wept and he fed.

"Mmm, such sweet, innocent, delicious life fluids. Much better than wine..."

Instead of drawing her blood out in a rush, he stopped after a short time and licked the fresh holes, lapping her life up while she tried futilely to fight him off.

Vlad laughed. "Ah, your struggles just make me want more! But I have had several deer tonight—not nearly as delicious as your blood—and am quite satiated. I need my rest."

He pulled away, and started towards the basement door.

Lydia lay on the couch, weeping. *When will this end?* she cried to herself. A tremendous thirst wracked her suddenly, which far outweighed the pain and fright she was feeling.

Vlad stopped, his back to her. "It will not end. Expect our...relationship...to continue forever." He paused. "Oh, do forgive me, I have neglected your thirst. I will be right back."

Take your time, Lydia thought, a bit of anger returning. She raised a hand to her throat, feeling the blood seeping from her new wounds. She cried silently, despair overtaking her like an ocean of darkness, from which she thought she might never re-emerge.

Vlad was back soon, with a cup of some sort of liquid. Lydia could tell right away that it was not water, but her thirst overwhelmed her; she took the proffered cup and downed it in a flash.

She immediately regretted it.

It was blood! The coppery, salty taste could not be mistaken for anything else, but what—or whose—was it? Then she noticed the blood dripping from Vlad's wrist. He had slit his veins and emptied his own blood into the cup!

Lydia immediately rolled over and threw up on the floor. The waves of nausea did not stop through several bouts of dry heaves. Finally, shaking, she laid back against the dusty cushions, pale and weak.

Vlad was standing over her, disgust and victory fighting for mastery on his face. "Our blood is mixed. It is done." He then turned on his heel and walked away.

CHAPTER 5

Lydia lay on the couch for unknown hours. Day followed night, apparent only by the dim light filtering through the single, draped small window high in one wall. Her weakness and despondency took away any will to move.

Thoughts and memories swirled through the blackness of her despair. Family, friends, good times—these were entirely lost to her. She knew that, even if she could escape, she could never return to her loved ones and her life. Steve and her kids would be in as much peril as any small animal in the wilds; Lydia's craving and hunger were growing, and she realized that her yearning was for blood, even though she still could not mentally bring herself to fully accept it.

Vlad would occasionally bring her small cups of his own blood, "to strengthen her," as he said, and at first Lydia fought and pushed the cup away. He would then pull her head back by her hair and force the liquid into her mouth. Always she would vomit it up again. Rats would then come out of the dark shadows around the room and swarm over the mess, fighting each other for every drop.

Enough of his blood finally got into her system, however, to cause her to have a yearning she didn't understand in the pit of her stomach whenever he approached her with a fresh offering. This caused her a lot of distress, as her strong sense of morality was still intact. To feed on the lifeblood of a fellow creature was abhorrent to her.

As time went on, however, Lydia's feelings of hopelessness, caused by her unceasing imprisonment despite constant prayer, were taking a toll on her faith. Added to that was the ever-growing blood cravings; the prayers became less and less frequent as she spiraled down and down into a black pit of despair. It was getting to be nearly impossible to believe that God was paying any attention. That Voice, so gentle and kind, was still. She had not heard it in days. Was she indeed cursed beyond redemption? Had God given up on her, condemned her for the monster she had become? Why? It wasn't her fault. She had fought Vlad as hard as she could, but still was cursed, like him, to walk the world, feeding on blood for the rest of the earth's days. Then what? Hell? It wasn't right, and she wasn't too sure she wanted anything to do with a Lord who allowed such injustice.

Therefore, the attacks by Vlad, which were becoming less and less frequent, did not cause her to fight like she used to. At the beginning of her incarceration, Lydia had run from him. She had continued to be repulsed by his touch, and had tried to make herself into as small a target as possible to avoid any more abuse on her mangled neck. It finally came to a point where there was no area on her throat that wasn't a purple mess. Vlad merely grabbed her arm and drove his fangs into the inner part, at the elbow. Lydia cried out, screamed, kicked, howled prayers at the top of her voice—and then went silent.

After that episode, she just didn't care anymore. Rarely did she get up off her filthy bed, even though it meant lying in a pool of her own blood. That is, until the rats came and devoured the fresh spills. At times they tried to bite her as well, but turned away in fright when she looked at them.

One evening, after Vlad had fed on Lydia's arm while she wept despondently into the back of the sofa, he pulled away and sighed. "I enjoyed you a lot more when you fought back. More of a challenge."

Lydia sobbed harder. Then, when she could pull herself together enough to speak, said in a hoarse whisper, "So kill me. Let me die!!"

"And let you have the chance to go back to your 'Lord'? I absolutely will not allow it!"

Lydia had caught the word 'chance', and clung to that thought as though a life preserver had been thrown to her in her stormy sea of despair. After he left, she summed up enough will to try and pray again. When no comfort came, she lapsed back into the familiar arms of despair. But this time, despondency was replaced by anger. *If God isn't going to pull me out of this*, she raged in her mind, *then I guess I am on my own. I'm damned and cursed anyway.*

Still, Vlad's parting words lingered in her mind...

Lydia slept again, and woke as evening approached. Her hours of sleep were becoming more and more the same as a nocturnal animal, or like that beast that roamed this empty house and kept her prisoner. As she lay there, staring up at the ceiling, she was aware of some new and odd sensations.

Her senses were much sharper. She could see her surroundings clearly in the dim light, whereas before she would trip over the various pieces of furniture scattered haphazardly around the room. The skittering of the rats and other creatures as they moved along the walls was much louder than it was the previous evening. As she rose from the couch, she noticed that her legs were much stronger. She also found that she was wanting to hunt.

For she was very hungry, and it was not a hunger for food. Her fangs were at least as long and sharp as Vlad's, and she had an all-powerful urge to use them. Like a cat, Lydia crept up to a wall and waited patiently. When a whiskered nose peeped out from behind a bureau, she lunged with a speed she'd never known before, grabbed the rat, and, without a moment's hesitation, bit into its furry neck and drained it completely.

Immediately the realization of what she had just done hit her, as did the wave of nausea and disgust she felt for having committed such a beastly act. The taste of blood in her mouth was disgusting; she looked frantically around for some way to get rid of it. Even an old rag would do. She opened various drawers to see if she could find one. However, nothing could wipe away the knowledge of the horrid thing she had just done. Or what she now knew she was capable of doing. It horrified her.

Then a sound: *plink-plink, plink-plink.*

She looked over towards the window and saw water dripping from the sill. It had rained during the day, enough for the water to build up around the window and leak into the basement. It wasn't much, but she felt it would be enough, if she kept her patience for the time needed to amass a small pool of water. Lydia found a small wooden bowl, dusty and covered in cobwebs and dead insects. She blew into it, scattering the debris into the air, and held the bowl up to the dripping water. After some time, seemingly interminable, she had about a tablespoon of liquid in the bowl. Raising it to her lips, she tossed the water into her mouth.

Pain! Searing pain!, as if she had swallowed lit kerosene! She threw down the bowl and writhed in agony, her eyes wild and her lips flecked with bloody foam. A strangled scream escaped from her throat, but it was a hoarse and nearly silent one; even in her pain, she didn't want that monster down here any more than he already was.

When the pain had subsided a bit, and Lydia sat panting from her exertions, she was suddenly overwhelmed by the need to take another rat. The need was so great that it far surpassed all other feelings; her revulsion, her morality, even her burned mouth. Nothing mattered to her frenzied mind but gorging on another rat. Or something else...

Once again, she took up her post by the wall, and when the opportunity came, she struck again. She had just finished that rodent, and was going to go on the hunt again, when she heard a low chuckle behind her. Whirling around, she saw Vlad leaning against the stairwell wall, watching her with a very satisfied look on his face.

"I'm certainly pleased to see that you are recovering. Fending for yourself as well! Good. I was getting tired of opening my veins for you. Feeding on you afterwards—pah! I might as well have fed on myself!"

Not a bad idea, Lydia thought. *Oops, he can read my mind. Now what am I in for?*

Vlad chuckled again. "Not to worry. We'll consider it a little joke. Now...I thirst!"

With no other warning, he jumped for Lydia, who managed to get out of the way just in time, leaving Vlad to grab empty air. His eyes widened in surprise, then he grinned. "I can see this is going to be a lot more exciting for me than our encounters for the past week or so."

Lydia hissed and bared her fangs at him. A red mist fell over her vision. She feinted away from his next lunge, and almost got away from him again. But she made the mistake of looking into his eyes...

With centuries of untold evils behind him, Lydia knew she was never going to win in any battles against him. His gaze rooted her to the spot, so that when he grabbed her shoulders and moved in to feed, she had no defenses. She once again felt her heartbeat slow as he pulled at her veins, swallowing her life fluids and causing her to almost lose consciousness...

Abruptly, he pulled away. With a disgusted look on his face, he spat on the floor. "Horrid! Ghastly! Rat blood has tainted the sweet taste of yours!"

Lydia glared at him, and spoke aloud for the first time in what seemed like days. Her voice was hoarse, both from disuse and from the scorching she had received from the water. "There's not a whole lot of choice around here! You make me into this *monster*, as hungry as you are, and leave me to rot in this basement! What am I supposed to do? It's not like I can order delivery from the Red Cross!"

Vlad arched an eyebrow. "This is more spirit and fire than I remember you having in a long time. Yes, you are correct; we must do something. But what?"

He paced back and forth, chin in hand, thinking.

Lydia raged at him, "Here's a thought. LET ME OUT OF HERE!" She waved an arm around wildly. "It's not like I can just go back to my family and my life! You ruined that for me! I can hunt on my own and just, I don't know..." She ran out of steam, and sank down in a chair.

Vlad looked at her, hard. She cringed, thinking maybe she had overstepped her luck, and tried to shrink back into the shadows.

"I'll tell you why, even now, I will not let you away from where I can readily find you. First of all, as I've said before, I want your blood above any other. Such sweetness I have never had in all of my centuries of existence! I will not risk your leaving me. Also, you are, shall we say, intriguing. Most of my victims—that is, the ones I've allowed to live—have lost all hold on their former lives by now, and are eager for the hunt. You...," he said, with a glint of admiration, "you seem to retain a certain innocence that I continue to find challenging. Whether it is a remnant of your misguided devotion to Him..."

Lydia stood up, and advanced on Vlad.

"Do you mean Jesus?"

Vlad slapped her hard against the side of the face. She reeled and fell on the floor. But surprisingly, she didn't feel much pain, only seething anger.

"You will NOT say that Name!"

Lydia rubbed the place where he had hit her. "Or what? Kill me? Go ahead! Or try! I seem to be in the same position, mortality-wise, as you. Seems you don't have as much control over me as you once had. Your mistake!"

An evil glint in his eye replaced the fire of his anger. "Maybe not, but perhaps...your daughter could join us. It would be...pleasurable...taking her. And in front of you, too! Maybe you could join in!"

Lydia gasped. "You leave my family alone!"

"YOU OBEY ME THEN!" Vlad spat.

Lydia fled back to her couch, wracked with grief. She sobbed hard into the cushions. Here she thought she had had a handle on him, and on this new existence of hers, but she had not figured in the fact that he knew about her family.

As Vlad was walking out, he turned to her, and said, "I will be back. I think I have what is necessary to keep you fed."

Fed! Like a dog! Lydia's anger flared again. Picking up the wooden bowl, she threw it at him as he climbed the steps and let himself out.

CHAPTER 6

Feeling restless, but not hungry enough to hunt, Lydia paced the room. She checked in old bureau drawers, looked into musty cabinets, and opened boxes, just for something to do. The storage spaces were empty, but the boxes contained old leather-bound books and documents made of parchment, all in a language she couldn't readily identify. *So much for occupying myself with reading...*

At one point, she pulled a chair up to a dresser that stood fairly close to the window, curious as to what the world looked like outside this enclosed space. She was getting cabin fever, and was burning to get a view beyond these walls.

Once on the dresser, she twitched open the drapes, but could only glimpse a wall of mud and grass, indicating that the window was only partially above ground level. There was a tiny well of space between the glass and the soil, but there was no way to see over the top. However, she thought maybe there would be enough space for her to wiggle up through the window and make her escape.

Now if only she could find something that would break the glass...

She was in the process of dismantling a leg from a partially hidden, upturned table when she heard a noise at the door. Quickly, she went and sat back down on the chair she'd occupied earlier, and tried to look as if she'd sat there bored all night.

As Vlad walked in, holding a burlap sack and looking quite pleased with himself, he stopped momentarily, flicked his gaze up at the window—*the drapes!* thought Lydia—then he looked back at her with a small shake of his head.

Lydia looked at the sack in his arms. It twitched.

"What is that?" Despite herself, Lydia was hoping it was some small animal, and that he would let it loose on the floor so she could pursue it. If she had to live this way, then she should at least have some control over how she sated her blood lust.

"I've brought you something. It took a lot of effort, and I was almost spotted, so I hope you appreciate it." He smiled, and Lydia could see that he had fed not too long ago himself. His fangs were still stained red.

Reading her mind, he answered, "I correct myself. I *was* spotted, but I took care of the...witnesses." He smiled again, and Lydia looked away, repulsed.

He started to unwrap the bundle, and Lydia came closer for a better look. The smell of living flesh assailed her nose, and she was fairly drooling with anticipation.

Finally, Lydia could see what he had brought her, and could not believe her eyes. He held out his prize to her as if he had found a box of rare jewels.

A baby! A human baby! A little boy, judging from the blue sleeper he was wearing.

She took him from Vlad, swiping the poor mite away from his deadly embrace. "How could you think I would attack and feed on this sweet little child? What have you...where are his parents?"

Vlad showed his blood-stained fangs again. That was all the explanation Lydia needed. Horrified, then furious, she shouted at him, "I hope you do get caught! I hope someone drives a wooden stake through your black heart!"

"Not that I have one. You do realize, don't you, that you would be destroyed along with me."

"Good! As I've said before, I'd be glad for an end to it!"

Vlad reached for the child, intending to take him away from her, but Lydia held the baby close. She turned away from him. "Poor little thing," she murmured down at the child, rocking him gently while he slept on.

Then she turned abruptly, and made to thrust the sleeping form back at Vlad. She was going to demand that he take the child back to where he had found him. But just as she opened her mouth to speak, she hesitated, and brought the baby back into her embrace.

Just one more look at that sweet, sleeping face. Once a mother, always a mother. Lydia smiled down on the baby. *Such a lovely little child,* she thought to herself.

Those long lashes against that smooth skin.

The little bow-shaped mouth.

The little baby breaths, carrying promises of the future.

And the...*Oh God help me!*...vein pulsing in his neck!

Now the sound came to her of the blood in his veins, rushing, calling to her! Her mouth grew parched, her own pulse quickened, and again her eyesight misted red. Nothing else existed but the pulsing, living, blood-filled...

She reared back to strike, but a sudden loud fluttering sound at the window caused her to jump, breaking the spell and almost causing her to drop the baby.

There was a bird at the window, hopping and fluttering. Apparently it had fallen into the recess of the window hole, and was madly trying to get out. It flapped and struggled, and finally got purchase on the surface of the ground and flew away.

Lydia turned back to her intended victim, sleeping gently in her arms. Just as the blood lust came over her again, she heard that almost-forgotten Voice in her soul:

No, Lydia, you mustn't!

Lydia was aghast at what she had almost done. Quickly, she put the child down on a safe, semi-clean part of the couch, and turned blazing eyes on Vlad.

"No! Never! Do you hear me? I'll put up with hunting rats and vermin, but I will NOT prey on humans! Get out and leave me alone! Take this child back as well!"

Vlad shook his head, as if at a student who had done poorly on a test. As he turned, empty-handed, to leave the basement, he once again took in the scene of the chair near the dresser, the uncovered window, and the footprints in the dust all around. Cocking an eyebrow, he headed up the stairs.

"Wait! Take the baby! Don't leave him here with me!"

He turned and gave her a long, hard stare. "The child stays. What you do with it is your business. I am going to my rest."

She watched him go through the door, and wondered briefly if she could flash past him. After all, she seemed to have all of the rest of his powers, so why shouldn't she be able to move as fast as him? Then again, what would happen if he was still faster? He seemed to have an endless capacity for making her life a living nightmare, so anything he did would be worse than the death she so wished for. Better to stay down here and practice for a while. Plenty of rats around to keep the hunger away.

Hmmm, a little hunting might be a good thing, she thought. *It would take my mind off the baby, and would tire me out enough that I won't be interested.*

Lydia crept over to her hunting spot, and soon came up with her first victim. She drained it, and then threw it on the ground near where she had heard tiny little vermin feet earlier. Immediately, several rats raced out to work over the carcass of their fellow, and Lydia caught two with one swipe. Finishing those off seemed to be just enough to sate her, and she headed back to lie down and get some rest herself.

The baby stirred in his sleep. Even though she had hunted and fed, the blood lust reawakened, and she walked slowly towards the little form. "Just a little," she murmured longingly to herself. "I won't even bite hard. He'll make it up in no time. I doubt he'll even feel it. Vlad seems to have put him into a deep sleep somehow..."

Lydia! Leave the child alone!

Lydia startled, and then threw her arms in the air, stared up at the ceiling, and let out all of the feelings of desertion and desperation that had been gathering like a storm for days.

"Oh, great! Now you show up!" she raged, finally getting a chance to let that Voice, whoever it belonged to - her imagination, her conscience, God, whatever - know just how she felt about the situation she was in.

"All right, now that you're back, for who knows how long, I want to know why the hell no one has come to my rescue! I asked, pleaded, prayed, and raged, to no avail! I'm not alive, I'm not dead, I'm...UNDEAD! Cursed! Horrid! I don't remember signing up for this when I said I wanted to be Your instrument. That is, if You are God speaking to me. This is not exactly how I wanted to live my life! Where's the justice? Why is this happening? Do you even care how much I'm suffering? Do you?"

Spent, she sat down on a couch a little further away from the baby, put her head down on the cushions, and immediately fell into a deep sleep.

CHAPTER 7

Lydia found herself in a huge crowd of people, all shoving and pushing each other down a dark street. The only lights came from torches on the sides of the buildings they passed, or carried in the hands of some of the men.

She was mildly surprised when she looked down at herself and found that she was clothed in a brown, coarse robe that covered her from head to toe. *Well, it's a whole lot better than that rag I was wearing*, she thought.

She had on brown sandals, and a white veil covered her head. Around her, everyone was wearing the same sort of attire, except for a group of men dressed in expensive-looking garments. They stood back and watched as the crowd surged by, the people shouting and pointing to some sort of activity up ahead, where the street widened into a large plaza.

"I'd better get out of here, or someone's going to get bitten," she muttered to herself.

To her utter surprise, however, her fangs were gone!

A woman shouted at her and pulled her by the arm. "They've taken him! Oh, what can we do? And his poor mother, she's right up there with him!" The woman was speaking in a strange language, but Lydia found to her surprise that she had no problem understanding what she said.

"Who are you talking about?" Lydia was surprised to hear herself answer in the same language.

The young lady looked wide-eyed in surprise at Lydia, but couldn't stop moving along because of the crowd pushing them towards the action up ahead. "The Teacher!" she wept. "They've taken him, and the Sanhedrin has sent him to the Romans! They will tear him to pieces, simply because he is a Jew! They won't listen to any of us!"

Teacher? Sanhedrin? What? Where? Lydia was thoroughly perplexed.

Until she came to where all of the commotion was. An understanding dawned on her of where she was; the reason behind her appearance here became all too clear.

A post stood in the middle of the plaza, and chained to it was a man, stripped of his garments from the waist up. His back was flayed so thoroughly that there didn't seem to be any skin left on it. Blood poured from his wounds, filling the cracks between the bricks in the street. Lydia felt for the wounds in her own neck—they were gone. But the memory of them was only too horribly real.

The Roman soldiers weren't through with their torture, however. Having run out of skin to flail on their victim's back, they were now whipping red welts into his legs. Not one sound did he make during the proceedings, which seemed to enrage the soldiers all the more. They seemed to have been drinking heavily before their grisly game, as some were staggering about, trying to grab nearby Jewish women, while others, whips still in hand, had passed out and were face-down, snoring in the blood-soaked street.

The women, and many of the men, were crying, shouting, and attempting to get to the victim. Guards, more sober and much more dangerous than the brutes with the whips, kept everyone at bay.

Lydia couldn't take her eyes off the scene in front of her, but certainly wished she could. She was relieved that she felt no blood lust, as she seemed to have reverted to her natural, living self. But the scene mesmerized her in a horrific way.

A disturbance around a fire in a nearby courtyard caught her attention, and she wrested her gaze away from the scene at the whipping post. Several people were pointing to a man dressed in traveling clothes. A large Roman official was also taking an interest in the scene, and was making his way over to the group. Lydia couldn't make out what people were shouting, but the traveler's words rang clear:

"I tell you, I do not know him!" He glanced nervously at the slowly-advancing Roman centurion.

Just then a rooster hopped up on a nearby wall and crowed. The traveler stood and gawked at the bird, terror filling his eyes. Then he ran out of the courtyard, past the man chained to the post.

Their eyes met, and the traveler seemed to lose all momentum. He looked as if he was shrinking into himself as he stammered wordlessly. Then he ran off through the city gates, and

Lydia could hear his anguished wailing echo off the walls of the town.

The chained man was finally pulled free from the post by the drunken horde of soldiers. They faced the crowd, pulling their victim around the circle. "Some king, eh? What, don't recognize him now?"

A curse went up as one of the soldiers ran carelessly into a thorn bush near the wall by the courtyard. After he'd pulled himself free, he was about to turn back to his fellows when he noticed that his own arms were bleeding. This seemed to give him a horrific idea.

He unsheathed his sword and hacked off a large amount of the dried brambles. He took the branches towards his comrades, carrying them on the sword's point, since the thorns were so long and sharp. Lydia thought they looked every bit as sharp and dangerous as Vlad's fangs.

The drunken soldier laughed, "Well, of course they don't recognize him! We forgot his crown!"

Catching onto the idea, the rest of the guards laughed as well. Then two of them wound their hands up in the discarded clothing of their victim, wove a crown from the branches, and brutally pounded the inch-long thorns into his head.

Lydia didn't think the brutalized man could possibly have any more blood to spill, but red rivulets flowed down his brow from these new wounds. He gasped, staggered, and fell. His torturers took this opportunity to pull him around the street by his ankles, leaving a red streak in his wake.

The crowd screamed and fought anew to reach him, but after a few of them were skewered unmercifully by Roman spears, they backed off and watched helplessly as their Teacher was practically torn to pieces.

A group of women were huddled around another woman who was nearly beside herself with grief. Lydia knew instinctively that this was his mother. She wanted to run to her, to tell her everything would be all right, and even better, once this day was over, but somehow she knew that the woman already had that knowledge. Still, seeing the physical torture of her son had to be searingly painful. Lydia didn't even want to think of what it would be like to be in her position. Her son Pat's face appeared in her mind's eye, and she shuddered to think of him as being in those soldiers' hands.

Just when it seemed the victim would be breathing his last right there on the street, a Roman soldier clothed in the garb of authority stepped into the midst of the brutes.

The centurion barked, "Enough! We want enough of him alive to crucify him!" Turning to a group of guards behind him, he commanded, "Take the prisoner back to Pilate!"

The man was half-carried away by a more sober group of soldiers. The drunks careened off toward the crowd, which parted before them. The Jews were loath to have these sotted heathens touch them, and no wonder. The soldiers were out to cause trouble. Their blood lust was not sated as yet, and the alcohol in their systems made them unwilling to show restraint.

The woman Lydia had met earlier touched her on the arm. There was a glimmer of hope in her eyes, as she spoke excitedly, "They've taken him back inside! This is good news! Because of Passover, Pilate will be allowing us to choose freedom for one of two prisoners! All we have to do is shout for Jesus, and we can free him!"

Lydia smiled sadly at her. All too well did she know the outcome of this night.

The sound of loud voices caught her attention. She looked over to the edge of the crowd and saw the well-dressed men she had noticed earlier. They were dispensing money to a crowd of milling townspeople, who thronged around trying to grab the coins.

Lydia's companion wrinkled her nose in disgust. She tried to look confident, but Lydia could see that she was starting to get worried again. "It looks as if our leaders are trying to sway the crowd by bribing those thieves, drunks, and layabouts over there to cause trouble. Well, we'll just have to be that much louder."

As everyone crowded into the courtyard where Pilate would bring out the two prisoners, Lydia could see earthenware bottles being passed back and forth, and men getting more and more intoxicated. Those who refused to drink from the bottles were shunted and elbowed toward the back of the crowd, no matter how hard they fought to hold their ground.

Suddenly, a hush fell over the jostling throng as a man dressed in Roman finery walked out onto the open area of the second floor. Flanked by guards, he took his seat and scanned the crowd. When all was absolutely silent, he spoke.

"People of Jerusalem, in accord with your Passover tradition, I am going to allow one prisoner to go free. This will, of course, be based on your decision."

The crowd started to murmur as he gestured at his attendant. The man clapped his hands twice; at this signal, soldiers brought out two men, one from either side of the viewing area. From the right came Jesus, staggering from the loss of blood, but mercifully dressed in his own clothes again. The crowd stared and spoke to each other as they looked at him, some in anger and sadness, and some in ribald mockery. He came out meek as a lamb, offering no insults. Instead, he looked down at his feet and offered no resistance to the pokes and prods from his captors.

Then, from the left, snarling and swearing, came another prisoner. The soldiers could barely keep him in check, even with the chains around him. Lydia knew immediately that this was Barabbas. He fought, kicked the nearest men, and cursed and threatened them. The crowd went wild at this; some started chanting his name. This was what they wanted, someone who would fight the Roman oppressors! Not the other, who just stood there quietly! What good was he? Such seemed the mindset of those Lydia could hear around her, but there was also an undertone of weeping and praying, which grew louder as events played out.

Pilate held up his hands. When the crowd didn't quiet down, he gestured to the soldiers. They responded by unsheathing their weapons—arrows, spears, swords, all in readiness to enforce the command for quiet. It worked; the people fell silent, knowing from experience that this was no mere threat.

When he could be heard, and all attention was on him, Pilate spoke again. "I give you the choice. On my left, Jesus of Nazareth. Personally, I do not find anything he has done that would be considered worth condemning, but your Sanhedrin seems to think otherwise."

Lydia glanced at the group of men who were doling out the coins earlier. They were speaking softly among themselves, looking highly pleased with what was transpiring.

"On my right, Barabbas. An insurrectionist and a sworn enemy of the Roman Empire. We consider him dangerous. I highly doubt that, if freed, he will stay that way for long.

"It is now your choice. Which one shall I set free?"

Lydia listened as the voice of the crowd grew. At first, Jesus' name was shouted louder than the other. The rich men hadn't had so much money that they could pay off everyone.

The opposition voice was growing, though, as many of the people became swayed by Barabbas' showmanship. He paced back and forth, dragging those holding his chains and shouting promises to the crowd. To a lot of people, he was much more alluring than Jesus, who remained standing quietly between two soldiers.

The woman beside Lydia tugged on her sleeve impatiently. "Why aren't you shouting? We have to save the Master!"

Lydia didn't know what to do. If she called for Jesus' release, and her voice was the last one needed to effect it, what would happen to the salvation promised by His death and resurrection? If she stayed silent, how would this woman beside her, and the rest of Jesus' followers, deal with her? She had no idea how long she would be among them, and she feared for her safety.

What happened next took care of her dilemma, but in a sinister and chilling way.

A new dimension seemed to take place in the midst of the crowd. From seemingly nowhere, but everywhere, came the sound of what sounded like a million voices. It filled the air, drowning out both sides of the divided crowd, yet blending in artfully.

Three words only:

"GIVE US BARABBAS!"

Lydia knew without hesitation that these voices came from all of humanity—past, present, and future—who rejected God's Way for an easier path. It was the voice of those who denied a relationship with Him in lieu of an easy life-style and self-centered living. It was the voice of the ages condemning and rejecting their Creator.

Knowing this, Lydia wept.

Pilate, upon hearing this statement, assumed it was the decision of the crowd before him. He called his attendant, who brought him a bowl of water and a towel. Then he looked on the crowd, who had gone silent, staring around to find the source of the loud voice they had all heard.

He spoke once again. "You have chosen Barabbas. Why, I cannot fathom. Knowing my soldiers, he will be dead within the week. But it is your choice."

He turned sadly to Jesus. "This man, who I have determined blameless, will be condemned to die as per your choice. As for me, I wash my hands of his blood." Saying this, he dipped his hands in the bowl and dried them with the towel.

From the silent crowd came an inebriated voice. "Let his blood be on us, and on our descendants!" he brayed. His friends, alarmed, tried to quiet him. He was still laughing as they dragged him out of the courtyard.

Lydia, her eyes welling with tears, shook her head sadly. Unfortunately, that statement would follow the Jewish people for the next two thousand years.

The crowd started buzzing, turned, and streamed back out to the street, as Jesus was dragged back onto the plaza.

Two burly men came through the crowd, sweating and grunting as they pulled a wooden cross between them. Jesus walked up to it, and, unbelievably, embraced the wood as if it was an old friend. The noise died in the crowd of onlookers as they watched him take the cross from the two men and place it on his own shoulder. He stood as if waiting for his next instructions.

The whole crowd moved as he was pushed and shoved towards the gate of the city. After he fell several times, Lydia saw a man being dragged from the crowd to help carry the cross. Not that the soldiers cared about their victim; they wanted to get this job finished and go off to get even more drunk. Some were uneasy; there was something about this man...

Another unbelievable thing! The prisoner stopped to talk to people along the way! Teaching and helping to the end! The crowd could only marvel at the sight.

The grief-stricken woman Lydia saw earlier went to embrace him, but was stopped roughly by one of the guards. The man in charge saw what was happening, and pushed the guard out of the way. "She's his mother—let her through!"

Lydia wept at the sight, thinking of her own family and how much she loved them. Would she be strong enough for a meeting such as this?

It wasn't long before they were all on the other side of the gates, and Jesus was pushed down on top of his cross. A few horrific hammer blows, and he was nailed to the wood. More blood flowed, *enough to cover the world for all generations*, said that Voice in Lydia's soul.

Not wanting to watch, but not being able to look away, Lydia stood and took in the sight for what seemed like hours.

Now, gasping for breath, Jesus looked about done in. He bowed his head, blood running from the ends of his hair and from his beard and nose.

Suddenly, he raised his head and shouted in a loud voice:

"My God, My God, why have You abandoned Me?"

Lydia suddenly recalled that she had said those same words the night Vlad took her away from all she had known and loved. Just before the scene faded to black in her mind, Lydia saw the Victim look directly at her. The Voice in her head softly, lovingly, gently said:

Yes, Lydia, I know your suffering. It is born of Mine. Once you swore to bear your cross for Me. Do not think you carry it alone. I am with you always.

CHAPTER 8

Lydia woke to light. Had she been asleep all that time? Or was it just a few minutes? She really couldn't tell.

Lydia. Remember.

The memory of what she had dreamt crashed down on her. It shook her, threatened to tear her very heart away. Lydia wept, as quietly as possible, but her necessarily silent actions betrayed her violent emotions. She pulled her hair, fanged her own arm, threw couch cushions, and pounded her fist into the surface of a rolled-up carpet.

Oh, how could I have betrayed my Lord? She was weak, cursed, exposed to the Light of Christ and found deeply in want. Prayer deserted her; she felt beyond salvation after the events of the dream and the important truths she had been reminded of.

Yet, even in her despair, there was some joy and hope mingled in as well. They were the first truly positive feelings she had had in who knows how many days. Would the Lord have shown her this only to condemn her at the last? The parting words from Him, in agony on the cross, gave her the first stirrings of hope for her own redemption, even with the transformation she had been forced to undergo.

Lydia looked over at the still-sleeping baby. From a distance, he looked like he still slept comfortably. That was a comfort; she felt she didn't dare approach the little thing. What if he woke up? How could she feed him, or minister to his needs? Most importantly, how could she get him back to his people? She was still victim to her own blood lust; that had not disappeared. Even now, she felt it growing in the pit of her stomach. To go over to him was asking for disaster.

Hearing the water dripping again, Lydia looked toward the window. The rains had come again, and water once more seeped in around the window frame. To her, that meant there was a weakness in it, and she thought maybe she could exploit that weakness and muscle the window open.

She paced, thinking.

Just as she came up with a good plan for getting the right leverage, the room went pitch black. Something was at the window, blocking the evening light. Looking up, she saw some commotion, as if someone was working right outside. She hurried over—maybe a gardener? Perhaps he could help her get out!

To her horror, it was Vlad! He was looking right at her, a large piece of wood in his hands. With an evil smile that turned her veins to ice, he put the board over the window. She yelled and begged him to stop, but to no avail. Presently there were thudding sounds against the other side of the wood, as if he was tossing large rocks down into the recess, then quiet.

Lydia rushed over and finally extricated the wooden table leg she had been working on earlier. She clambered up on the dresser and, with all of her strength, she swung the club against the window. Shards of glass rained down, and Lydia tried her hardest to push the window covering away. But it wouldn't budge. Too many rocks kept the board in place.

Screaming in frustration, she jumped down from the dresser and raced back and forth, trying to come up with another plan.

Lydia.

The Voice again!

Baptize the child, and quickly. His soul is in peril. The demon wishes to destroy him tonight.

"Umm, okay, but with what?" Lydia felt pity for the little mite, so innocent and undeserving of Vlad's cruelty.

Her eyes fell on the wooden bowl where it had landed after she threw it. She ran over and scooped it up. Taking it over to where the water still dripped from the window hole, she waited for it to fill to about a tablespoon's worth.

She then flew to the baby's side. He was beginning to stir, making little baby whimpers in his throat. Trying to ignore her raging need for blood, she prepared to pour the water on him. She stopped momentarily and looked up at the ceiling.

"Um, Voice? Sorry, I'm still not sure who you are. I mean, I think I know, but I don't dare...well...um..."

She couldn't help but stammer. The very thought of talking to Almighty God, her Creator and Savior, and having Him answer in a clear voice, was more than staggering. "This baby—I mean, is he okay? He's been asleep so long..."

He is safer this way.

"Um...okay." She wasn't going to question it.

Careful not to splash the water on herself, Lydia poured a little on his forehead, while saying the ancient words of the Rite of Baptism:

"I baptize you in the name of the Father..." another couple of drops, "...and of the Son..." the last of the water, "...and of the Holy Spirit."

With that, she put the bowl down and went to sit opposite the baby, just to watch him sleep. Her night vision was now so acute that, even without the light from the window, she could see as clearly as if it were day. It was a pleasure to watch the little chest rise and fall. She noticed that the hunger she had had earlier was gone, for which she was grateful.

The quiet was shattered by the sound of the basement door being slammed open, and Vlad's feet running down the stairs. Lydia turned to look at him and almost fainted from fright. Rage distorted his face, and he came at her swiftly and menacingly, fist raised.

"WHAT HAVE YOU DONE???"

"What? Wha...what do you mean?" Lydia was nearly gibbering with fear. She raised her arms over her head to protect herself. "I'm...I'm just sitting here...just sitting..."

"I heard you down here! Remember, we are connected mentally. What did you do to that child?"

"He's still asleep. If I'd done anything, wouldn't he have awakened?"

With a glance that could have cut diamonds, Vlad strode over to the baby and picked him up. He noticed the water still fresh on the child's head and whirled on Lydia. "Water! Those words! You've baptized this baby into your useless faith! I heard you! I left this creature here for you to feed on, not to adopt! You and your disgusting hold on that useless belief!"

He stopped his ranting and came at her with eyes narrowed. "I truly regret having brought you here."

Lydia matched his glare. "No more than I do, believe me!"

Vlad tossed the now-squalling infant back onto the couch as if the little boy was a sack of potatoes. Then he turned and lunged at

Lydia, mouth wide and fangs ready to tear her throat out. Lydia screamed and threw an arm up to protect herself.

Just as he reached her, he pulled back. His voice lost some of its rage, but he still seethed. Lydia could tell by the low, controlled way he was now talking. "No, that would be too easy. I knew you were going to be a challenge when I met you. This whole incident actually makes you a little more...intriguing. I would not want to lose such a precious supply of pure blood."

As he had been talking, half to himself, he had reached over in a flash and now had Lydia in a grip just strong enough to keep her from getting away. Terror-stricken and struggling, she found herself gasping and nearing hysteria, as he brought his head slowly closer and closer to her throat. He nuzzled her collarbone, working his way up to the most vulnerable area in her neck. She shut her eyes tight, grinding her nails into her hands, whimpering at the knowledge of the imminent attack.

"Oh, but wait, I forget." He pulled back, pointing to her throat. "Rat-tainted." He went over to the still-crying child and picked him up. Before Lydia could move, he had put two fang marks into the baby's chubby neck. Then he held out the screaming little boy to Lydia.

"There. You don't even have to work at it. Just lap up the blood, and we'll leave some life in him for later."

At first, Lydia backpedaled furiously in disgust. Then, realizing Vlad would destroy him, she rushed forward, intent on saving the baby's life. Blood streamed down his neck, pooling on the floor.

"NO! Nononono, don't! Don't hurt him!"

Vlad paused. He seemed to be thinking about something. After a moment, which seemed to be an eternity to Lydia, he turned and put the baby back down. "Very well. Perhaps that daughter of yours, tucked up so safely in her dorm room tonight; maybe she would like to join us. I wonder how she would taste..."

Lydia's eyes widened in surprise and horror. "No! Leave her alone! I'll do...I'll do anything. Just...don't hurt my family. Please!!"

Vlad picked the baby up again and thrust him at her. "Feed."

Lydia started crying. "Why? I don't understand why it's so important. Why this child?"

"Its blood will purify yours, and maybe I can stand you again."

"Oh, dear G—oh, no!"

Vlad's eyes sparked fire at the near-mention of the Name. "FEED!"

Crying harder, Lydia shakily put her tongue to the baby's open wounds, and, praying forgiveness, lapped up the blood welling in the fang marks. Immediately, she turned away and was sick.

Vlad looked on, disgusted. He made some sort of gesture, and the baby went quiet. He put him back down on his makeshift bed.

"Lydia, what am I to do with you? You do realize, don't you, that even if you don't feed, you cannot die. You will just go mad."

Lydia fell on her knees, begging. "I don't want this! Please, just let me go away from here!"

"And what do I get in exchange? Why should I let you go?"

Lydia didn't have an answer. She curled herself up on the floor, sobbing.

Suddenly, she realized he hadn't said anything for several minutes. Curious, she looked up at him. Her breath caught in her throat...

The leer on Vlad's face scared her more than his rage had when he had roared down the stairs earlier. He moved closer to her, and she scrambled backwards, away from him. She cringed as his eyes roamed over her.

A slight look of surprise replaced the leer, and he said, almost to himself, "This is interesting. I'd heard of this happening but have never experienced it myself."

"Wh...what..." Lydia tried to crabwalk backwards, away from him, unable to get far enough so that she could stand up and have a chance of fleeing from him. He kept coming closer, not allowing her the slightest possibility to get away.

He continued as he advanced, staring at Lydia with a strange look in his eyes, "I have fed almost exclusively on you for weeks, and in turn have given you of my blood. Our life fluids are now so mingled that, as you have changed, so have I. Not in my immortality, but in...other ways..."

Lydia gulped. "Meaning?" she barely whispered. Her whole being shook. *What new hell was he suggesting?*

Vlad leered again. "Meaning, my dear, that I find myself rather, shall we say, stirred up by your presence, your essence...your physicality..."

Oh, no, not that! Lydia shrank back again, whimpering high in her throat, and found herself against the hard surface of some piece of furniture.

"Oh, yes, Lydia, that! I was once mortal, and there are things one simply does not forget."

With a movement Lydia did not see coming, he reached over and tore off her gown.

Hours later, her entire body bruised and violated, Lydia lay in the darkness of the basement and wept. There wasn't a single part of her that didn't hurt. Vlad had been thorough; fang marks were everywhere. Even though she had attempted to wrap the remnants of the torn gown around her, she still felt vulnerable.

She looked up at the boarded-up window. A little sliver of moonlight was still able to get through. Looking at it reminded her once again of how she had felt when looking at the night sky as a child. Now her strong, sure knowledge of God's care had replaced her childish fantasies, and it gave her the strength to get up and stop feeling sorry for herself. Now was a time for action, she knew, although she didn't know what that action was going to be at the moment.

Even though she didn't need light with her new visual abilities, the light coming through still helped her to navigate the maze of furniture. She checked on the baby, who was still in whatever thrall Vlad had put him in. Then she went over to the window to pray. If there was going to be "action," she needed to be prepared for it.

She wasn't sure how it happened, but hours later she found herself prone on the floor, face down, her arms straight out from her sides in the form of a cross. Also, when she put up her head, she found that she had smeared blood on the wall in the shape of a cross. Looking alarmed, she glanced over to the baby, but saw to her relief that she had fanged her own arm and used that blood to draw it.

There was a strangled sound behind her, and she looked around. To her terror, she found that she had discovered what she had done at the same time as Vlad, who had come down to see if her blood was palatable again. He stood stock-still at the foot of the stairs.

Then, in a towering rage, he boomed, "WHAT IS THIS???" in a voice so loud even the rats scattered for refuge.

Lydia thought to join them, and had indeed gotten halfway up, but Vlad caught her by the arm. He yanked her roughly up off the floor, which caused many of the wounds on her exposed skin to open up again.

She just stared at him, wild-eyed.

He shook her hard. "I've given you all the chances I'm going to!" he screamed at her, his face inches from hers.

With that, he plunged his fangs into her jugular and drank without stopping, until there was not a drop of blood left in Lydia's poor body.

He tossed her to the floor and strode over to the baby. As the light faded from Lydia's eyes, she had to behold one more atrocity. Vlad took the child, reared back, and tore out the little throat. He drained the child's body and tossed it over at Lydia.

"Dessert," he sneered, and with that he marched back up the stairs, not even bothering to close the door this time.

CHAPTER 9

The darkness in the silent basement was absolute. No light came through the space at the top of the boarded-up window, as clouds obscured the night sky outside.

After a time, a dim glow seemed to seep through the ceiling, and suddenly it turned into a brilliant light. It shone brighter than the day, sending the shadows to hide wherever they could. Swiftly it came, and parted into two columns of light, as it came to rest beside the two deathly-still figures lying blood-soaked on the floor.

The columns quickly became human in shape; light-filled beings of indeterminate age and gender. They bent over the mutilated forms of Lydia and the baby, deftly picked them up, and disappeared with their burdens, leaving the cellar as dark and sinister as before.

What woke Lydia from her near-death coma was the feeling of the wind on her face and the coldness of the night air. Her eyes flew open, and she looked into the face of the being carrying her.

She felt as if she should be trying to get away, since the events of the past...what, week? Month? Eternity?...should have caused her to believe the worst, but the being gave off such a feeling of love and peace that all fear fled from her mind.

However...

"Who are you? Where are you taking me?"

The being looked down at her and smiled. "The Master has need of you. We are taking you to Him."

Lydia trembled a little. "By 'Master', who do you mean, exactly?"

Then her guide looked into her eyes, and Lydia could see the joy of eternity in its gaze. Happiness flooded her; was she being taken to Heaven?

Suddenly, a horrible thought occurred to her. She found herself overcome by fear; what if this was the only time she would witness and experience eternal happiness? What if...?

She put a tentative tongue up to explore her teeth. *Oh, no! Still fanged!*

She started to cry. "No, no, no, oh please! Oh please! I can't see Him like this! I'm cursed, unclean, disgusting!"

An even worse memory finally claimed its place in her mind. She could hardly contain her horror. "The baby! Oh, the poor child! I...I didn't want it to happen! I was weak! My family! I'm so sorry...so sorry!"

The being smiled gently at her. "We have the baby. All will be well," it assured her.

Lydia's mind faded out, and she slept.

The first thing she noticed when she woke again, even before she opened her eyes, was that she was once again lying face-down on a cold, hard floor.

A dream! she thought. *I'd only dreamed about being spirited away from this hellhole!*

Right before depression engulfed her, she noticed something else; the smell of years of incense, furniture polish, and spent candle wax. Opening her eyes, she found herself inside a church, lying prostrate in front of the tabernacle. The only light came from two candles on the altar and the candle in the red sconce beside the Tabernacle that held the Sacrament. No one else was in the building, but two orbs hovered unseen near the ceiling, as though watching the scene below.

Lydia was so relieved at where she found herself that she almost laughed out loud.

Unfortunately, her joy was short-lived. A bundle lay cold and still beside her, the poor little baby, torn asunder by Vlad and left to die.

At the sight, she began to weep, softly at first, stroking the now-dead little face. Then the events of her captivity and mutilation, her horror and loathing, both of Vlad, and what she had become, overtook her. She wailed and screamed, tearing at her hair and beating on the floor with her fists. She lay before the tabernacle, howling with pain and desperation born of her brutal incarceration. "Dear God, my God, please! I didn't want this! I am so sorry! I was weak! Weak, and because of it, this little boy died! Oh, God, forgive me! Help me!"

She went on for some time, and in her pain did not notice a figure letting himself in at the side door.

The parish priest had noticed the candlelight from his residence next door, and, believing that intruders or transients had somehow gotten into the locked building, had come over to investigate.

He was a good man; he would do whatever he could to help in whatever way he could. If the intruders were thieves, well, perhaps their break-in could be forgotten if they would be frightened off by his intervention.

Never in his wildest nightmares did he expect to see what his eyes beheld. A woman in a torn, blood-soaked gown, hair wild and her skin torn in a million places that he could see, bent over a...a what?

He stepped closer.

A...dead child??

Was this woman an escapee from some dreadful ogre of a husband or boyfriend, seeking sanctuary in the church? How did she get in? He had checked all the locks that night himself.

Also, why had she lit the altar candles?

He came closer, stepping out of the shadows, intent on helping her. Lydia heard him as he came closer. What was worse, she smelled him. Smelled his blood. Heard his heartbeat, faster because of his surprise at seeing her here. Her throat went dry, and she felt her stomach knot as the now-familiar red mist clouded her vision.

The priest reached out to touch her shoulder, and was almost paralyzed in fear by the shock when she whipped her head around.

Mouth gaping, fangs bared, her eyes glowed red, and she leapt up. With super-human speed, she grabbed him and forced him up against the altar. As she went for his throat, the orbs of light flew down from the ceiling and passed between Lydia and her intended victim. Sparks flew, and Lydia shrieked and fell back.

The priest, scared beyond sense, fled toward the door.

He was stopped short by her cry. "Father! Please! Don't leave me! I...I won't hurt you! Just...keep your distance! For the sake of your life, please! But stay...I need you to help me!"

He turned around, but stayed where he was, horror-stricken at the visage he was seeing. Such a thing didn't actually exist, he was sure of it! He knew they were only stories! Was she play-acting? Insane? What was her intent in playing such a horrid trick?

No, he could see that her wounds were very real. And her throat! How could she be that...that...pulverized, and still live?

The baby! He looked at the small form in alarm...then looked back at Lydia. A horrible understanding came over him, and he turned deathly pale. It looked as if he would run again.

Lydia had to stop him. She needed him to stay, if she was ever to return to a normal life.

"No! No, Father! I didn't do this! The one who cursed me destroyed this child! I wouldn't do this! Please believe me!"

The priest relaxed a little, but still backed away, trying to put more distance between him and this...this...what? Poor cursed woman? Or she-devil?

"Please, Father, don't leave! I..." She cocked her head, as if listening. Then a look of sheer panic came over her face. "Oh, no! Oh, sweet Jesus, no! He knows I'm here! Oh, Father, please!" She looked at him imploringly. "You must help me!"

Swallowing his fear, the priest finally found the ability to speak. "What...what can I do?" He really didn't know what to say or do, since he was so overcome by panic and fear. However, being the good soul that he was, he knew he had to at least stay long enough to hear what she had to say.

He watched as the woman looked toward the tabernacle as if listening to someone. Then she turned to him with a new resolve in her eyes. It was as if an unheard voice was giving her direction. The panic and fear were still there, but they were accompanied by a determination and hope that were missing before.

He was truly surprised by her next statement.

"Father, you must hear my confession."

His mouth opened and shut without the ability to reply. This was certainly not what he had expected!

Lydia tried to explain. "I don't know how long I've been held captive, but I do know that, before this time, I did have a life. I lived. I have a husband and two grown children. I went to church, received the Sacraments. I am now...undead! Cursed!" She started crying again, despair etched in her face. "Please! The Sacraments must be made available to me now! They are the only path I have to salvation and freedom!"

The priest moved a little closer, but she held up a hand in warning. He could see that it was covered with what looked like bite marks, like the rest of her visible skin, but how old the wounds were or who had done them he had no way of knowing. He did, however, know that it was not his place to decide. He had taken a sacred oath as a priest to care for all of God's people, and he knew that vow must extend even to this strange, mutated, and mutilated creature.

"Yes...yes, of course!" He sat down in the front pew and waited for her to begin her confession, as if she was a regular parishioner on a regular day. It all seemed so unreal to him, but he felt somehow that it was imperative that he comply with her request.

Lydia began, but not in a way that the priest had foreseen.

"Under pain of the loss of my very soul, I swear to you that I did not kill this baby."

She put her face in her hands and wept. "Oh, Father! I was weak, and so hungry, and overcome by bloodlust! I am so ashamed; I did lap up some of his blood after my tormentor opened the child's veins! I...oh dear God!...killed rats and consumed their blood as well! None of this did I want to do! And now I am here, and I almost killed you! I don't know why this is happening, or why I am here now, or even *where* I am! I don't know what to do anymore!"

Lapsing into silence, Lydia hugged herself, trying to keep out the nightmares that flooded her mind. She rocked back and forth, moaning. Occasionally she would stroke the dead child, as if comforting him.

He tried to wait for her to go on, but his curiosity soon got the better of him. In the silence, he couldn't help but ask. "How did you get in here anyway?"

She looked confused. "I'm not really sure. I remember being carried through the night, and a beautiful, peaceful face looking down at me, but everything else is too fuzzy to remember..."

They both looked up as the silent orbs floating above them flashed a brief, bright light, and then they remembered how those lights had broken up the perilous lock Lydia had had on the priest. Did these orbs have something to do with how she got here? They both gazed and wondered silently.

The lights above them flashed golden, dove down, and circled around them. An aura of gentleness and peace emanated from them, a feeling that was relayed to the humans watching in wonder from the semi-darkness of the church below.

Lydia bowed her head as the priest spoke the ancient words of absolution. He wanted to put his hand on her head as a blessing, but a look from her warned him to continue keeping his distance.

Instead, she moved away to the other side of the altar, away from him and the tabernacle. He knew what she was going to ask for next, even before she spoke. "Now, Father, please allow me to receive the Eucharist. Only the Sacred Body and Blood of Jesus can save me from this curse."

Once again, she got that look on her face, as though she could hear something he was not aware of. Then, she stared in abject terror towards the darkness at the back of the church. She looked wild-eyed at the priest. "Please hurry! He's coming! You must get away and hide before he gets here; I know he'll kill you if he knows...oh, no, he already does! Quickly! Hurry!"

The priest was himself near panic. He stammered, "How...how can anyone know...?"

Lydia started breathing in short gasps as fear spread throughout her body, not so much for herself, but for the man so valiantly trying to help her in spite of his own shock at the events of this night. "Our blood is mingled, and somehow it joins our minds also. My connection to him is weak, but when he is angry, as he is right now, I can read him all too easily!"

Upon hearing this, the priest sped to the tabernacle doors and extracted the paten, which holds the Bread of Life during Mass. He brought out a wafer of unleavened bread and quickly said the words of consecration over it.

A chalice was on a side table, as preparation for the early Mass in the morning. He picked it up, along with the cruets of water and wine. Pouring the wine into the chalice, he mixed some of the water in it, said the consecration, and made as if to bring both the Bread and Wine to Lydia.

She shrank back. "No! I can't trust myself not to attack you. When anything that has blood running in its veins comes near me, all I want to do, all I can think of doing, is to drain it of its life force. I will not do that! As God is my savior, I will not!"

The priest cautiously set the paten and chalice on the side table and hurried back to his seat. Lydia moved towards the table, but then stopped and looked at him, desperation in her eyes. "Leave! Now! He'll be here any minute!"

"But...the paten! The chalice! The...the baby!"

"Leave them for now!" Lydia's voice had taken on a voice of command, one he felt he had to obey, and God help him if it was the wrong choice.

"Go!" she said. "But don't let me see you leave; if I don't know where you've gone, he can't follow you from reading your whereabouts in my mind. And he *will* look for you, believe me!" She closed her eyes. "Leave! Please!"

He hurried off into the shadows as quietly as he could, exiting though a different door and making his way quickly back to his house. Poor frightened man that he was, the moment he got inside the door, he called the emergency number for the police.

Meanwhile, Lydia had approached the Eucharist. Falling on her knees, she prayed, and, picking up the Host, quickly put It into her mouth. The sudden pain throughout her body was horrendous. The touch of the consecrated Host to her tongue burned it as if she had swallowed fire.

Trying to pay no heed to the pain, Lydia held up the chalice. Through teared-up eyes, she put the cup to her lips, noticing briefly that she did not reflect in its surface. Swallowing the Sacred Blood, she had just enough time to place the cup back on the table before she fell to the floor in a fit of convulsion.

Her eyes bulged, her throat constricted, and she found herself unable to breathe for what seemed an eternity. A horrible blackness rose in her, filling her sight, and she screamed out in terror and pain.

The blackness poured forth from within her, and she saw the orbs above her quickly dive down. They expanded and surrounded the evil emanating from her. The light swirled for an instant and then consumed its captive. It transformed again into the two orb shapes, which wafted back up to the ceiling to continue their vigilance.

At peace for the first time in what seemed like a lifetime, Lydia sat up. Almost afraid to look, fearing what she might, or might not see, she slowly turned her gaze to the surface of the chalice.

She broke out in tears of relief. She could see herself! Opening her mouth, she saw only normal teeth in her reflection, and her skin was as fresh and new as if she had never been mutilated!

Best of all, she no longer felt a connection between her mind and the vampire's. Her mental imprisonment was over also! Forgiven in Reconciliation and safeguarded against the forces of evil with the Eucharist, Lydia prostrated herself towards the altar and praised her King and Lord.

"Thank you, Heavenly Father! Thank you, my Lord Jesus! Thank you, Holy Spirit!" She lay on the floor, repeating those words over and over, and basking in her return to normal existence.

Then, His Voice again:

Prepare, Lydia. The demon is here.

Lydia couldn't believe it! She was still in danger! She almost envied the dead little body on the floor by the altar. At least he was beyond Vlad's grasp...

The Voice cut into her thoughts:

Remember, you are Mine, paid for with great cost. Remember that, Lydia. No one can take you from Me. Not your soul, not who you really are! Only if you turn from Me will you run the risk of losing Me!

Lydia looked up, eyes filling with tears. "No, Lord! Heaven help me, I don't ever want to lose You!"

Suddenly a jolt of pure, joyous energy shot through her. It poured through her very soul, causing an ecstasy that she had never felt before. It strengthened her, fulfilled her, made her very being come alive.

Then, almost immediately, came a cold voice from the shadows behind her. "Did you really think you could get away that easily?"

CHAPTER 10

Lydia spun around, still on her knees. Vlad was halfway up the aisle of the church, slowly and deliberately making his way to where she was.

She scrambled up and ran towards the altar, diving under it as Vlad got to the bottom of the steps leading up to where she cowered. He did not venture any further, however; instead, he paced back and forth in front of them, staring at Lydia as if she was an animal in a cage. Finally, he spoke.

"I can understand how you would be able to get out of my house, had you been in any shape to move. I did leave the door open, but where did you get the strength? Furthermore, how did you get here?"

Lydia kept silent, not knowing if he could still read her mind. Somehow, she felt that he should not know about the beings, which she now knew were angels, that had transported her here (wherever "here" was), and that they were even now hovering above them.

He glanced toward the floor in front of the tabernacle. "And you brought the child as well." Then he glared back at Lydia. "Did you really think that hiding in a church would do you any good? I tell you, your pathetic devotion to this, whatever it is, is useless."

It was apparent to Lydia that Vlad could come no further than where he was in front of the altar. She was protected in this area. It was sacred ground, and the demons that had such free rein over the earth still could not approach it. God was worshipped here, and the Body and Blood of Jesus was miraculously present on this very altar at every Mass. No wonder Vlad could not come up and take hold of her!

Empowered by this realization, Lydia came out and stood up in front of the altar. She looked him in the eye. And she felt—nothing. No weakness, no loss of consciousness, no being drawn into his thrall. He no longer had control over her!

Vlad, in turn, noticed that Lydia's skin was as smooth and clear as on the first day he saw her. Being who he was, there was no room in his mind for the idea of divine intervention as the reason for this miracle. He believed himself to be more powerful than any other force in the universe, or beyond. Such are the allures and lies of the ways of evil. Instead, he said, "Well, you do heal quickly. Good. You were running out of fresh areas for me to feed on.

"Now, I thirst. Come down from there."

He smirked as an idea came to him. "Actually, this is an ideal place to get, shall we say, reacquainted. At the feet of your plaster Savior!"

Lydia stood her ground. "No," she said firmly. "Not anymore. In God alone is my strength, and in my weakness, God has made me strong. You have no more power over me."

Vlad howled, beside himself with rage. He leapt up onto the first step, only to fall back, hissing, his fangs bared.

Lydia watched as he paced again. Suddenly he stopped, and an evil smile came to his lips. He turned back to Lydia and, pointing toward the side door, said, "You leave me no choice. I am hungry, and do not wish to go any longer without feeding."

Lydia looked towards the door, which seemed to open on its own.

She gasped as the priest walked in! He made his way slowly towards Vlad, his face expressionless.

"Father! No!" Lydia screamed, but he didn't seem to hear her. He merely continued walking toward the vampire.

She watched helplessly, shaking in fear for the poor man. "Father! Don't look at him! Look away, close your eyes, anything! You're in danger! Don't you see?"

Heedless to her words, he just kept his slow, steady pace forward.

Lydia acted at the same time as the orbs of light. They dove down as she sprinted out of the altar area and shoved the priest out of the way of Vlad's hungry grasp. He landed on the floor, blinking, surprised and confused as to where he was. The orbs circled him like watchdogs guarding their Master's treasure.

Lydia glared at Vlad. "He is not yours either!" she hissed at him. "Leave this place!"

Vlad pushed her, and she landed hard on the stone floor. He tried to leap on the priest, who, horrified at what had almost happened to him, was attempting to get as far away as he could. The lights stayed right with the cleric, one on either side, although he did not realize it.

Lydia got up and ran at Vlad, pulling on his arm in a vain attempt to stop him. However, she no longer had the demonic strength she had had when the curse was on her. "Leave him alone!" she screamed.

Vlad turned quickly and got her shoulders in a vise-like grip. He snarled into her face. "I will not leave until my hunger is satisfied!!"

Lydia, who had been fighting his hold on her, suddenly went limp. She closed her eyes for a moment, then opened them, stared at Vlad for a moment, then quietly said, "Then take me. Don't destroy this man's life."

Vlad was surprised for a moment, and then he started chuckling deep in his throat. "Am I to understand that you would give yourself to me, just to keep this man safe? Do you honestly believe that your 'sacrifice' would keep him alive? After all I've done, do you really think I would keep any sort of bargain? You should know by now that the only promises I keep are the ones I make to myself! What would keep me from tearing out your throat, again I might add, and then doing away with him?"

Lydia sighed and nodded. "Yes, I realize all of this, but what choice do I have?" Her eyes shone with a new resolve. "But if I didn't at least try to help him, to protect him, I'd be as damned as you."

Vlad shook his head. "Poor misguided Lydia. You have no idea what you can be at my side."

"I do know what I cannot be, and that is saved! To feel the warmth and love of Jesus Christ as I walk with Him in eternity. That is worth dying for a thousand people and more!"

Sirens could be heard in the distance. As they got nearer, Lydia knew in her heart that the approaching emergency and police units were on their way to this place; she could see the priest moving towards the back of the church to intercept them.

Vlad knew as well. He turned his head to listen. Then he turned back to Lydia, in a full rage. "Fool!" he sneered. "Many lives will be lost tonight, and it will be your fault!" He stared coolly down into Lydia's eyes, whose gaze met his without fear.

He whispered as he pulled her closer, "Yours will be first, and I will make sure you stay dead this time!"

Lydia turned her head, exposing her throat to him, and said, "You might be able to kill this body, but my soul lives forever!"

Enraged, Vlad bared his fangs and struck her as hard as he could, puncturing skin and sinew, rending her flesh and tearing a great hole in her throat. Once again, he drained her of every drop of blood.

Then he dropped her, feeling only vaguely sorry that he would not taste her blood again. Still, there was another option waiting innocently for him...

The police entered first through the back doors of the church, the EMTs waiting outside until needed. What their eyes beheld made even the most seasoned veteran shrink back in fear. There, up at the front of the church, at the very front of the altar, two figures were locked in an embrace of death. Then, one of them slumped to the ground in a heap, while the other turned and faced the officers at the door.

What they saw terrified them beyond anything they had ever witnessed before. Some were so frightened that they ran back outside, but a few of them stayed, guns pointed, arms quaking, too shocked and stunned to move.

The ghastly figure started toward them, covered in his victim's blood. His sharp fangs gleamed red as he hissed. Spitting out the shred of flesh he still had had in his mouth, he showed his teeth in an open-mouthed grimace, bore down on the trembling police officers...

...and disappeared!

The officers blinked and looked at each other. Had they imagined all of this?

No! The woman slumped in front of the altar was still there. They moved cautiously up the aisle to have a closer look.

She had to be dead...there wasn't enough left of her throat to be able to breathe.

The officers were about to call in the EMTs when, incredibly, they saw her move!

Incredulous, they saw the mutilated victim stretch herself prone on the floor and reach both arms toward the tabernacle. They could see a puddle of blood under her head. She again lay still, and those present were sure that she was beyond help.

Two orbs of light caught their attention; they swirled seemingly randomly, and then touched down on either side of the altar. The lights shimmered and stretched, forming themselves into humanlike figures. The police officers fell onto their knees, dumbfounded at the sight.

The two glowing shapes suddenly went down on their own knees as well, facing the tabernacle. New light filled the room, blazingly bright, scattering and obliterating all shadows in the church. The officers, now joined by the EMTs and the priest, who had all walked, amazed, up to the front of the church, could only kneel and look on in wonder.

The beings of light fell to their faces as a third Figure took shape before the altar. It was a Man, but none such as the group had ever seen before. He gazed on them all with love, but also with a power and authority that exceeded time and eternity.

He was Eternal.

He was Jesus.

This knowledge was overwhelming; the mortals present knew Who this was in their hearts and minds without a doubt. Why this was happening, they did not know. They just knew it for what it was: a miracle.

They watched as He bent down and took the woman up in His arms. He kissed her forehead, and she stirred.

Lydia heard voices. She felt warmth, and peace, and absolute relief that her trial was over. She was happy and content to just float with her eyes closed forever.

Then, it all crashed around her as she became conscious in her body once again. The pain from her ravaged throat was excruciating, and she worked her mouth, trying to scream. But since she had no way of using her throat, there was only silence as she writhed.

Hands. Gentle hands, lifting her. A Voice, calling her name.

It was understandable, considering the torments she had gone through, that Lydia's first instinct was to fight the embrace she felt herself in. She squeezed her eyes shut, refusing to look, and twisted, trying to break away. No more lies! No more deceptions!

She suddenly stopped.

The Voice! That Voice again! Calm, beckoning, pleading with her.

"Lydia! Quiet, please, quiet. You are safe. I am here."

It was not coming from within her! Incredibly, she seemed to be hearing it from outside her spirit! Were her ears deceiving her?

Lydia felt that sweet rush of peace within her soul again. Still, she was confused and afraid. Did she dare trust? The soaring hope, always followed by despair, fear, and horror as she found herself back under Vlad's power.

Through the red, searing pain, she felt she just could not bear any more, and she prayed for death.

"Lydia. I am Life."

At these words, she opened her eyes, and found herself looking into the Face she had longed to see for as long as she could remember. It was a Face that had seen all of eternity, all of mankind's rises and falls, had been one of His own people for a time.

She could only stare in wonder, only vaguely aware that she was alive and yet unable to breathe. Her heart, freshly beating with the new life with which He had infused it, was throbbing so wildly and ecstatically with love that she thought it would burst.

He smiled gently at her, and as she gazed back into His eyes, she could see the majesty and power that belonged only to her Lord and Savior. A new happiness welled up in her as she realized: He had come for her!

Lydia felt a gentle, caressing hand on her torn throat, and the horrible pain was instantly gone. She wanted to laugh, to sing, to shout His praises. Instead, she merely put her arms around His neck, like a child safe in its parent's embrace. He silently held her close, His head against hers.

Unaccountably, this loving gesture caused her to start crying. She thought of all she had done, and hadn't done, in her life, and her relationships with the people who had come in and out of the scope of her existence.

Was this her personal judgment day? She was still not wholly aware of where she was. She had the horrible notion that she was about to lose Him due to the deeds of her lifetime that she was ashamed of, and her sobs grew harder. They came to a keening crescendo as she thought of what had happened ever since she had met Vlad.

"Oh, my Lord! I'm such a wretch! Less than nothing! I've been weak! I'm a loss! That poor baby!"

He caressed her, rocking her back and forth as they stood at the altar. Then He gently pushed her back so that she had a clear look into His eyes. "It is forgiven, Lydia. Do you not trust My words? My priest, my son, has given you absolution in My Name. Believe in that, and forgive yourself on the strength of My having forgiven you. If you do not forgive yourself, you will never fully heal."

"But...but...the little boy..."

"He is safe, where no evil can ever touch his soul. You made that possible by baptizing him. If nothing else has saved you, your actions and obedience to My command, even at the risk of the loss of your mortal life, has done so."

Then He pulled her back into His embrace, and she stayed there, hoping to never part from it.

"Lord," she whispered, "let me go home with You. Please! It's all I've ever wanted since I chose You above anything that this life has to offer."

She could feel Him smile, and He held her closer for a moment. He kissed the top of her head, and she felt as if she was going to melt with love. She could hear him whisper, "Yes, and I have not forgotten that. I never will. It is what has drawn Me to you. It is why I have a mission for you to fulfill as My chosen messenger."

It became clear to Lydia that her existence on earth would continue, and it was almost too much for her to bear. She started crying again, clinging to Him. "Lord, don't leave me! I can't possibly exist without you!"

He put His hands on her shoulders and once again looked at her with all the beauty and goodness and peace of eternity. "My daughter, you never have. Your life has always belonged to Me."

He let go of her shoulders and took her hands in His. She watched, incredulous and scarcely breathing, as He kissed both of her wrists, then her forehead. "I have sealed you against the trials to come. Don't be afraid. Trust in Me."

Giving her one last embrace, He looked towards the people before Him. "My son, Father Samuel!" he called.

The priest came forward from the group. He could barely speak, so stunned was he at what had occurred. "Y-yes, Lord?"

Jesus looked at Lydia, then back at Fr. Samuel. "Take her to your house and give her something to eat. Then find her husband. He has been searching in desperation, and he will be overjoyed to have his wife back."

Then He held up His hands, and light shot from the nail scars on His wrists. It fell on all those assembled, and all felt the blessing of the Eternal One of God.

The light dimmed as He disappeared, escorted by His angels. At the same time, the sun came over the distant mountains, bathing them with the rosy hue of a new day.

CHAPTER 11

Steve stared vacantly out the kitchen window, a cup of coffee on the table in front of him. Another night without sleep. Another morning rising, alone, to another bleak day of watching and waiting.

Where was she? It was so frustrating! The police, the search and rescue teams, the—he hated to think of it—forensics teams, they'd all looked diligently. Airports, train stations, state borders, hospitals of every type. They'd all been alerted, and every passenger and patient scrutinized.

Nothing.

Over a full month since he'd last heard her voice, and that only briefly. Remorse filled him; he hadn't even listened to her! Had she been in trouble even then? He couldn't remember how she had sounded when he had called her that night. He'd been so full of his own excitement and news, most of which he hadn't shared with her, confident that he would be able to fill her in when he got home. In that short call, in which he'd told her that he was being re-routed to Austria, he'd been so distracted by what was going on around him that he had cut her off. Now he deeply regretted it.

He raked his fingers through his hair in frustration. Thoughts of guilt were ramming their way back into his conscience.

The night she'd disappeared, he had gotten the word from corporate that he was getting a raise and a promotion, and he was just heading out to celebrate when he called Lydia. Now the happiness he had felt was gone, replaced by hollow regret.

Three days later, he had gotten a call from their local sheriff's office. His neighbor had noticed Lydia's car had been absent, and there were a couple of newspapers in the driveway. There was no answer when she had gone over to check on her, and she had grown worried and called the police. Lydia never went away overnight without telling someone, either her family or her neighbors. Usually both.

Her co-workers had not seen her either. They remembered that she had worked late on the last night she'd been at work, but no one was too worried about her safety. After all, they reasoned, Ned had been on duty, and he was the best security officer they had.

Then Ned had turned up missing as well, and suddenly the possibilities took on an entirely different angle. Now there was a hunt on for two people. Had they gone off together? Willingly, or did someone take them both by force? No one seemed to have any leads.

Steve had flown home immediately, where his kids, Trudy and Pat, were waiting for him. The police filled the three of them in on what little they had come up with so far. There wasn't much to go on. Lydia's car had been found in the parking lot at work, undisturbed. There were no signs of trouble; no torn bits of clothing, no scratch marks on the car, no signs of breaking and entering, and certainly no personal items. However, the forensics team had found crushed greenery and broken branches in the woods surrounding the parking lot. It looked as if someone had run through them in some haste.

Then the worst; a great deal of blood at the base of a tree. Alarms went off in everyone's heads until the team turned up another poor mutilated animal nearby. The team took blood samples, hoping against hope that the two findings were related, and that they were merely dealing with another mysteriously savaged animal.

However, and this was what sickened Steve now, the blood samples turned out to be human, and of the same blood type as his wife's. But if it was from Lydia, where was she? With that much loss, how could she have made it out of the woods? More to the point, where did she go? The only thing he could hope for was that, since her body had not been found, she would be found alive somewhere.

Since this discovery, he had been scarcely eating or sleeping. Work was out of the question, as he could barely concentrate on even the most simple of tasks.

The only news in the past week was a mixed blessing. The finding of the security guard in a hotel room several hundred miles away solved the question of the connection between Lydia's and Ned's disappearances. The manager of the hotel had called the police, having heard on the news that Ned and his car were being sought.

The police knocked on the door, and, when there was no answer, had the manager use his key to gain entrance. They found

Ned, cowering in a corner, gibbering to himself. When they approached him, he screeched in fright and tried to duck under a table. They finally had to call an ambulance and a special team to bundle him out of the hotel and get him checked into a nearby hospital.

What was even more disturbing than Ned's behavior were the marks on his throat. It looked as if a large predatory animal had attacked him. The marks were scarred over, but he wouldn't let anyone near enough to have a good look at them.

Steve's thoughts were disrupted by the sound of floorboards creaking upstairs, and was once again grateful that the kids were with him at this time. What would he have done without their support? He wondered briefly if they were able to keep up with their studies while at home, and shook his head briefly at himself in irritation. How could he expect them to do so, if he himself could hardly concentrate on the day-to-day aspects of living?

He poured his coffee down the drain, rinsed his cup, and put it in the dishwasher. Then he went into the family room and did what he had been doing every day for a month—he flopped down in his chair, turned on the TV, and flipped through the channels without really noticing what was on.

Lydia'd pitch a fit, he thought. Then a sharp jolt of pain and loss hit him, and his eyes filled with tears. Choking back a sob, he reached over and picked up the phone to call the sheriff. He should be at his desk by now; it was time to get the latest information on what they had found out about Lydia.

Pat lay awake, staring at the ceiling, where the posters from his childhood still stared back at him. He had not had much luck sleeping either, but he was used to it. Being in college meant that sleep was a rare commodity. Thank heavens for modern technology! He had been able to attend lectures from home via the school intranet. So far, he had been able to keep up with the classwork and lectures; fortunately, his teachers all said that he could make up any lab work any time before the end of the term. Since that was several weeks away, Pat felt confident that he would be able to meet that requirement.

That is, if Mom is found, he thought.

The thought jolted him.

No, WHEN she is found!

He was shocked at himself. Was he already giving up? No, he wouldn't do that, but what hadn't already been tried? The only thing Pat knew for certain was that his mother had to be alive. She had to be! He refused to believe anything else!

He shifted to get a little more comfortable on the bed he'd outgrown, and heard something slide off the bed to thump onto the wood floor. Looking over the edge, he saw that it was his cell phone. Picking it up, he noticed that there was a message on it.

His hopes rising, he stabbed at the message icon to see who had called, hoping that it was his mom, and that everything would be okay now. It was a short-lived optimism, however; the message was from his baseball coach. The team needed him to play the first few games of the season while one of the members nursed an injury. The coach knew of Pat's circumstances, though; he said he would put in a temporary substitute until Pat could get back, but he also said that he couldn't hold the position for him for long. In other circumstances, the call would have thrilled Pat, but it all seemed so trivial now.

He sighed. The chance of his college sports career! However, he was not about to head callously back to school while Mom was still missing. That was one resolution he would not go back on! Even if he had to take an extra term to make up for his absences, he was not leaving his dad and sister until...whatever the outcome.

Blinking back tears, Pat sat up. *No sense dwelling on things here in bed. Time to get moving.*

He thought of his dad. He was probably down there with the TV going. Pat shook his head sadly. *Poor Dad,* he thought, as he put on his running clothes.

Pat had tried to get his dad interested in going out for a run or a walk, the way they used to when Pat was still living at home. *It would be good for him to get some fresh air and get his mind off things he had no control over, but Dad won't have anything to do with it. Pity...it would do him a world of good.*

Pat ran down the stairs and into the family room. *Yep, Dad, TV, chair, phone. All present and accounted for.*

"Hey, Dad."

Steve looked up from staring blankly at the TV screen. "Oh, hi, Pat. Sleep well?"

"No."

"Hmph. Me neither."

Same conversation, but what else was there to say?

Pat fidgeted. "I'm going running. Dare I ask if you'd like to come along?"

Steve slowly shook his head, his attention turned back to the screen, where the local news was relating a story about a fire on the east end of town. "No, the sheriff is supposed to call in a few minutes. He was a little late getting in today, so I'm waiting for him to call me back."

Pat squeezed his dad's shoulder. "Okay, Dad. See you in a bit."

As he turned to go, Steve looked up again. "Pat?"

His son turned back. "Yes, Dad?"

"Remember there's a special Mass tonight, to pray for your mom."

Pat almost rolled his eyes but thought better of it. Any means to get his dad out of the house for awhile. He had lost hold of his own faith while away on his own, and when his mom went missing and remained gone, he had given up almost entirely. He thought to himself, *well, if it gives Dad comfort...*

"Okay, Dad. I'll be here."

Steve smiled. "Thanks. It means a lot."

Pat smiled at him, turned toward the door, and trotted out of the house.

Trudy watched her brother jog down the street, then turned away from her bedroom window. Wearily, she walked back to her bed and lay down. She picked up a book, thumbed through a few pages, and put it back on the nightstand. Then she got back up and paced the room.

She wished she had gone running with Pat, but knew she wouldn't be able to keep up with his long-legged stride. The exercise seemed to help him deal with this nightmare they were all in; Trudy used what little yard work she could do for the same reason.

For the last few days, after trimming and pruning the landscape to within an inch of its life, she had started digging up the area where her mom usually planted a vegetable garden every spring. Ever optimistic, Trudy thought it would be a nice surprise when her mom got back from wherever she was.

This morning, though, Trudy was almost too weary to move, much less work in the garden. Although she had slept fairly well, she had had nightmares that had left her exhausted by the time the sun came up.

She managed to finally get up enough energy to put on her bathrobe, and trudged downstairs. Her dad was on the phone with the sheriff; once again, he didn't sound too encouraged.

After shuffling into the kitchen and pouring herself some coffee, Trudy came back out and sat across from her dad. She watched his face as he spoke into the phone.

"Okay, Sheriff. I'll sit tight and wait. Oh!" Steve thought of something. "Remember to check where those two sisters thought they...oh, that's right, you did. Sorry, it's just that...right. Okay," he sighed, "talk to you later."

He hung up and rubbed his eyes. Then he noticed Trudy. *How much she looks like her mother! Especially in the morning, before all that procedure with the makeup.* His heart lurched with love and sorrow.

Trudy smiled and reached out a hand to him. "'Mornin,' Dad."

He reached across as well. "'Mornin,' love. How was your night?"

Now it was Trudy's turn to rub her eyes. She pinched the bridge of her nose, then shook her head to clear out the cobwebs. "Not so great. Bad dreams."

"Care to share?" Steve looked concerned.

Trudy thought a moment. "It's all rather fuzzy now. But I know they were bad enough to wake me a few times."

Steve patted her on the knee. "Well, at least they were only dreams," he said.

Trudy sighed and nodded. She looked at the phone. "Any news?"

Her dad sat back in his chair. "Nothing since yesterday. They found a cell phone in a dumpster that matched your mom's, but it turned out to be someone else's."

"The owner was probably glad to get it back."

Steve gave a small laugh. "Not likely. The thing was covered in spaghetti."

"Eww!"

Trudy got up and stretched. "Think I'll go get dressed now. I guess I'll spend some time turning over more of the vegetable garden." She looked at the bare patch of mud outside of the living room window. A noise from her dad made her turn around. He had an amused look on his face. It lit his features for only a moment, but she was glad of even a moment of happiness for him.

Making a face, she said, "Yes, I know. The rains will just flatten it down again, but it's something I want to do."

Steve waved his hand. "Don't let me stop you."

She smiled at him and headed back upstairs to get dressed. Halfway up, she heard her cell phone's texting ringtone. Her heart skipping a beat, she ran to her room and picked up the phone.

Yes! It was him!

Trudy spun in delight. The only bright spot in her universe! The guy who had made her year, and her life, the night he had introduced himself, and the guy she missed terribly, even though they had known each other for such a short time...

She gazed out the window at the buds forming on the trees. Soon she was lost in the happy memory of that night. It had been a rather strange encounter, but the entire night had turned out rather odd as well. Even so, thinking about that meeting sent a thrill up her spine.

CHAPTER 12

It was towards the end of her evening class, and she and her friend Martha were finishing up some paperwork. Suddenly Martha, whose attention tended to wander if there wasn't a conversation going, poked her in the shoulder and giggled.

"Ow! What's that about?" Trudy rubbed the spot.

"Don't look now, but I think your fan club is here..."

Trudy rolled her eyes. "What are you talking about? Come on, we have work to do."

Martha gestured with her head towards the back of the room. "There's a guy standing in the back doorway, and he's been staring at you for like five minutes!"

Trudy turned quickly, and saw one of the most handsome men she had ever laid eyes on. Curly brown hair, beautiful brown eyes that seemed to stare straight into her soul...she couldn't look away.

It was Martha who startled her out of her trance. She nudged Trudy again, laughing. "Quit staring! You look like an idiot!"

Trudy turned abruptly, staring straight ahead, a blush creeping over her face. She turned towards Martha with a giggle of her own. "Oh, Martha, he's gorgeous! Oh, is he still there? I can't look. I'm so embarrassed!"

Martha sneaked a look behind her. "Yep, still there. Ya know what, Trudes? I think I'll go over and introduce myself!"

Trudy gave her a playful punch on the arm. She only half meant it. "You will not! You already have a boyfriend!"

"Well, to paraphrase a certain sentence, 'What happens on campus stays on campus'."

Martha gave Trudy one of her sly smiles, which was all Trudy needed to get motivated. She got up and gathered her books while Martha sat and grinned at her.

"Um, I think I'll go do some research at the library..."

Martha snorted. "Uh-huh. Sure. Catch you over there in a few. And I want a full report!"

Trudy blew a raspberry at her friend and headed toward the back of the room. She stopped short when she saw that her mysterious admirer had disappeared.

Once outside, she looked up and down the walkway to see if he was anywhere in sight. In the twilight, she could not see anyone except for a couple of students making their way across the campus.

Her heart sinking, she headed towards her dorm room, deciding that she would just spend the evening watching TV and eating pretzels. *Living the life...*

As Trudy walked through the lengthening evening shadows, she suddenly felt a presence, as if she was being followed. With no one else around, she knew she was on her own. However, she also was confident in her abilities to protect herself. Her experience in martial arts training had given her the means necessary to fend off any attackers.

She turned on her heel to confront the person following her now.

It was him. That same handsome man who had been watching her! He was now about three feet away! Trudy didn't know what to think...was he stalking her? What were his intentions? She didn't trust him, and yet...

She could only stand there, speechless.

He stepped back, seeing the look on her face and her balled-up fists ready for battle. He smiled at her and held up his hands in a gesture of surrender.

"Do forgive me, miss. I did not mean to frighten you. I saw you back there in the classroom, and wanted to introduce myself then. But you were so busy with your friend..."

Trudy relaxed a hair. His voice was as mesmerizing as his eyes. She detected a slight accent, but couldn't place it. She kept up her defenses, though, just in case.

He spoke again. "May I accompany you? I would like to get to know you better, if that isn't too forward of me."

Trudy raised an eyebrow. Such quaint manners! Did he talk like this all the time? She found herself being drawn into his charm.

She gave him a small smile. "Um, sure. I was just heading for..." she almost said 'my dorm room' but caught herself, "...the library."

He looked puzzled, and pointed hesitantly back over his shoulder. "Isn't the library back there? I'm new here, so I may be mistaken..."

Trudy blushed again. *Smooth, girl,* she thought to herself. *Now he's going to think you're a total idiot!*

She laughed nervously. "Right. I'm, uh, going by way of the wetlands area behind the bio lab. It's so beautiful, even at night. I love the sound of the frogs."

Never mind that it's the wrong time of the year for them to be out...

The young man shrugged. "If that is what you desire."

He suddenly looked pained. "Oh, my manners!"

Trudy looked startled as he made a small bow. He said, "My name is Victor. And who might I have the privilege of addressing?"

Trudy stifled a giggle. "My name's Trudy."

Victor lifted her free hand and, to her wonder, kissed it ever so gently. She felt a slight tingle where his lips met her skin. "I am very pleased to make your acquaintance. Now, if you will allow me..."

He took her books, and carried them as they walked the path that led around and back to the library.

Well, at least he can't try anything without having to drop my books first, Trudy told herself. She refused to let her guard down, however. It was not in her nature to trust anyone outright.

As they passed the marshland, which was very wet due to the recent heavy rains, she felt a sharp prick on the back of her neck.

"Wow!" she exclaimed, swatting at the spot. "Those mosquitoes are early this year!"

She drew her hand back; there was a smear of blood on her fingers.

"Got the sucker! Must've been there awhile. Look at how much it got!!"

She stopped and turned around.

Victor had stopped a few paces behind. She looked back at him, curious.

Curiosity turned to alarm; his eyes seemed to glow with a light of their own! The only light on this part of the path came from the moon, which flitted in and out among the clouds. Trudy blinked; *what an imagination!*

Still he stood there, unmoving. She was again drawn into his gaze.

He came slowly towards her, his gaze unwavering, mesmerizing. She was riveted to the spot...

The next thing she knew, they were in front of the library! She blinked in surprise.

"I hope to see you again," Victor was saying. Smiling, he handed her books to her, and, with a bow, turned and walked back down the path.

Trudy felt dazed as she watched him leave. A tap on her shoulder brought her back to herself.

It was Martha. "I've been waiting for you for an hour!" she complained.

Trudy could only stare at her friend. *An hour!* She'd just left the classroom not fifteen minutes ago!

She looked at her watch. *Martha's right! What happened to the time?*

Trudy scratched at the back of her neck, and was shocked to find that the skin was broken in several places. Suddenly she felt unaccountably weak; all she wanted to do was go back to her room and go to sleep.

Martha was pulling her into the library. "I want to hear every detail!"

Trudy shook off her friend's grasp.

"Uh, Martha, I think I'll just head off and go to bed. I'm really tired."

"What?" Martha's eyes opened wide. "On a Friday? I thought we were going out clubbing!" A thought occurred to her. She narrowed her eyes and gave Trudy that sly smile of hers.

"He really must be special. Wow, that's some fast moves!"

Trudy got Martha's meaning and gave her friend a push on the shoulder. "No, it's not that! You know me better!"

Martha pouted. "Yeah, but you could've changed. Handsome guys can do that to a girl." Then her voice got excited again. "So, come on, spill! Tell me about him! What's he like? Where's he from?"

Trudy gave Martha an exasperated look. "Okay, okay! Walk back with me, and I'll tell you all about him. Or at least what I know so far, anyway."

The two girls started toward the dormitory, talking and laughing. As they approached the building, they got quiet, then stopped walking. Both felt as if they were being watched. This was a somewhat deserted stretch of the pathway, and led under a thicket of low, overhanging trees that came right up to the edge of the concrete. Neither girl had ever been in this area once the night had taken over, and now they were feeling a bit spooked.

The girls looked around. No other students could be seen; everyone was inside studying or having a late dinner. They stood looking down the path towards the light spilling from the dorm's front door. It was so close, but with the darkness and the way they were feeling, it could just as well have been on the moon.

"Isn't there another way to the building?" Martha whispered nervously.

Trudy thought a moment. Her nerves were a bit jangled; this evening had been really strange. It was hard to come up with any ideas. Finally, she remembered an alternate route.

"I suppose we could go through the science hall. It's only about a half-block from the other dorm; we could get in there, walk the length of the building, and my dorm would be only about fifty feet away once we got back outside. And no trees!"

Martha shivered. "Let's do it."

They hurried off, looking nervously over their shoulders.

Trudy's plan worked, and they made it safely to her room in a very short time. Martha's enthusiasm for going out had disappeared, and Trudy invited her to stay the night, an invitation she gladly accepted. She was not about to go out there again until daylight.

Trudy and Victor spent several more evenings together, and she really felt that they had a serious relationship started. The strange events of the first night seemed unimportant as they got to know each other better. They went everywhere together, but Victor really seemed to favor the pathway beside the wetlands. Trudy was very happy that he liked that area as much as she did.

Then the call came that brought her back home to her dad and brother. She had quickly packed a few things and was just headed out to her car, when Victor was suddenly at her side.

"Where are you going, Trudy?" His look of concern caused her to lose the control she had had on herself ever since she had hung up her phone.

She turned to him, her eyes brimming with tears. "Oh, Victor! My mother's missing! She hasn't been seen in three days!"

"Oh, that's terrible!" He looked shocked.

Trudy went on. "Dad's flying home from his business trip, and Pat's on his way back to the house too. Oh, Victor, I'm so scared!"

Victor pulled her close, and she clung to him. He caressed the back of her neck. "Oh, Trudy, I'm so sorry. Do you wish me to come with you?"

Even in her pain, her heart melted at his concern. She held him tightly, and then pulled back, looking up at his face. Those eyes...

She wrenched her gaze away and fumbled for her keys. "No, but thank you. It's really best if it's just the family right now."

"I understand." Victor sighed and put a hand on her face. "Go, then, but I will keep in touch. I want you to know that I care."

Trudy smiled at him, and then quickly got into her car before her knees gave way in sheer delight at his words. He leaned in and gave her a quick kiss on the top of her head. Wiping her eyes, Trudy started the car and pulled away. He watched as she drove off.

As she left the parking lot, she took a look in the rear-view mirror so she could wave good-bye.

He was gone.

Now, in her room at home, she read the text message.

"Miss you. Victor."

She sighed. Then she got into her gardening clothes and headed downstairs again.

As she headed towards the garage, she noticed that her dad was once again on the phone. There was no noise coming out of the kitchen, so she surmised that Pat was still out pounding the pavement.

While gathering her gardening tools in the dark garage, she felt a familiar prick at the base of her neck and swatted at it. *Stupid mosquitoes!*

Right after Mass that night, Steve, Trudy, and Pat snuck out the side door. There were a lot of people in attendance that night; Lydia had many friends in their parish. Right now, however, her family just couldn't face the sympathetic faces and concerned voices.

Steve and the kids had a quiet dinner that night, each lost in his or her own reverie. No one wanted to stay up past 8pm, so exhausted were they from the trial they were enduring. Not expecting to sleep, they went to their respective rooms to lie down and contemplate their ceilings.

Thus it was that, when the phone rang at around 4:30 a.m., they were all awake, and raced to answer it.

CHAPTER 13

Lydia sat at Fr. Samuel's kitchen table. She'd had some coffee and a ham sandwich, which she would have thoroughly enjoyed if she hadn't still been in a state of shock. Now the EMTs were checking her over; no one present could see the point of an exam after what they had all witnessed, but they also knew they had legal responsibilities to satisfy. Besides, who outside this group would believe such a thing had happened, if they hadn't seen it themselves? Best to have all the paperwork taken care of.

Fr. Samuel had found some clothes in the donations cupboard that would fit Lydia. She was now wearing a pair of faded jeans and a warm sweater. He'd also found some shoes, but without socks, they slipped and slid on her feet.

Without saying anything to her, Fr. Sam had also slipped silently out the back door of the residence, carrying the filthy, bloodied rag she had been wearing. Living out in the country, he was allowed to have a burn pile; he threw the horrid reminder onto the smoldering ashes, and was pleased to see that it caught fire right away.

The police had called Steve, and he was on his way. Lydia just hoped he wouldn't get in a car accident in his haste to get to her.

She learned that she had been gone about a month, and she was currently only about thirty miles from home. The story that was given to the reporters, who had somehow found out she had been found and had been clamoring around the door to the priest's house, was that Lydia had been found wandering in the nearby wooded hills, dazed and disoriented.

No one who had been there that night wanted to try to account for what had happened in the church, and all were happy when Fr. Sam used his remarkable communication skills to satisfy the media. The officers and EMTs had no proof to back up what they had experienced; the braver souls who had tried to take pictures of the events in the church found that their cell phones yielded only the regular walls and furnishings. No floating lights, no people. Nothing out of the ordinary.

The EMTs left at about the same time Steve roared into the drive. They took the little broken body of the child with them; they would attempt to identify him, but they didn't think they would have much luck. After a short time, they would simply bury him discreetly, but none would ever forget.

Steve rushed into the parish house, ran into the kitchen, and joyfully swept Lydia up into his arms. "Oh, sweetie! Lydia! I thought I'd never see you again!"

She couldn't answer him, as she was overcome with emotion. They fell into each other's embrace, crying and laughing at the same time. Fr. Sam looked on from his seat at the table, his own eyes brimming with tears as he watched them.

At last, Steve pulled back, lifted her chin, and gazed lovingly into her eyes. She gazed back, and the love she saw there was a bright, shining mirror image of the love she had seen in her Lord's eyes.

"What happened to you, Lydia? Where have you been? When I'd heard you'd gone missing..."

He choked back a sob.

She put a hand to his lips. "Not now," she said. "I can't even begin to explain. I'm just so tired. When we're alone..."

"I'd heard you were found wandering out in the woods. Can you remember anything else?"

Lydia sighed and put a trembling hand to her throat. "Wish I could forget..." Her voice trailed off.

Steve looked troubled at these words, and seemed about to question her further, when they heard someone behind them.

It was one of the police officers. "Um...ahem... I hate to bother you, but we have some paperwork to fill out. The APB on your wife has to be closed."

Steve looked at Lydia, who was swaying with exhaustion. He looked back pleadingly at the officer. "Could we do this later? It's..." he looked at his watch, astonished. "Seven a.m.! I didn't know it was so late! We promise we'll go to the police station later and take care of it."

The officer looked at the two of them. Neither one looked as if they'd had a wink of sleep in at least a week. He smiled. "Yes, of course, but today is Sunday, so you'd be better off waiting until Monday. We don't have a lot of personnel in the office today."

"Good...good, we'll do that. Right now I need to get my wife home."

Lydia smiled at those words, her eyelids drooping as she leaned against Steve.

The officer turned to go. "Best medicine for all ailments, a good seven or eight hours' sleep." As he passed the yawning priest: "Get some rest if you can, Sam. Your associate can handle early Mass."

Fr. Sam managed a smile. "Thanks, Jim. I didn't realize you were my bishop now, too, to give me the day off!!"

The officer raised his eyebrows. "Oh, you're not getting the day off. I'll be at the evening Mass, and you'd better be there!"

The two men laughed, and the officer joined his team outside. The patrol cars drove away, one by one, leaving only Lydia, Steve, and Fr. Sam.

Lydia and the priest exchanged a long look, and Steve sensed that something had gone on far beyond what he had been told. There was some sort of bond that had formed between the two of them, a relationship born of some shared experience. He hoped that Lydia would soon let him know what had actually happened; right now he felt isolated, and he didn't like the feeling.

He looked on as Lydia hugged the priest. "Good-bye, Father. I'll be in touch."

"Yes, do that. We need to discuss what happened here."

Steve's curiosity was really up now. Fr. Sam had found Lydia out in the woods, hardly knowing which way to go....hadn't he? What needed discussing? Why couldn't she just talk to their local pastor?

He thanked the priest, who laid a hand on his arm. "Don't worry, you'll find out everything you need to know. Just give her a chance to rest right now."

Steve nodded, and took his wife's arm to help her out to the car.

Lydia was already on her way to being asleep by the time Steve had driven out of the parking lot. He touched her leg, and she pulled away in a quick jerk, whimpering and holding herself close, as if trying to get away from him.

"Lydia!" he whispered, alarmed. "Are you okay?"

All she got from her was a strange, murmured answer. *Something about vampires...?*

The next thing Lydia knew, the sun was shining full on her face, and she could hear the glorious sound of the birds singing in the trees. She lay in bed, just luxuriating in the sights and sounds of her life returning to normal. Stretching, she was gratified to realize that she was not sore anywhere. It was so wonderful! *Thank you, Lord*! she prayed.

Getting up, she was about to walk into the bathroom when the sight of her own reflection in her full-length mirror halted her.

Her reflection!

She just stood there, staring at herself. What a marvel mirrors were! So were sunlight, and birdsong. And showers...one of which she was going to take right now!

Lydia turned on the shower, tentatively sticking a finger into the stream of water. She felt a little foolish doing so, but the memory of the last time she tried to touch water was still raw in her mind.

"Sorry, Lord," she prayed silently. "Human mentality. I should have more faith. You healed me, and I should remember that and move on."

She could have sworn she heard a faint laugh in her heart, and she smiled.

Standing in the shower, she watched the water as it fell, running down her body and pooling at her feet. It was a joyful experience. She lifted her arm, and found herself amazed at the way her muscles and ligaments obeyed her. Everything, large and small, was new and wonderful to her this morning.

Lydia stepped out of the shower, dried off, and put on the softest, warmest clothes she could find. When she opened her bedroom door, her nose was greeted by the smell of bacon and coffee.

Oh, wonderful Steve! Oh, wonderful food!

Then she heard voices downstairs, one light and happy, the other so like Steve's but with the tenor of youth.

Her kids! She practically ran down the stairs and into the kitchen, where her three most favorite people in the whole world were sitting at the table.

"Mom!" Trudy and Pat leapt up from their seats and ran to her. There were excited hugs and kisses all around, as everyone competed to be heard above each other.

"Oh, my family! I'm so happy to be home with you!"

"Where were you?"

The questions didn't take any time to start coming. Lydia wasn't sure how to answer them just yet. She looked to Steve, who got the message she was sending him: please run interference here!

Steve pulled out Lydia's chair with a loud clearing of his throat. "First, breakfast. Then, answers. Maybe. Keep in mind that your mom has been through a lot and may not be able to tell you much of anything. There could be some shock and memory loss possible."

Nice job, love, thought Lydia gratefully.

Steve brought her a meal fit for a queen: eggs, toast, bacon, and coffee. She looked up at him and grinned. "Oh thank you, thank you, my love. I am so hungry!"

A dark memory ran across her mind at the word "hungry;" the memory of Vlad's look just before his attacks on her flashed into her mind. She shuddered, and then shook her head to clear the thought.

The kids, watching her, looked concerned.

"Mom, what's wrong?" Pat asked.

Steve turned from the sink where he had been rinsing dishes. "Lydia?" he asked worriedly.

Lydia smiled shakily. "Oh, I'm fine. Just...a little tired still."

Trudy, her wonderful girl, stroked her mom's face. They both felt tears welling up. "Mom, it's beyond words to have you back!" Then she wiped her eyes. "Just relax, have some brekkie. That'll help a lot!"

Lydia had to translate in her mind. *'Brekkie'? Oh, 'breakfast'. Duh!* "Thanks, Trudy."

Lydia gazed at her lovely family. They looked back expectantly.

"What?" She was puzzled by their stares.

Steve said, "Well, I guess it's just that we're so glad to see you with us again, and of course we are kind of curious as to what happened to you."

Oh boy. How to tell them? What *to tell them?* She closed her eyes and sighed. "I'll tell you what I can remember, but let me eat first, okay?"

Then she remembered it was Sunday. She looked at the clock over the sink. "Oh! Church!"

Steve and the kids looked at each other, smiling. Trudy giggled.

"Now what?" Lydia was truly baffled by their reaction.

Trudy spoke through her laughter. "Mom, it's Monday! You've been asleep for over 24 hours!"

"Oh, good grief! I had no idea! No wonder I'm so hungry!"

With that, Lydia dug into her breakfast.

CHAPTER 14

As Lydia ate, the kids and Steve filled her in on the month she had missed.

She was very surprised and happy that Steve had gotten a raise. They tossed some ideas out as to how to spend their newfound "wealth," and then laughed at the very idea. With two kids in college, they knew full well where that extra income was going to go!

Pat told her about the coach's call, and she urged him to get back to school as soon as he could, so he wouldn't miss out on any more practices than he had to.

"It can wait," he assured her. "Coach knows you're back, but he said to take as much time as I want."

Lydia smiled at him. "Okay, do what you think is best."

She glanced over at Trudy, who seemed about to squirm out of her own skin with her news.

"Mom!" she exclaimed, her eyes shining, "I have a boyfriend!"

"Psh!" Pat mumbled, just loud enough to be heard. "Whoop-ti-do!" Still, he grinned at his sister, who swatted him with her napkin.

Lydia raised her eyebrows and glanced at Steve. He was curious as well; apparently this was news to him.

"Do you now? Do tell!" Lydia was all ears. Trudy was not one to attach herself to any particular boy, so this one must really be special.

"Well, he's really good-looking," here she punched her brother, who was pretending to gag, "and we met at school not too long ago. His name is Victor."

Lydia's wrists tingled briefly, and she absent-mindedly rubbed them. "How long ago is 'not too long ago'?"

"A few weeks. He is so sweet, Mom! He always wants to be with me!"

"So, you've gone out a lot?"

"No, not all that much." Trudy's voice reflected her disappointment. "We've gone to a couple of movies, and a lot of walks around campus. He's only available in the evenings because of his work schedule. A lot of weekends, he has to help on his parents' estate.

"I love it when we can get together. All the girls are so jealous when they see us." She grinned. "I've never had that before."

"'Estate?'" Steve teased. "Where is it? I'd like to get to know these folks better!"

Lydia nudged him. "Uh-huh..." She looked back at Trudy; she had some teasing of her own to do.

"A workaholic, eh? Sounds like someone else we know..." She rolled her eyes toward her husband. He made a face at her.

"He's paying his own way through college. He actually is a bit older than the usual student; he started late due to family concerns."

Trudy scratched the back of her neck. "Ugh! Mosquito bites!"

Lydia laughed. "Well, you can blame that swamp by your lab. They ought to bomb it with bug killer and drain the darn thing."

It was Trudy's turn to roll her eyes. "Mom! It's not a swamp! It's a marsh! It also doubles as a bioswale. Rain from the grounds around it drains into the marsh and then down into the gravel at the bottom. That way the water gets cleaned and filtered before it passes into the groundwater reserves. Besides, it's never really boggy unless we've had excess rain. And, ya know, I'm getting skeeter-bit here, too!"

Lydia held up her hands, laughing. "Okay, okay, you win!"

As she picked up her fork to start eating again, Lydia noticed her wrists were a little sore. She looked at the hand she was eating with.

Is that a scar? Why wasn't it there this morning when I was in the shower?

Then it disappeared, as rapidly as it had come. *Huh. Trick of the light. Well, whatever.*

"When can we meet this Mr. Wonderful?" Steve was asking his daughter. "I'm sure you have at least one picture of him on your phone..."

"No...no pictures. He doesn't like his picture taken. Some sort of phobia. How about if I have him come here for dinner some time? Maybe next month? That's Spring Break, and I think he can get time off then."

"Certainly. Just decide on a night and we'll plan accordingly. And, if you don't mind a bit of advice," here Lydia looked seriously at Trudy, "do yourself a favor and get to know him better before you fall for him completely."

Trudy sighed. "Yes, Mom, I know. It's just that we don't always have the same free time. You know how college is. He did say that once he got the estate's affairs in order, we could be together a lot more!"

"Okay, as long as you know what you're doing."

Lydia stood up and cleared off her dishes. As she put them in the dishwasher, she didn't think there was a happier person than herself at this moment anywhere in the world.

Except, there was still the fact that she had to tell her family something about why she had disappeared for a month, and what happened during that time. She couldn't ignore the fact that they were still waiting for her to tell them.

"I'll, um, be right back. I want to see if the crocuses are out yet." She hurried past them and out the door.

As she wandered alone in her garden, she prayed. "Lord, what do I tell them? How much do You want known of what happened?"

A gentle voice stirred her soul. His Voice. Oh, how she had missed it!

"Tell them only that you were taken. You escaped, but did not know where you were. That is the truth they are prepared to accept right now."

"But I told Steve that I remembered everything!"

"When you are alone with him, you can tell him everything. He won't understand right away, but he will in time."

"Yes, I'll do that. Thank You."

She walked back into the house. Sitting her family down, she related the bare bones of her ordeal: how she had been kidnapped in the parking lot at work, woke up in a dark room, and had been able to break a window and escape. She told them she had wandered through the woods, not knowing where she was going, and having to eat whatever was available. Nothing else was really clear to her mind. Not out-and-out lies; more like incomplete truths, for their protection.

Steve frowned and looked like he was about to say something, but Lydia gave him a slight shake of her head. He glanced at the kids and back to her questioningly. Lydia nodded almost imperceptibly. It made him wonder even more--what had happened to her while she was missing? And why couldn't the kids know?

CHAPTER 15

As they were driving to the police station to close out the missing persons report, Steve asked, "So, can you tell me a bit more as to what went on?"

Lydia looked uncomfortably out of the passenger window. "Not while you're driving."

"Huh?"

She turned to him. "Steve, I can hardly believe what went on myself. You would have to be in a position where what I have to tell you will not end up in your losing control of the car."

Now Steve was thoroughly curious, and not just a little distressed. "Can we stop and get a coffee then? Maybe discuss it at our favorite café?"

"Not in public either. I've been told I can tell you, but no one else."

"Told?" Steve was getting exasperated. "Told by who?" He tried to lighten the mood. "Are you involved with some secret organization?"

Lydia bit her lip. This was not going to be easy. "Um...not in so many words."

Steve hit his hand on the wheel in frustration. "Okay, I'll have to assume the worst, since you won't be direct with me." He was quiet a long moment.

A horrid thought hit him. Although it was something he did not want to ask, it had to be done.

His voice trembled. "Lydia..."

She looked at him, then down at her hands. "Yes?"

"Are you, um, did the EMTs suggest going to the hospital, you know, for, um, testing?"

Lydia looked confused. "Testing?"

"Um, yeah, people who have been missing, sometimes they block stuff, they need someone to help them come to terms and get it all out in the open. Plus other stuff, you know, physical..."

What he was suggesting finally hit her. She grabbed his arm—lightly, since he was still driving—and said, "Oh, Steve, I remember clearly everything that went on. I wish I could forget, but it's with me every moment. As to the 'physical,' no doctor would believe anything I said as to what happened to me."

She sighed. It was getting too tricky to dance around the facts any longer.

"Pull over, Steve. This parking lot is fine. Shut off the engine, and promise me you won't go ballistic. It would be best if you gave me the keys."

Steve complied; his heart was now pounding with such anxiety and confusion at his wife's words that he didn't think he'd be able to drive further anyway.

Steve sat and listened as Lydia related her story, alternately incredulous, angry, and fearing for his wife's sanity. How could he believe any of it? It disgusted and enraged him that anyone would abuse Lydia, who was infinitely precious to him.

What she told him was very hard to take seriously. Vampires? Divine intervention? Voices in her head? Maybe she did need to go to the hospital for psychological evaluation...

Lydia could see that he was passing through all the stages of emotions that she had expected. When she finished telling of her harrowing experience, he sat back, staring out the window.

For the longest time, neither of them spoke. Then Lydia quietly took his hand. She turned his head to look directly into his eyes. "My love, these are not lies. I am perfectly sane. Please believe me. I would not lie to you, or make up some absurd story."

Steve grunted, but he was able to give her a small smile. "I would have preferred that you had told me you had gone on a spur-of-the-moment shopping spree to Paris."

Lydia smiled as well, although it was a sad one. "I wish that was the case."

A thought occurred to her. "Let's continue on to the station. If any of the officers are there who were in the church that night, perhaps they could back up my story. At least that part of it."

Steve touched her face. "I believe you, dear, no matter how unbelievable this whole thing is at the moment. I just can't believe such a thing could happen. As in," he hurriedly said, seeing that Lydia was going to object, "everything is so out of the realm of general realities. I will have a hard time processing it. You'll have to give me some time."

Lydia nodded. It was to be expected, considering.

Her phone suddenly rang.

It was Fr. Samuel.

"Lydia? I need to talk to you. Face to face. We need to go over what happened here. I'm having a hard time believing what I saw and experienced, and I want to make sure I wasn't hallucinating."

"Understandable, Father. Do you mind if I bring my husband? I just told him the whole story, and I think it would help everyone sort things out if we all discussed it together."

"Of course. Can you come by this afternoon?"

Lydia covered the phone and asked Steve, "Can we go to Fr. Sam's parish? He needs to talk about this, too."

"Oh, I'd forgotten he was a witness also. We can go right after we get the paperwork done at the police station. Are you up for the long trip?"

"It's not that far, I don't think. I really don't remember, but I should be fine." Into the phone, she said, "Sure. We'll be there in a couple of hours."

She clicked off, and then held out the car keys to Steve. "Are you sure you'll be able to drive?"

He passed a hand over his face, still in some shock. "Yes, as long as I don't think about anything." He took the keys and started the car, and they drove the few short blocks to the station.

As they walked in, heads turned. Most turned back quickly. Lydia could see that those present who had witnessed the events in the church were not going to get involved. She couldn't really blame them; it had been worse than any horror movie, then abruptly it had gone into an experience more glorious than any human imaginings. What could she expect? It wouldn't be surprising, she thought, if most of them went into denial about the whole experience. Just too much to take in, especially for those without faith.

The officer at the front desk looked up. "Can I help you?"

"Yes," said Steve. "We have some paperwork to fill out. My wife had been missing, and..."

"Oh, yes. The Lydia Bronson case. We were expecting you this morning. How are you feeling, Mrs. Bronson?" He smiled softly at her; he had not been there that night, and so had no trouble meeting her gaze.

Lydia was mildly surprised that he knew who she and Steve were, but then again, the police probably didn't have a lot of missing-persons cases where the person who was gone came in and closed out her own paperwork. "A little tired, but none the worse for wear, I think, thanks."

"Ah, good. Well, just a couple of signatures, and you're free to go. Don't be surprised if you hear from the detective bureau. They would like to ask some questions. We haven't had any other abductions, and we don't want any more either. Your input may help us keep others safe."

"Umm, sure. Of course." *And what do I tell* them? she thought.

On their way out, Lydia said, "That took a lot less time than I thought. Maybe we could stop and get that coffee." She was thinking to herself how wonderful it was to have coffee, and food, and all those wonderful things she had taken for granted. No rats, either...

Then she noticed Steve was hanging back, watching her rather carefully. She looked at him, puzzled. "Steve?"

He looked as if he was at a loss for words. Scratching his head, he stared, first at the ground, then at her.

"What is it, Steve? Are you okay?"

He really looked uncomfortable now. She went to take his hand, but he moved away slightly.

She looked shocked and troubled. He'd never done that before, even on those occasions when he'd been angry with her.

He saw the look in her eyes and softened. "I'm sorry, Lydia. It's just that, well, it occurred to me just now... Well, if you had been, um, changed...into a, um...Doesn't that mean...they don't change back, do they?"

Lydia got what he was trying to say, and looked lovingly at him. Poor confused man.

"Steve, listen to me. Look." She opened her mouth and pointed inside. "No fangs." She waved her arm at the sidewalk. "I'm throwing a shadow. Also, my make-up sure would look awful if I didn't have my reflection to look at this morning." She smiled at him.

He relaxed. "Right...right...okay. But..." He looked away.

Lydia put a hand on his arm; this time he didn't flinch or pull away. He looked at her and said carefully, "How can you be so...so casual about it now? Making jokes, talking about going for coffee..."

Lydia stopped him. "My love," she said soothingly, "I lived this hideous experience. I also experienced God's healing power. Steve, I saw our Savior! I saw His angels! He healed me! And I'm still here! What's not to rejoice about?"

Steve slowly shook his head. "I wish I could believe all of this as you do. But...it's hard."

Lydia pulled him gently towards the car. "Then let's go see Fr. Samuel, and find a way to help both of you to see the Light."

Fr. Sam was more than gracious. He had had his housekeeper make raisin scones that morning; they tasted wonderful with the hot tea with which she kept refilling their cups. While she hovered around, making sure everyone was satisfied, the three others made small talk about the weather and the coming spring season. The priest, like Lydia, was an avid gardener, and they talked animatedly about their plans for the coming growing season.

Once the tea things were cleared away, and the housekeeper had gone into town for groceries, they got down to more serious subjects.

First, Lydia again recounted what had happened from the time she was spirited away until Fr. Sam had found her in the church. Together, Lydia and the priest took turns repeating and clarifying what they both had experienced. It was a comfort to the two of them to go over what had happened.

For Steve, it was a different experience. He was still somewhat bewildered. He found it difficult to believe that Fr. Sam had no trouble believing his wife concerning those events that had led to his finding her.

The good priest caught the look Steve was giving him and felt the need to explain. "Steve, I saw what your wife looked like when I discovered her in the sanctuary. Never have I been so frightened. I felt her supernatural strength when she attacked me," Lydia winced at the memory, "and I saw the...creature...that tried to destroy her. And now that I see her again," he eyed her smooth, unblemished throat, "I can now safely admit to myself that I saw all the rest as well.

"Now, this is the part I don't understand." He turned to Lydia. "What do we do now? Why did this happen? I remember His parting words to you...something about 'a seal against the evil to come'?"

Lydia shook her head. "I have no idea, but I'm sure when the time is right, we'll know."

She wiped some sweat from her brow. Funny, she didn't feel all that warm...

Then she stopped short, as she noticed both men looking quizzically at her forehead. She laughed nervously.

"I seem to be sweating. I hope I'm not getting a fever...what?"

She was getting perturbed at the concerned looks the other two were giving her.

Steve's mouth opened and shut, but no sound came out. There was a look of shock on his face. Fr. Sam, not taking his eyes off of her, reached over with a napkin to wipe her face. He drew it away, and Lydia could see what had stunned them.

There was blood smeared on the napkin! Lydia stared, unbelieving, and then looked at the hand she had used to wipe her face.

Blood!

Now her wrists suddenly gave her such pain that she cried out. She put her hands up...and almost fainted.

Her arms were bleeding from holes just below her wrists! "What...what? I'm...what's this?" She panicked, trying to wipe it all off and get the blood flow stanched. Fortunately, it wasn't pouring out, just seeping.

Then, as suddenly as it had started, it was gone, and with it any signs that what they had seen had happened at all. Even the napkin was clean once again.

Lydia felt that same electrifying jolt through her soul that she had experienced before, so strong that it almost drove her to her knees, followed by that serene peace throughout her being.

And the Voice of One so dear...

Lydia, you must go to the bishop. I have a message for him.

CHAPTER 16

The three of them were silent as Steve drove them to the cathedral. They were having a hard time absorbing yet another supernatural event. The question was the same in each of their minds: what, or who, was the author? They all knew the rules about "private revelation". It has been proven throughout history that such events as this could be used for ill or good, and sometimes years can pass before the truth is known. This was why the Church made it a point to look very closely into any and all "miraculous" events, not declaring its truth or falseness until the events were long over, or until there was even the tiniest seed of untruth. If there was anything spoken or observed that was against Scripture or Holy Writ, the Church made swift moves to condemn the events. Otherwise, people would continue to follow the extraordinary happenings and be led down a path unintended by Scripture. This was a situation that none of the three wanted to see happen.

Not to say that people didn't go against the Church's condemnation, unfortunately. Thousands would still rather follow and believe a supernatural "apparition" than the beliefs handed down through the ages. Regardless, the Church says what it has to and holds its position, and merely prays for the return of these souls before it is too late.

It was a short ride to the bishop's house near the cathedral. The bishop himself met them; the call from his old friend Samuel had been rather frantic, and he thought it best to give the staff the rest of the day off. He knew his friend, and Sam didn't get panicked like that without good reason.

He shook hands with Fr. Sam, then with Steve and Lydia as Sam introduced them. He smiled at them and asked, "What can I help you with? I must say, that was quite a phone call."

The three visitors looked uncomfortably at each other. Fr. Samuel spoke first. "I...think you need to sit down for this."

"Oh, of course. Please, come into my office."

After they were all seated in chairs around the bishop's desk, he looked at them each in turn. *What was this about? A marriage problem? No, their faces show too much shock to be merely that.*

And besides, Sam is too good a priest to need help untangling marriage issues—and he looks as pale as the other two.

After a short silence, he cleared his throat. "So, what is the problem?"

Fr. Sam spoke up. "Your Excellency..." The bishop gave him a look. "Oh, sorry, I mean, Frank. This is probably the most awful, the most incredible, but maybe the most wondrous thing you will ever have related to you."

The bishop made an impatient noise. "Don't speak in puzzles, Fr. Sam. Just say it plain and let me decide."

So, the three of them took it in turns to tell the bishop of all that had gone on, including what had happened in Fr. Sam's house that afternoon. When they had finished, Bishop Frank sat back in his chair, mulling over what he had just heard.

While they had been relating to him the ordeal Lydia had gone through, he had found himself getting more and more tense. Why did all of this sound familiar? Yet he hadn't heard any of it before...A dream? Perhaps.

No one spoke for a time. No one wanted to interrupt the bishop while he was deep in thought. The three of them knew how hard it was to believe any of this.

Finally, he looked at Lydia. "This is a lot for me to try to understand. Yet it's difficult to think any of it was made up, especially since I know the mind of my friend Sam here. So...this message you spoke of. What is it?

Lydia said, "I...I really don't know. There's been nothing else, although I keep asking for..."

She stopped.

The bishop had that same shocked look on his face that Steve and Fr. Sam had had earlier, and she knew it must be happening again. She looked at her wrists. The scars were back, but no blood seeped this time.

Suddenly, her mind went blank.

The men saw Lydia raise her hands from her sides and speak, although she didn't look as if she was conscious of her words:

Hear Me, My sons. I have seen the self-destructive ways of My people, and the way that they follow the evil that the Adversary pours into the world. They have overwhelmingly forgotten who is the Keeper of their lives. The time has come to purge My creation of the demons that feed upon it.

There will soon be a war waged between My angels and the subjects of the Father of Lies. I will use My people to warn of the coming days. My daughter Lydia has begged to be an instrument of My Grace...a tool I may use for the salvation of souls.

A time is coming when My angels will be loosed upon the world. There will be three days of darkness, at which time those committed to My Reign must hide themselves. If they do not, or cannot, they will still be saved, but their time on the earth will be over.

When My time is right, Lydia will be one of many to be a sign and symbol for all of My people to hide themselves. They must not look to see what is happening outside, for their hearts would not be able to withstand it. They must keep hidden until the sun shines again, at which time the Tempter and his cohorts will have been purged for a time.

Peace I leave with you. Do not fear. Remember I am with you always.

After these words, Lydia slumped unconscious to the floor.

The three men sat agape, hardly believing what they had just witnessed.

Steve moved first, rushing to his wife's side. He felt for a pulse. "Lydia! Are you alright?" He gulped, swallowing the panic and fear that was rising in his heart.

To his utter relief, her pulse was strong; soon her eyelids fluttered, and she sat up slowly. "What...what happened? I seem to have blacked out..."

The bishop spoke quickly, before the others could say anything. "It seems you fainted," he said, shooting a quick look of warning to the other men. "This has been very difficult for you. I suggest you go home and rest. I appreciate you sharing your very strange experience with me."

"But...the message! I'm supposed to deliver a message! Did I? I don't remember anything."

"Perhaps the message was just in your experience. Let me give the matter some thought. It will take awhile to absorb all of this."

As the group made its way out of the office, the bishop called his priest back in. "A word, Sam."

"Yes?" Sam moved back into the room.

The bishop closed the door. Suddenly he looked about ten years older. "Please do not let Lydia know what she said here today. Pass that request on to her husband. If she truly doesn't remember it, then the message stays within these walls until the time is right. If she's making any of this up...no, don't look at me like that; I know you witnessed some extraordinary events, and I believe you, but if she's made up this 'message', it will pass without anyone else knowing."

Fr. Sam thought about this. "Of course. I'll pull Steve aside when he drops me off at my house."

Lydia rode in the back of the car on the return trip; the efforts and events of the day had tired her out. Steve was trying his hardest not to question her about what had happened at the cathedral office. Fr. Samuel could tell he was bursting to discuss with her what the message had been, and prayed that he could get the bishop's request to him before Steve lost control and started asking questions.

They turned in at the parish house. Fr. Sam turned to say good-bye to Lydia, but she was sound asleep. He beckoned Steve to get out of the car, and related to him what the bishop had instructed. Seeing the sense in his words, Steve swore to secrecy concerning the message.

"But for how long? What happens next?"

Fr. Sam sighed. "Who knows? We just have to get on with our lives the best we know how. What else can we do?"

"Pray. A lot."

CHAPTER 17

Lydia woke in her room, feeling refreshed. She remembered being led into the house by her husband, but she had been so groggy from sleep that she couldn't remember climbing the stairs and falling into bed. However, here she was, and it was another glorious early-spring day. Her husband lay asleep beside her, and the alarm clock showed that it was 6:30 a.m.

Stretching and yawning, she turned on her side and closed her eyes again, luxuriating in the fact that she didn't have to get up to go to work. At least for now. It was far too soon to be going in and acting as if nothing had ever happened. She still needed time to process everything.

She wasn't even sure she still had a job. And there were all her friends to inform of her return. It was going to be a busy day, so she was in no hurry to get out of bed.

There was that question again: What to tell everyone? It seemed to her that what she had relayed to the kids was enough for everyone else as well. Yes, there had been media people hanging around Fr. Sam's house the night she...*oh, don't go there....*

She took a mental side street to get away from what she was about to send through her consciousness. Media...yes, they had been there, but had been told that she was found wandering in the woods. She hadn't seen anything in the papers, so they must have lost interest in the story due to lack of exciting information. That suited her just fine. That only meant that her friends and neighbors had not bombarded her. Now, however, she felt that it was time to let them know...

Lydia thought over who to tell first. Who could she depend on to not only get the information right, but also to get it spread like wildfire so she wouldn't have to be on the phone all day?

She finally settled on calling her church, and then the folks who ran the prayer chain. She knew that was the best way to get her return known by her parish friends. Her neighbors, of course, already knew, but were waiting respectfully for her to make the first move; Steve had told them that she had been exhausted.

After breakfast, Lydia took a stroll around the neighborhood. It was a tonic to feel the spring breeze and see the green shoots poking out of the ground. Occasionally she would see someone she knew. Then there were excited cries and hugs, a bit of conversation, and then she would move on. Although she only walked about a mile or so, she was very tired when she got home.

As she rested, she made the calls she needed to make to her friends, and then felt refreshed enough to take a trip over to church. She hoped to find someone who could open the church for her, so she could go in and pray for a bit.

The church secretary met her at the door to the rectory. "Lydia! It's so good to see you back! We all prayed so hard for your safe return."

"Thanks, Agnes, it's good to be back." She gave Agnes a hug.

"Can you come in for a bit?"

"Actually, I was hoping someone could let me into the church."

"Well, you could go in, but they're cleaning right now. Would you like to come in and have some coffee or tea or something?"

"That would be wonderful, thanks!" *Just don't ask a lot of questions, or this will be a really short visit,* Lydia thought nervously to herself.

It proved to be a very nice visit; Agnes did not ask any questions, but let Lydia talk about whatever she wanted. The secretary had learned a long time ago that it was best to just let people who had experienced trauma talk about whatever came to mind. She would be there for Lydia if she ever needed to tell someone the whole story.

After her visit with Agnes, Lydia went home and called her supervisor, Wanda, at work. She knew there was a good chance that they had filled her job; after all, business does not stop merely because someone drops out of the picture. Thanks be to God, however, her position was still open.

"We just kept hoping you would come back. Mr. Pederson said he would give it another month, and then he would have to get someone else. Gotta tell you, though, he was not looking forward to it. You know how he likes your work." Wanda was so happy to hear from Lydia that she could not stop talking.

"Wanda? Oh, Wanda?" Lydia was trying to get her attention.

"Oh, sorry, Lydia, I'm just so excited!"

"Thanks, but when should I start back again? Would it be okay to take the rest of this week off, and start on Monday?"

There was a slight pause on Wanda's end. "Are you sure? Do you feel up to it?"

"I will be by the time Monday rolls around. Right now I'm really tired, but I'll be going stir-crazy by next week. You know me!" Lydia laughed.

"Okay, that should be alright, if you feel up to it. What happened to you anyway?"

Oh boy. Wanda never pulls any punches. And, of course, there has to be something to put on the paperwork. There was always paperwork...

"Not sure. I was kidnapped..."

Lydia heard Wanda's sharp intake of breath. "From here? Our parking lot?"

"Probably just one of those freak happenings." *Too right,* Lydia thought. "I doubt something like that would happen again. After all, the lights had all gone out."

"That's what Ned told us. We weren't really sure what to believe from him, though."

"Yes, I heard about him." Lydia made a mental note to herself to look Ned up as soon as she could. She really needed to know what happened to him that night.

"He was really bad there for awhile. He's back to work, but refuses to work the night shift. The only reason he is allowed to stay on is because he's been with us for so long."

"Poor Ned. I'm glad he's doing better, though."

There was a short pause in the conversation.

Then Lydia said, "Guess I'd better go. Lots to be done around here. Like taking a nap..." *And getting out of where this conversation is going...*

Wanda laughed. "You do that!"

She did.

In the next few days, it seemed the whole town learned of her return. Her friends threw her a welcome-back party, keeping the festivities low-key due to the circumstances behind why she was away in the first place.

She was called in to the police station to answer more questions, but she couldn't provide them with much more information than she had given them previously. When asked for a description, she gave them the story that she had been knocked out and had awakened in a dark room.

What was the sense of giving them a description of a vampire?

Lydia almost laughed at that thought. *"Just bring in anyone that looks suspicious and parade him past a mirror. If he doesn't show a reflection, that's your boy."* Yeah, right.

That Sunday, the family could hardly get out of the church for all the people swarming around them. Lydia was grateful to hear of all the prayers on her behalf; she felt terrible when she thought about how she had almost fallen into a spiritual place from which she may not have returned, if it hadn't been for the intercessions of those around her now.

She pushed that out of her mind. There was simply no way she ever wanted to revisit the agony she had gone through. Instead, she concentrated on the happy faces around her.

That night, Lydia went to bed early. Morning would come soon enough...then it was back to work, and back to normal. She hoped.

CHAPTER 18

BZZZZZ!!!

Six-thirty...Lydia yawned and sat up. Morning already!

She felt really rested for the first time since her return, and what's more, she felt truly healed, at least physically. Memories of her imprisonment and treatment surfaced on occasion, and she knew someday she would have to face them down. Some other day, but not now...

The only thing she did insist on when she got to work was to be moved to a different cubicle. She couldn't look out her doorway without remembering *him* standing there, that small smile on his lips.

"But why? I like having you here next to me so I can throw things at you!" her co-worker, Kim, teased her.

"Right, like extra work. No, really, I guess I just need more light. That end cubicle is still close enough. You just have to walk further to use me as target practice!" Lydia grinned at her friend as she started to box her things up.

Once she had her new cubicle the way she wanted it, and the tech department had sent someone to set up her computer, she settled in to work. After logging on, she brought up the accounting file she had been working on, hoping against hope...

Oh, wonderful. She looked at the screen and sighed. *So nice to know that everyone sidestepped that accounting problem just for me.* She smiled ruefully. *Oh well, nothing like a challenge. Now where was that shipping document...?*

At lunchtime, Lydia felt that she simply could not stay inside any longer. It was one of those days when summer seemed to extend its regime into the spring season. In other words, the weather was unseasonably warm, which made it difficult for Lydia to concentrate on her work.

"I'm going for a walk," she told Kim. "Shouldn't be long. I just have to go out and soak up that sunshine."

"Oh, yeah, wow, I should do that, too. But here I sit, just me and my lunchbox." Kim grinned; she liked exercise like a rabbit likes coyotes.

Lydia smiled back. "Ta-ta! I'll bring you back a ray of sunshine!"

Outside, she walked along the tree-lined path, taking in the sights, sounds, and smells. Far-sighted civic authorities had mandated that every building complex in town had to either provide a greenscape or leave some of the surrounding wilderness standing when the buildings were constructed. It was not unusual to see rabbits and the occasional deer around the campus. Lydia loved this area; she even walked it on the days when she wasn't at work.

Turning left, she inadvertently took a path that came out, to her dismay, right about where she had been attacked that awful night. She quickly turned around and ran back the way she had come, her heart thudding in her throat. She couldn't get out of there soon enough.

When she finally stopped to catch her breath, she heard a rush of water somewhere down a path she didn't remember seeing before. Curious, she took the short walk down and came across a lovely little fountain splashing in its own tiny alcove. It was such a delight to see the sun sparkle through the water as it splashed down a series of concrete leaves into a pool bordered by small purple flowers. The sun shining on the side of the building across the path from it made the area even warmer and more peaceful than the surrounding foliage.

She watched, entranced by this delightful surprise, until suddenly a shadow seemed to pass over.

She looked up.

Odd...no clouds in the sky. Must have been a tree branch. She looked up at the area above the fountain. *No, there was no wind to cause any of the leaves or branches to block the sunlight in any way.*

Now she had the odd feeling she was being watched. Was someone standing at a window in the nearby building, peering out at her?

Lydia shaded her eyes and looked up at the rows of windows. No one seemed to be at any of the windows, at first glance. Then she noticed that, on the fourth floor, the closed drapes on one of the windows were moving, as if someone had just been looking out.

She also suddenly realized that she'd never been on this side of the complex. That frightened, headlong run must have taken her a lot further than she had thought. Uneasiness fell on her like a cloak; suddenly she had the feeling she ought to be getting back to work. Although she would have loved to sit by the fountain, she knew she wouldn't be able to come back. It was all too unsettling, thinking that someone was watching her.

"Here ya go!"

Kim came into Lydia's cubicle and dumped a fair amount of paperwork on Lydia's desk. "Boss-man says he wants a copy of each page. Sorry about all the staples."

Lydia made a face. "If you were all that sorry, you'd have pulled them out for me."

Kim snorted. "Are you kidding? You should see the 'gifts' he gave me! Makes your pile look like a dream. And get this...he wants the copies all stapled like the originals."

Lydia grumbled, "Oh, I'll give him staples..."

"In his backside, no doubt!" Kim laughed and went back to her own cube.

Lydia pulled all the staples, making sure to paperclip the correct pages together, and headed for the nearest copier...and stopped.

There was a sign on it: "Broken – AGAIN!"

Nuts! That left only the copier in the hallway.

Rounding the corner into the passage, Lydia happened to glance up. She saw the mirror there, and shuddered at the memory of when she had first realized something was wrong with the "man" she had met.

She shook off the thought. It was just a blessing that she could see her own reflection!

As she stood at the copier and watched the paper pass into the machine, she suddenly felt a cold wind brush past behind her.

"Oh, who left the door open? It's not that warm yet!" Cursing menopause and the heat these older ladies had to deal with, Lydia marched down the hall to the door.

To her surprise, it was closed, and no one was anywhere near it. She looked around, puzzled; perhaps someone had gone out. Uneasily, she turned around and went back to the copier. She hastily gathered what she had completed and hurried back to her cube. Ah well, she had plenty of other tasks that were more important than making copies.

She realized that her heart was beating fast, and her breath was coming in short gasps. *Oh, what a time for an anxiety attack! Maybe I should have stayed home another week...*

That weekend was as glorious as the rest of the week had been, and Steve was outside trimming the still-bare rosebushes; "giving them their spring haircut", he liked to say.

The kids were home, and Lydia was busy getting lunch. Pat and Trudy were playing a video game, and their laughs emanated from the family room. As Lydia walked in, the game was drawing to a close. Suddenly, Pat's character made a sneaky dive, and Trudy's character disappeared in a puff of smoke.

Trudy howled, "Oh, that sucks!"

Now Lydia had heard this saying many times from her kids, and in fact had used it quite often herself, but now the phrase brought back horrendous memories from when she was held captive.

She asked, "Uh, Trude? Can you use a different phrase?"

Trudy gave her mom a "what's gotten into you?" look. "Why?"

"Uh, it's...well, it's overused."

Trudy rolled her eyes. "How about 'bites'?"

Lydia winced, and her stomach did a flip-flop. "Worse. Even more over-used."

Trudy shook her head in disbelief. "Whatever..."

Pat rolled his eyes in agreement with his sister. "Okay, how about 'stinks'?"

"Yeah, that works."

The kids looked at each other and shrugged. No doubt about it, Mom was getting weirder every day.

Just then, Steve rushed in, cursing a blue streak, and headed straight for the kitchen sink.

"Steve? What happened?" Lydia joined him while he ran his finger under running water.

"Rotten thorns! Roses have to be the most ungrateful, miserable plants in the world. Ripped my finger wide open!"

"Oh, ouch! Keep it under the water. How bad is it?"

Steve held up the digit, still bleeding.

Suddenly he stiffened and looked around slowly at Lydia. She caught his caution and understood. Rather sadly, she realized he still wasn't sure she wouldn't revert to...

"I'm fine, honey," she whispered. Then, realizing Trudy had come in behind her, she turned around to ask her to get the bandages.

The words died in her throat. Trudy was staring at her dad's finger, eyes bright and tongue showing ever so slightly between her lips. It moved slowly back and forth over her teeth.

"Trudy!" Lydia screamed, shaking her daughter by the shoulders.

That brought Trudy back to wherever she had gone. "What? Wha'd I do? Mom, what was that for?" She shrugged away from Lydia and rubbed her shoulders.

Lydia blinked and shook her head. Had she been hallucinating? "Your dad needs a bandage," she said in a normal voice.

"Yeah, I see that." Trudy opened a cabinet and tossed him the box. "But I don't think screaming at me is necessary. It doesn't look like we'll need to call the paramedics."

Lydia rubbed her eyes. "Sorry, Trudy. I was...just...really concerned."

Then to change the subject: "Okay, lunch is ready. Who's for a turkey sandwich?"

While the kids were washing up and kidding each other about the game they'd just finished, Lydia turned silently to look at Steve. With a lurch to her stomach, she could tell by the look on his face that she had not imagined anything. Steve's worried gaze followed Trudy as she went to the table.

It hadn't been Lydia's reaction he had been concerned about. It was Trudy's!

As they sat eating lunch, Lydia took the opportunity to ask her daughter some offhand questions, designed to try and make some sense out of what had gone on at the sink.

"So, how are classes going, Trudy?"

Trudy sighed. "They've been tough. We just had a mid-term in my phlebotomy class, and it about wore me out!"

Lydia felt a little relieved. That must be the reason for the interest in Steve's cut finger, and also for the way she reacted to the incident. She had an interest in the workings of the human circulation system, and she was worn out from a tough test. Had to be it! Nothing else made sense, and Lydia wasn't about to let any other possibility come to mind.

Trudy went on. "But Victor did wonderfully well on the test. I'm so proud of him!"

"Oh. Right. So how are things with you two?"

"Terrific! We see each other almost every night!"

"I thought that class was during the day."

"I switched to the night class." Seeing her parents' worried looks, she said, "Don't worry. Victor escorts me back to my dorm after class. He's such an old-fashioned type! I feel so safe with him!"

He'd better stay 'old-fashioned', Lydia thought to herself. She could see the same sentiment reflected in the faces of the two men at the table as well. Aloud, she said, "I hope he can make it to dinner some night during spring break."

"Yeah," Pat said good-naturedly. "I'd like to know what his intentions are with my baby sister!"

At this, Trudy stuck her tongue out at Pat. He threw his napkin at her, and lunch dissolved into a four-person napkin war.

CHAPTER 19

Things were not as happy at work, to Lydia's dismay. Every day she felt more and more apprehensive, although she couldn't put her finger on what the problem was. Nothing had changed with her work relationships or the amount of tasks she was assigned, but there was just something in the air. She felt cold much of the time, no matter the weather or how warmly she dressed.

She stopped taking walks outside; she was constantly tormented by the tiny pricks of mosquitoes, although she never seemed to slap any. Walking indoors instead wasn't nearly as interesting. She continued to wander the halls anyway, just to keep her muscles from atrophying due to long periods of sitting in front of a computer.

Then came the voices. Or voice. She couldn't tell for sure. She knew it came from outside of herself; unlike that warm, safe one that she now firmly believed was the Lord speaking from within her very soul, this one was cold. It was accompanied by cold spaces of air as well. She never understood any words, just an indistinct whisper.

A man's laughter, innocently coming from across the room, would cause her to jump in fright. She started avoiding shadows, and again wondered if she was losing her sanity. Her co-workers were starting to worry about her; she could tell from the looks on their faces. No matter how she told herself that she was imagining things, and to stop acting so ridiculous, the situation seemed to only get worse.

One morning, after an especially uneasy night of horrid dreams, she awoke to the feeling of lips on her bare shoulder. She panicked, and shrieked.

Steve, shocked, backpedaled to his side of the bed. "What? What's wrong, Lydia?" He reached for her, but then quickly drew his hand back.

"Oh!" she gasped. "I am so sorry, Steve. Just a bad dream."

"You sure you're okay?" Steve still looked worried.

Lydia knew she had to make him feel better, so she cozied up to him. "Yes, I'm sure. Now," she said in her best come-hither voice, "was there something you wanted?"

Steve was dressing for work when his cell phone went off. Frowning, he picked it up. Why would anyone from work call him now? He was within twenty minutes of the office. Couldn't it wait until he got there?

Actually, it was a text from his secretary. "Steve, you're needed in Atlanta ASAP. I've got your plane and hotel reservations taken care of and sent the info to your laptop. Head straight for the airport. You won't need anything from here. All the reports I've sent ahead should suffice."

A text? Lou never sent texts...Oh well; maybe she was in a hurry.

He called Lydia, and then reached into the closet for his travel bag.

Lydia sat at her desk, trying to fight down her apprehension. In two days, the kids would be home for spring break, and they had arranged with Trudy to bring her young man to dinner on Saturday. Now Steve would be gone! She'd miss his input; Trudy seemed to be so serious about this guy. Lydia wanted more than just her own opinion about him. Sure, Pat would be there, but he lacked the years of experience that Steve had.

To take her mind off things, she walked over to Kim's office to have a chat.

"What's doin'?"

Kim turned from her monitor and smiled, happy to have a reason to take her eyes off the screen for awhile. "The usual slog. What're you up to?"

"Oh, just taking a break. Want to go for coffee?"

"Sure, let's go!"

The two friends headed for the break room. As they got near, Lydia spied a familiar figure coming out.

"Ned! Hey, how are you?"

Ned didn't answer; instead, he gave Lydia a startled, almost frightened look, and dashed back to the security office. He looked back at the two women once, and then closed the door tight.

Lydia looked at Kim, amazed.

Kim just sighed as she returned Lydia's gaze. "Yep, that's pretty much how he acts any more. He is seeing a counselor, but I don't see any difference. For awhile, it seemed he was getting better, but lately, he seems to have reverted."

Lydia had a thought. "When do you figure he started reverting?"

Kim thought for a minute. "Not sure. I don't see him all that much, but I started hearing people say they thought he was getting odd again maybe, oh, a week or so ago. Why?"

"Just curious." However, it was more than mere curiosity that had Lydia asking that question. The strange things she was experiencing seemed to have started again at about the same time. Suddenly she had a real need to talk to Ned.

"I'd like to say hi to Ned, since I haven't seen him in such a long time. I'll catch up to you in a few."

Kim looked doubtful. "Good luck..."

She went into the break room, and Lydia walked the rest of the way to the security office.

What a difference between now and the last time she had visited him! She had to wonder what happened to him that night. Hopefully, she would get some answers, but she promised herself that she wouldn't try too hard. He was pretty tightly strung, from what she had been told.

She knocked on the door, calling quietly, "Ned?"

No response.

"Ned, it's me, Lydia. Do you mind if I come in?"

Nothing.

She tried the door; of course it was unlocked, since he wasn't allowed to lock it during the day. Going in, she noticed the lights were dimmed.

"Ned?" She saw him behind the desk, wringing his hands nervously as he watched her movements.

"Are you okay?" He had never been like this. As she got closer, she noticed that he had lost a lot of weight. His skin was pallid, as if he had not been outdoors in a long time.

He finally spoke; his voice was faint and tremulous. "Lydia? Is that you? You're back??" He looked slightly more animated now that he recognized her.

"Yes. I've been working for a couple of weeks. Hadn't you heard?"

"Maybe. I...I don't know anymore. Nothing is right. I'm feeling so...there's something going on." He looked terribly uneasy.

Lydia started around the desk to try to comfort him, but he scuttled quickly away, looking sidelong at her as if he was a wild animal being hunted.

"Ned," she said softly, "can you tell me what happened the night the lights went out here?" She didn't want to say "the night I was abducted"; she thought maybe that would send him over the edge.

Ned got still and quiet, staring ahead. Finally, just as Lydia was going to repeat the question, he spoke.

"How can I forget?" he said, almost too quietly to be heard. "After you left my office, I turned the TV off and got my stuff ready to leave. Just as I was powering down the computer, the lights went out. I got the flashlight and went to the back of the building. It was so dark..."

He swallowed hard. His eyes grew wide with fright as he thought about that night. Lydia reached out, but thought better of it and drew her hand back.

"Ned? You don't have to go on..."

He looked at her as if seeing her clearly for the first time. "Oh, but I do. You're the only person who has heard this. Now that you're back, I can finally share this with someone I think might understand!"

Lydia nodded. "You're probably right, Ned."

He looked a little surprised at her quick agreement, but went on with his story. "I got to the fuse box, and then my flashlight went out. I heard some weird noise, and then I was pushed up against the wall. There was a hand around my throat, and then…" He shut his eyes, visibly quaking. There were tears running down his cheeks.

He was having trouble breathing as he gasped out, "I saw a…a…face. Then…the teeth! Oh God, help me, the teeth! Sharp…fangs…it…"

Now he was crying, rocking back and forth. This time, he let Lydia hold him. She made soothing sounds, as if he was a frightened little boy waking from a nightmare. He grasped her arm tightly as he let the pain and fear he had held within himself for so long wail out of him.

She thought over what he had just disclosed, and a horrifying thought occurred to her. *If Vlad was with me the whole time the lights were out, who…or what…attacked Ned?* Were there two of those monsters? Or more? She tried to quell her own rising panic and fear as she comforted her friend.

At length, he quieted, and Lydia let go of him. As she straightened up, his collar came away from his throat, and she gasped at the healing puncture wounds. He noticed her looking at them and pulled his collar back around his neck.

"The next thing I knew, I was in a hotel room, and someone was dragging me out the door and into a patrol car. I spent some time in a hospital, where they treated this," he pointed to his neck, "calling it 'an animal bite of some kind'." He squeezed his eyes tightly shut again. "As if that description even comes close. I never told anyone what happened. They already think I'm nuts."

"What has happened since then?" Lydia spoke gently; it was imperative that she find out, since her own sanity might hinge on what he was experiencing now.

"Everything was going okay, except for my recurring nightmares." Lydia nodded in agreement. "But just lately I've felt cold spots, and I can't bear being outside. I also feel a need to be home before night falls. I'm just too scared to be out anymore."

He looked imploringly at Lydia. "Is it over? Am I imagining things?"

Lydia was surprised. Here she was trying to get that affirmation from Ned, and he needed it from her! Suddenly the need shifted; she felt Ned had to hear something positive in order to get on with his life. She knew she had to provide that optimism.

She looked levelly and steadily into his eyes. "Ned, listen to me. I am sure that, now that you've let all this out to me, you will start to feel much better. Think about it; there have been no more instances of attacks, either to animals or humans, since that night. I am absolutely certain that whatever that was, is now gone."

"Do you really think so? What about you? Did you see anything that night? I never did hear what happened to you."

Lydia gave him her rote explanation. He still looked doubtful.

"But what about those cold spots?"

Lydia thought something up quickly. "Probably this old heating/air conditioning system. The company's too cheap to get it fixed properly." She hoped she was right. The idea of a second vampire turned her veins to ice.

Suddenly another thought occurred to her, and it was all she could do not to panic: *What had happened to Vlad? Where was he?* Those were questions that had neither been asked nor answered.

Lydia put those thoughts out of her head; she couldn't show panic in front of Ned in his fragile state. She had to get back to her desk, where she would have some privacy to think things over.

She leaned over and gave him a kiss on the forehead, trying her best to look cheerful and optimistic. He showed some of his old self as he smiled and said, "Don't do too much of that. I might get used to it!"

As Lydia smiled and turned to leave, Ned's voice, trembling again, made her turn back. "Lydia? Do you know more than what you are letting on? You didn't seem to be shocked by what I told you." His eyes held a look of fear and uncertainty.

She thought quickly. What should she tell him? What would he do with the information?

In the end, she simply said, "Yes. There is a lot more, but I can't bring myself to discuss it. Suffice it to say, what I experienced makes it very easy to believe what you have just told me."

He opened his mouth to speak, but Lydia held up a hand. "I really can't bring myself to talk about it. Please. Just know that we're in this together. I do believe we are safe now, that's all I can tell you."

She turned and left, walking back to her office. Kim had gone back a lot earlier, so she decided not to get coffee after all. Her stomach had knotted up from her conversation with Ned, and she felt like she wouldn't be able to hold anything down anyway.

As she headed slowly back to her cube, she felt as if a dark cloud of fear was following her.

Was he gone? Were they safe?

She certainly hoped so.

Back in her cube, Lydia tried to fight the fear rising in her, threatening to tear away the fragile peace she had finally built up. A sense of foreboding washed over her, and she realized with a start that she had had a feeling of dread for a couple of weeks. She just hadn't acknowledged it, preferring to hide it under her daily activities.

By all accounts, Vlad had simply disappeared that night in the church. This meant that he was still out there terrorizing someone. Lydia couldn't stand the idea of someone else having to endure what she had endured.

"Lord," she prayed, "please get rid of him, and the other one, too, if there is one."

In her heart, she felt one word.

Soon.

CHAPTER 20

As Lydia got back to her pile of tasks, she heard a soft knock on the metal joining on her cubicle. She turned to see a young lady, dressed in a turquoise skirt and jacket. The woman smiled and put out her hand.

"Lydia? I'm Denise, from HR."

"Uh, hello." Lydia shook the proffered hand, confused. *Why would someone from HR want to talk to me? Have I missed getting some paperwork done? I'd been told everything was in order for me to go back to work...*

Denise's words interrupted her thoughts. "We've received your résumé for the admin position in East Four, and it looks like they would like to interview you."

"My résumé?" Lydia was really confused now. "I didn't send it in.

Kim!" she directed down the hall, "did you do a funny-ha-ha and send in my résumé to HR?"

Kim poked her head out of her cube. "Heck no! I'd be the last to do that! Who would I dump my extra work on?"

Denise cleared her throat. "Well, nonetheless, the executive in charge of this team would like to see you. All you have to do is talk to him and tell him there's been some sort of mistake. I'm sure he'll understand."

"Okay, I guess. When is the interview?"

"Now."

"What? But...but I look a wreck! Can we reschedule for tomorrow? I promise I'll look less ratty!"

Denise looked at Lydia's jeans and beer-joint T-shirt. She raised an eyebrow. "No, he wants to see you now."

Lydia stood up and reluctantly followed Denise out of the room. She knew this was a golden opportunity, but at the same time, she couldn't figure out why her résumé had even been considered.

Well, here's some time I'll never get back, Lydia thought to herself as she followed Denise down hallways and from one building to another. *I hope my interviewer at least has some candy on his desk that he'd like to share...*

They finally came to a stop in front of an elevator. The doors opened and they entered. It was a short, swift ride up to the fourth floor, where they got out.

"Just this way now." Denise led Lydia down a carpeted hallway to a pair of heavy wooden doors. They entered a wood-paneled room with several desks spaced generously apart. Another door opened off from this one into a private office.

Lydia saw that there were two other admins in the room, and that they were getting their things together to go home. She frowned and looked at her watch.

Six-thirty already! She had lost all track of time this afternoon. Her stomach growled; now she was hoping her interviewer would have sandwiches!

She looked at Denise, who was busy writing something in a notebook. "Isn't it a little late in the day for an interview? I have to go home and make dinner."

Lydia then remembered; she was flying solo at home; who would she be making dinner for?

She sighed. *Okay, fine, I'll eat later.*

A figure caught her eye. There was one other person in the room besides the admins and Denise and herself. A young lady with a housekeeping cart was busily emptying the trash. She looked up at Lydia, and they exchanged smiles and nods.

Denise opened the door Lydia had noticed upon entering. Inside, it was very dark, as the curtains were drawn over the windows. A small light on the desk threw shadows behind the pieces of furniture arranged neatly in the room.

"Please take a seat," Denise told her. "Your interviewer will be in shortly."

"What is his name?" Lydia suddenly realized that information had not been provided.

Denise looked down at her notes. She looked puzzled. "His name? It's not on here. That's strange!"

Lydia almost rolled her eyes. *Typical.* "Well, who works in this office?"

"He's new, and I don't handle the executive positions. You can ask him when he comes in."

Well, that's weird, Lydia thought.

She looked around. "What's with the dark? Don't you think he'd like a little light to see by so we can carry on a conversation like two normal people?"

"His admins tell me he's had a migraine today, and insists on the dark so that he can work."

"Ah. Understandable." Lydia nodded. "My daughter gets those."

Denise smiled. "Good luck, Lydia. Please let us know how it goes." She went out, closing the door behind her.

Lydia walked around a bit, rather nervous about this turn of events. Passing the windows, she became curious as to what she could see in this direction, and from the fourth floor. She hadn't been up this high in the complex the whole time she'd worked here.

She peered out, then down. Startled, she found she was looking straight at the fountain she had discovered just a few days earlier!

Ah, so that was it! She knew she was being watched that day! So, some lonely executive had seen her and was now trying to get to know her better...Although she was flattered, Lydia knew she would have to tell Mr. Whoever-it-was that she was happily married, and that was the end of it.

The opening of a door behind her interrupted her musings. Before she even turned around, she suddenly had two distinct and very unsettling sensations.

The first was a near-frosty coldness in the air that raised the hairs on the back of her neck and on her arms. The second was the sudden fire-like pain in her wrists. Heart thudding, legs threatening to melt beneath her, she knew without looking who it was that stood behind her.

She whirled to face him, and almost screamed.

"Lydia," Vlad said with a cold smile, "we meet again."

CHAPTER 21

Her first terrified thought was *Oh, no, not again!*

She backed up against the wall, shifting ever so slightly to the right and away from Vlad's angle of approach. Moving very slowly, her legs were in rabbit mode, ready to leap away at the first opportunity. Her heart hammered in her chest, and she had to fight the urge to panic and bolt. He would be on her before she could get halfway across the room, and she had learned early on that he was more inclined to attack her when she was running away from him.

Lydia watched Vlad warily as he walked slowly around the desk. He came towards her steadily, smoothly, like a leopard stalking its prey. His eyes locked onto hers, and she suddenly felt drawn into his gaze. Her mind whirled; her memories were fading, and she was beginning to doubt that her ordeal had ever happened. *Such a handsome face...how could I think he would have ever done any of those things...*

Her reverie exploded as the pain in her wrists intensified, and she shook her head. Her mind cleared from whatever power his gaze had had on her, and she inched away as he approached. The throbbing pain was unrelenting; she tried to look at her hands without being obvious, to see if they were bleeding. It didn't feel as if they were, but she hid them behind her back nonetheless. She didn't know what Vlad would do if he saw the scars, and she didn't want to find out.

The door was only a few feet from where she stood. She kept edging toward it, knowing it was probably a futile maneuver but feeling like she had to do something. She wasn't going to just take his awful treatment of her, like a sheep before the slaughter.

Vlad could see what she was trying to do, and he shook his head as if to say, "You know you won't get away."

Then he smiled...

Lydia found all of her nightmarish memories returning at the sight of those fangs. She could feel her body tensing and her face twitching with revulsion. Her body shook as she braced herself for the inevitable.

To her utter surprise, however, he stopped walking towards her. Instead, he became seemingly interested in a chair, gazing down at the upholstery as if it was the most fascinating thing he had ever seen. He ran his hand nonchalantly across the expensive brown leather on its back. Lydia glanced again at the door, then back at Vlad, trying to figure out what he was planning.

Finally, he turned and spoke to Lydia, who was in about Stage Red of takeoff mode. "You know, you are deucedly hard to kill."

Lydia's voice cracked, and she said through a dry throat, "Guess I have friends in high places."

Vlad peered at Lydia's neck, and she shrank under his stare, trying to protect her throat without using her hands, which still pained her tremendously. "Your surgeons certainly did a good job. Not a scar anywhere."

She hated this casual assessment of her condition, as if he was commenting on a minor operation.

She narrowed her eyes. "No thanks to you!" she spat at him.

Vlad looked as if he was going to start towards her again, and she readied herself for an escape attempt, but instead he began to pace back and forth in front of her. He spoke again, amusement in his voice.

"I'm so glad you were able to come in for this little chat. When I saw you down there at the fountain, I must say I was very surprised. Especially since I'd left you for dead."

A sudden revelation hit her like a thunderbolt: It had been right after the day she'd discovered the fountain that she had started feeling cold. The apprehension, the feeling of being watched...

Her hand suddenly shot to the back of her neck. *It hadn't been mosquitoes!*

And Trudy'd felt them too...! No...!

He smiled broadly, and to her horror he ran his tongue over his sharp teeth.

Lydia swallowed her terror and tried to look in control of herself. She crossed her arms, relieved to see that the scars were still invisible.

"So you arranged this...'interview'? Well, sorry," she said sarcastically, "but I already have a job that I would prefer to keep. Find another chew toy."

With that, her legs finally released their pent-up energy, and she bolted to the door.

Vlad was faster. He caught her and pinned her up against the wall, pushing her chin up with one hand, tilting her head one way and another. She dug her nails into his arms as she struggled to get away.

It didn't seem to faze him a bit. He calmly stroked her throat with the index finger of his other hand, especially where her pulse beat fast. His eyes caressed her flesh almost lovingly. She pushed at him, feeling a scream welling up from her deepest self. As it rushed up, she took a deep breath and...

He stopped its onrush by putting his hand over her mouth. His eyes were like stone as he whispered near her ear, "If you scream, I will kill anyone who comes through that door. Have I made myself clear?"

Lydia's eyes widened in terror. Would he really do that? Yes, of course he would. Her past experience with him proved that out.

She nodded slowly, and he released her mouth. He returned to stroking her neck and collarbone, gazing down at the flesh as she trembled under his scrutiny.

Lydia knew for certain now that this creature was far more than just a vampire. In her soul, she knew he was much more dangerous than that.

A mere vampire stole lives. This demon stole souls.

He bent down, and she could feel the pain as he bit into her throat, felt the pull as he fed on her. She expected to fade and collapse, but he drew back after a short time, licking his lips. He could read the terrified look in her eyes, and he laughed as he let go of her.

"No, Lydia, I am not going to take you into my world again. I have found someone else for that purpose. No, you are far too valuable as you are."

From somewhere deep within herself, Lydia found the courage to respond. She drew herself up and almost shouted at him, "No! I will not allow this! I am leaving!"

So saying, she turned towards the door, heedless of the blood seeping down onto her shirt.

Vlad grabbed her, whirled her around. "Think seriously on this, Lydia. Remember," he growled menacingly, "I know where your daughter is."

Her heart felt like it had stopped. She almost shrieked, but swallowed the impulse with some effort. Tears sprang once again to her eyes, and she pleaded with him, "No, please! I'll..." she sobbed, her heart sinking, "I'll stay. Just leave my daughter alone!"

Vlad smiled triumphantly. "Much better. I'm sure we'll get along fine."

He released her again, and she wobbled shakily toward the door. She could feel her world collapsing around her.

"Oh, and Lydia?"

She turned to face him once again, and jumped. He was right behind her, although she hadn't heard him move.

She stared at him dully. "What?"

His eyes blazing, he said mockingly, "Welcome to the team."

That was the breaking point. Lydia gave him a long, hate-filled stare, and spat at him. Then she turned on her heel and stormed out, slamming the door on his derisive laughter.

CHAPTER 22

In the main office, Lydia noticed that everyone else had gone for the day. She sat down at an empty desk, put her head on her arms, and cried. It was possible she was taking a great chance being in such close proximity to him; after all, he might come after her again if he knew she was still there. There just wasn't enough strength left in her to get up and flee the room.

She became aware of soft footsteps behind her, and braced herself for yet another onslaught...but the hand on her shoulder was small and gentle. Lydia looked up into the concerned eyes of the cleaning lady.

"You are okay, madam?" the young woman asked. She had a foreign accent that Lydia couldn't place.

"Yes...I mean, ...no...um, I don't know..." Lydia wiped her eyes and tried to pull herself together.

The young woman smiled, a sad look on her face. Her eyes filled with compassion and concern as she noticed the blood on Lydia's neck and T-shirt, but said nothing about it. This puzzled Lydia; why didn't the sight of it cause a reaction?

"You are tired? No food? I will bring you some."

Lydia tried to protest, but the woman was already at her cart. She brought back a parcel wrapped in a linen cloth.

Lydia's curiosity overtook her fear of the demon in the adjoining office. Why would she wrap her dinner in linen? Wasn't that kind of strange for a cleaning lady to do?

Lydia gave her companion a shaky smile. "No, really, I'm...I'm okay."

It seemed her words fell on deaf ears, as the woman continued to unwrap the parcel. Lydia watched silently for a moment, then asked, "What's your name? I haven't seen you here before." Lydia was warmed by this stranger's presence and care, and, although she felt escape was essential, she also felt somehow drawn to this young lady, and safe in her company.

"I am called Teresa." She finished uncovering the parcel and stepped back. An almost bite-sized loaf of bread and a covered cup rested on the desk.

Lydia looked at the small repast, then at Teresa. Was this her gracious friend's only dinner? Once again, she protested. "I couldn't, really. You'll go hungry. I can just go home and..."

Lydia tried to rise to her feet and found that her legs were too weak to support her. She fell back into the chair, her head spinning. Vlad must have drained her more than she'd realized.

Teresa stood silently, looking as if she was listening to a voice only she could hear. She nodded briefly, and then closed her eyes for a moment, her face tilted toward the ceiling. Opening them again, she brought her gaze down to stare directly into Lydia's own puzzled eyes.

Lydia couldn't believe what she saw. Teresa seemed to glow; her eyes held a fire of love and warmth that seemed to draw Lydia into them.

Teresa spoke. "Lydia, what is before you is the Bread of Heaven and the Cup of Salvation. You must strengthen yourself for the trials to come."

Lydia was unsettled, to say the least. Was this true, or was it blasphemy? With all that had gone on this day, she couldn't tell what was real and what wasn't anymore.

"You're saying this is Eucharist? My Savior's Body and Blood? How am I to know what you're saying is true? Who are you, anyway?" Lydia narrowed her eyes and looked suspiciously at Teresa.

"You will know me here as Teresa. This is not a lie. It is the Spanish translation of my real name. I have taken on a persona that reflects a Spanish heritage, although in life my home was in France. You have known me as Thérèse."

Lydia looked more closely at Teresa, and realized with a shock that she did, indeed, look familiar. Those eyes...that smile...put her in a nun's habit, and...

"Thérèse? Thérèse of Lisieux?" Lydia was agape.

Teresa nodded. "You took me as your patron saint many years ago, and so I was chosen to be your protector and provider in these coming days of trial."

Lydia shook her head as if to clear up her thoughts. If only she could believe...

Teresa smiled gently. "You must believe. If not in me, then in the Gifts before you."

Lydia shot a brief, panicked look at Vlad's office door.

"He is gone," Teresa assured her. "Do not worry. We are alone."

Lydia suddenly realized two things in the same flash. One, Teresa could read her mind. And two—miracle of miracles!—even though he'd attacked her again, Vlad was not able to hold her in his thrall.

With this last realization warming her heart, Lydia reached for the Bread and Wine. As Teresa looked on, Lydia partook of the Eucharist. As the Sacrament went down her poor wrecked throat, she could feel the electricity she now always received when she communicated with her Lord.

Unfortunately, the sensation was not as long-lasting as it had been. Nor did it heal the marks on her neck. Lydia could tell when she felt at her throat.

"Teresa, what about this?" Lydia pointed to the puncture wounds.

"They will subside. No one will see them. However, the demon will. If they are not visible to him, he will become suspicious, and our plans will be thwarted."

Teresa lovingly packed away the empty cup into the linen. When she returned from her cart, she said, "Please do not be afraid. Have faith in Him Who loved us before we ever knew Him. He will not leave you unprotected."

Then she added, "Know that you are not alone in this ordeal."

Lydia's eyes opened wide in surprise at this revelation. "Oh? Meaning?"

"There are thousands of good souls like you who are undergoing great trials at this time. The Father of Lies has sent his minions out to attack God's people, and your suffering is joined with these others for the salvation of souls."

Lydia said, "So you're telling me that I'm not the only person with a demonic remora..."

Teresa smiled gently. "No. You have many brothers and sisters being tormented in this way, and in other ways. Some worse than you."

Lydia leaned her arm on the desk, supporting her forehead in her hand. She sighed wearily, then muttered sarcastically, "Oh goodie. Maybe we should form a support group. Get matching T-shirts. Start a bowling league..." At the moment, she was too tired and discouraged to feel any kind of sympathy or optimism.

Teresa put her hand on Lydia's head. "I know this is distressing, but God does have a plan. That is why I am here. I will stay here to support you and help with your struggle to stay faithful."

Lydia sighed again and stood up. "Thank you, my dear sister. I feel that I'm really going to need you."

"God be with you."

The two women embraced. Then they parted company. Lydia left the room and headed to the building's exit doors, almost running in her haste to escape the memories of Vlad and his torments.

As for Teresa, she disappeared in a soft ray of light, cart and all.

CHAPTER 23

Lydia woke to a very bright morning. She felt almost too numb to move. At least it was Saturday. No going in to work, which was now a den of Hell as far as she was concerned. *If I survive this trial,* she thought, *I'll never complain about regular work again!*

She rose and peeked into the mirror with some trepidation, not all sure of what she would, or would not, see.

Phew! Her reflection was still intact, and, heaven be praised, her throat was once again unblemished! She sighed in relief and put on her robe.

Her footsteps made a lonely echo through the empty house as she walked down the stairs. She felt so alone, what with the kids well on their way to their own adult lives and Steve out and away so much. Lydia thought again how nice a small cottage would be instead of this huge "stuff-holder".

As she passed her cell phone lying on the kitchen counter, she noticed that there was a new text message. She picked it up.

It was a text from Steve.

That's odd, thought Lydia, *he usually calls when he's gotten to his destination.*

She read the text: "Made it! Getting a hotel room. Call you later. Steve."

Lydia was puzzled. Why would he text her with such a short message? And what texts he did send usually ended with "Love, Me." Why was he being so formal? *Oh well, probably just in a hurry. Not thinking.* She texted back, "Okay, love you," and set the phone down. She'd call him later. Right now, she really needed some coffee.

As Lydia sat outside in the warm sunshine drinking her coffee, she anticipated the events of the day. Pat and Trudy would be home sometime this afternoon. Spring Break had started, and she knew they were eager to be back at the old homestead. Nothing like Mom's home-cooked dinner, and Mom's washer and dryer!! Well, at least they knew how to wash their own clothes...

At some point today, Lydia knew she'd have a trip to make to the grocery store; she hoped Trudy would be home early for that.

The two of them shopping together made the trip quick and easy, and Trudy was really good at finding a bargain.

Then Lydia and Pat would prep the dinner ingredients. She had decided on chicken; ever since her captivity at the hands of Vlad, the sight of raw beef left her nauseous. She couldn't afford that feeling, especially since Trudy's beau would be coming to dinner that night.

She reasoned that it would probably be a good idea to get to Mass that evening. Pat was not very attentive to his weekly responsibility, and Lydia felt that he would not have time to plan some activity away tonight. Tomorrow, who knew? She felt bad about making him a "captive audience," but was of the opinion that it was her duty as his mother to do everything she could to keep his soul safe.

Especially now...

A shadow passed over her heart as she remembered Vlad's threats against her family. Could he really hurt them? She prayed about it, trying to leave the problem in God's capable hands.

Then she shook herself, got up, and went back into the kitchen. *Get busy,* she told herself, *and get your mind way from...all that.* Time to get stuff done; after all, they were safe there. As far as she knew, Vlad did not know where they lived.

Yet...

Ack! Go! Get busy! Now!

Lydia quickly gathered the laundry and shoved it into the washing machine. She figured that, with the piles of laundry the kids were probably bringing home, it would be a good idea to get hers and Steve's out of the way.

She sighed. *Oh Steve, why did you have to be called away right now? Ah well, we soldier on. Hopefully, this friend of Trudy's will be a nice kid.*

Lydia was in her room, and had just gotten dressed, when she heard the front door open.

"Mom?"

"Zat you, Trudes?"

"Yep." There was a thud, as she dropped her stuff in the hallway. "Pat's here too."

"Terrific! I'll be right down!" Lydia took one last look at herself, stroked her clean neck appreciatively, sent another grateful prayer heavenward, and headed back downstairs.

"Guess what, Mom? Victor's going to try to get here early today so he can go to church with us!" Trudy was standing at the foot of the stairs, practically vibrating with excitement.

"Oh, good!" A Catholic kid, or one who was willing to be supportive of Trudy's faith? Point One in his favor!

Lydia kissed her daughter on the cheek. She looked at the bag of dirty clothes, then at Trudy. "Laundry room will soon be cleared and ready for the next assault. Major hint here, meaning don't leave all this in the hallway."

"Yes, Motherrrr."

Lydia smiled. "And you're in the house now, dear; you can take off your sunglasses."

"I will. It's just that I've been kind of, well, headachy lately. Just during the day, though." She removed them and squinted, obviously affected by the daylight in the room.

Lydia looked concerned. "Should you see a doctor? I'm sure they can work you in this week."

Trudy shook her head. "No, I'll be okay. It doesn't happen all the time. I feel fine towards the evening. It's just that the days get so bright as we go towards summer."

Lydia had to agree. Not long ago, they'd had cool cloudy days, which was common for spring. But just recently it felt more like summer. She looked out the window. "It does seem like spring and summer are fighting for supremacy early this year."

Turning to Trudy, she asked her, "Do you want to hit the grocery store with me? The earlier we do this, the more time we'll have to make sure the house is in good order for our guest."

"Yeah, alright. You know, Victor doesn't care what the house looks like."

"Well, I do."

Pat walked in at that moment, after having spent some time in conversation with one of the neighbors outside. He was about to dump his backpack and laundry beside Trudy's, but at a look from his mom, he sighed.

"Hi, Mom. Yes, Mom. Going, Mom."

They laughed as he lugged his dirty clothes to the laundry room. Then he dropped the rest of his stuff on the kitchen table.

"Pat!" Lydia fixed him with her best "mom" look.

"Oh, I'm not going to leave it there." He gave his mom a kiss on the cheek, and punched Trudy playfully on the shoulder. "So what's for lunch?"

Lydia snorted. "Stick your hand in the fridge and see what jumps into it."

Lydia and Trudy ambled their way through the market, chatting about Victor and the anticipated meeting that evening. As they approached the meat counter, Lydia said, "Oh, gotta get some chicken. Should we grill? I'm not really sure how to use that behemoth in the back yard."

Lydia prattled on as she passed the beef section of the counter, studiously avoiding the sight of the red meat that always seemed to sicken her nowadays.

Then she suddenly realized that she was walking by herself. Looking behind her, she saw that Trudy had stopped beside the area she herself had quickly bypassed.

"Mom," asked Trudy, "Aren't we having steak? I kind of have a hankering for a good hunk of cow."

Lydia felt a little queasy. "Chicken's better for you."

Trudy made a face. "I always have that at school. Come on. Please??"

Lydia sighed. "Oh, all right. Pick something out, but bag it up so it doesn't leak on everything." The truth was, she felt as if she wouldn't make it through the register line if she had to look at that bloody red meat.

She pretended to be engrossed in a display of chutney while Trudy picked out what she wanted. Once she heard the "plunk" of product hitting cart, she turned to her daughter...

...whose eyes seemed to be a bit glazed over as she stared down at the bag of beef.

Lydia felt a little panicked. What was going on with her daughter? "Trudy?' she asked worriedly.

"Huh?" Trudy snapped back into reality. "Oh, sorry. Lost in thought."

"Ah, no wonder," Lydia jibed, "since 'thought' is a land you rarely visit. Hard to find your way back?"

"Ha ha. I am laughing. Ho ho."

The two of them giggled and started off down the aisle, looking for the other items on their shopping list.

Lydia felt at peace, as she always did during Mass. Since she couldn't be in the arms of her Savior, the time she spent in church plus the sacraments were the closest she could come. Also, her children were with her. This did not happen as often as she would like. She knew they would eventually settle down and get to Mass regularly on their own. Also, college life was hectic, and although she knew how important regular Mass and reception of the Sacraments were, she also knew she couldn't regulate her adult children's lives as she did when they were little. She just left them in God's hands and knew He wouldn't allow them to be lost.

The only dim spot was that Steve wasn't with them. She hadn't heard from him either, besides that one text. She had called him and left a message, but that was earlier in the day. Hopefully he had called home while they were at church, and she could quell her growing uneasiness.

When Mass was over, they left the church, talked with the priest for awhile, and headed for the parking lot. Lydia noticed Trudy was looking a little disappointed.

"Dear? Is there a problem?"

Trudy sighed. "Oh, I thought Victor would have shown up by now."

"It's possible he got caught up in traffic. You know how the freeway can get."

"Right," said Pat, "I heard earlier that there'd been a stall out there a few miles away. Traffic had to be diverted, not because of that, but because of the two car accidents caused by rubberneckers."

Lydia shook her head sadly. Then she asked, "Were there any injuries?"

"Not that I'm aware of. Just fender-benders," Pat answered. He pulled out his keys as they approached the car.

"Well, that's good anyway."

This gave Trudy something else to worry about. "Oh, what if Victor was in the middle of that?"

Pat sighed dramatically. "Odds are he wasn't."

Lydia, following at a short distance behind, stopped abruptly. She'd suddenly gotten very cold, and her wrists were tingling. Looking around, she thought she saw a shadow move behind a tree in the woods just off the church property.

"Oh Mother dear, the coach is leaving," Pat shouted from the driver's seat, startling her and causing her to look away. "You can look for squirrels at home."

Lydia rubbed her eyes, clearing the image of what she thought she had seen. *Here? At the church? No, it couldn't have been...him. Could it?*

"Muh-ther!" Trudy was getting impatient. "Victor could be waiting for us at the house! Come on!"

"Right, right, okay. Just thought I saw a...a...deer."

"Well, let's say 'bye bye' to Bambi and get back to the house."

Lydia got into the car and, grinning, poked Pat in the side. "Smart aleck."

CHAPTER 24

The dinner was just about ready, and Lydia was washing up some prep dishes when the doorbell rang. Trudy, who had been wound up tighter than a spring the whole day, jumped up from where she had been trying unsuccessfully to read a book, and dashed to the door. Lydia smiled as she heard her exclaim in a loud voice, "Victor! Finally! Did you get caught up in that freeway accident?"

Lydia couldn't hear what Trudy's boyfriend was saying, but something about the timbre of his voice suddenly caused her to tense up. The world suddenly froze in place, and her wrists started that familiar feeling again. She stood with her back to the kitchen door, not wanting to believe what her senses were trying to tell her.

"No, it...no! No, no, no! It couldn't be!" she whispered to herself. "Oh God in heaven, no!"

She shook as she stood at the sink, unable to turn around, her stomach in knots and her entire body trembling with terror. Now it all made sense! All those weird things about Trudy: her fascination with blood, her sensitivity to light, her singular devotion to her "boyfriend"! The "mosquito bites", same as hers!

"Mom! Victor's here!" She could hear Trudy behind her, and another set of footsteps with hers. Yet when she looked at the reflection in the glass of the kitchen window in front of her, Trudy was...alone...! It was dark outside, so everything behind her was in sharp detail in the window.

Lydia willed herself to turn around, and, for Trudy's sake, to put on a pleasant face, as if seeing "Victor" for the first time.

All of her nightmares were nothing in comparison to the way she felt when facing Vlad in her own house. She felt ultimately violated, and she knew without a doubt that the entire family was now in danger because he now knew where they lived.

Trudy was smiling, heedless of the energy that passed between Vlad/Victor and her mom. "Mom, this is Victor. Victor, meet my mom."

Trudy was so proud and happy. It broke Lydia's heart to think of how this relationship would end.

Or would it? Oh Lord, was this who Vlad spoke of when he'd said he'd "found another"? The revelation made Lydia want to scream and run at him with all the power she possessed. Where were a sharp wooden stake and a mallet when they were needed??

Victor smiled, the look in his eyes mocking and triumphant. Lydia wondered how he could smile without the fangs showing.

He took Lydia's trembling, outstretched hand, proffered for a handshake. She curled the fingers of her other hand into a fist, her nails biting into the palm, as he raised the hand he held up to his lips to kiss it, Old-World style. She gasped as she felt his fangs prick the back of her hand ever so slightly. The sensation caused her to sway on her feet, nearly fainting from terror.

"Mom? What's wrong?" Trudy looked worriedly at her mother.

Vlad/Victor tried to look concerned as well. He was a superb actor. "Is everything okay?" he asked.

"Um, yeah." Lydia wiped her forehead, hoping those wounds hadn't started bleeding, giving her stigmata away. "Blood sugar problem."

Victor looked somewhat amused at what Lydia used as an excuse. He put his hand on the back of Trudy's neck, giving it a little massage. To Lydia's horror, he bent over and nibbled at the area behind her right ear, looking at Lydia all the while. Lydia was one frayed nerve ending away from screaming and flying at him, and he knew it. He also knew that she wouldn't do so, out of love for her daughter.

"Oh, stop that, Victor!" giggled Trudy. She looked at her mom's blanched face, worried again. "Mom, you sure you're okay?"

"Yes," Lydia quavered, "I'll be fine."

"Then we'll just go out to the dining room and wait for dinner." She took Victor's hand and started to pull him back out the door into the rest of the house.

"Which has arrived!" shouted Pat, as he came through the doorway to the patio, carrying the main course on a platter. "Sorry, sis, these steaks were pretty thick; I know you like them well-done, but they would have been on that grill until Christmas."

"No worries. Hey, Pat, this is Victor."

Lydia turned away as the two shook hands, so no one could see the anguish on her face. How long would it be before Vlad would attack her son as well? She couldn't bear to think of it.

"Victor's heading to Europe in a few days to check on his family estates," Trudy said. "Mom, do you mind if I go with him? I'll be back at the beginning of the term. He's paying my way." She looked adoringly at the monster beside her, all innocence and light.

Lydia listened to this as she kept her hands busy washing dishes. She would have gone for his throat otherwise. That path, she knew, led to certain death, not only for herself, but for Pat and Trudy as well. She felt as if her entire universe had just been demolished by this...*devil*.

How to tell Trudy to run screaming from this demon? What could she possibly do or say that would make sense? As far as her kids were concerned, vampires only existed in books and horror movies. If it was up to her, she would prefer that it stay that way. Anyway, whatever she said, they would probably want to have her committed; she'd been acting a bit derailed for awhile, in their eyes. Especially if she turned around right now and tried to reveal Victor for the vile creature that he was.

"Mom! Earth to Mom!"

Pat laughed. "Gone to Neptune or somewhere. She's hard to talk to sometimes."

Gathering her strength, and praying for more, Lydia turned away from the sink. She felt sick to the depths of her very soul. "Well, we can discuss that later," she said, trying hard to sound normal. "Let's go have dinner."

As they turned towards the dining room, with Pat in front and Trudy following, Vlad turned towards Lydia with the most evil leer she had ever seen. Lydia looked back at him with a mixture of disgust, terror, and, above all, primal hate.

He just laughed softly and allowed himself to be led by Trudy out to the dinner table.

After they'd sat down, Lydia said, "Well, let's say grace!"

Pat and Trudy looked a little uncomfortable, but said the dinner prayer while Victor looked on. Then they all piled into the food.

All but Lydia, who had lost any interest in the grilled meats or the salad, the steamed veggies and the rolls that she and the kids had been working on most of the afternoon. She picked at a few things and listened in on the conversation around the table.

She was startled when Victor asked, "Lydia...may I call you Lydia? I see your husband isn't here. I was hoping to meet him."

That look in his eyes...as if he already knew. Lydia sucked in her breath.

"Yeah, where is Dad?" asked Trudy. "I mean, I know he's gone," she gave her brother a look; he'd made a "Duh!" face, "but where this time?"

"I actually, um, don't know. Must be awfully busy, since he hasn't called. I've tried to call him, but I always get his recording." She tore her eyes away from Vlad's gaze.

"Well, that's weird. Not like him." Pat looked concerned.

"I know. Hopefully, we'll hear from him tonight." Lydia worked very hard not to burst into tears. Her worries about Steve had intensified once she knew who they had invited into their home. It was even worse now, with that look Vlad had given her...

The conversation went back to school matters, and Lydia put a forkful of carrots into her mouth. They tasted like dust.

"Mom, you'd better get some dinner in you," Pat interrupted her reverie.

"Yes, you really should take care of your...blood sugar." Vlad tried to sound concerned, but Lydia had the appalling, fatalistic thought that, at some point tonight, she herself would be his dessert.

He was actually eating real food, which for some reason didn't surprise her. All the fables she'd heard about vampires hadn't turned out to be completely true as far as her experience had shown her. Then again, Vlad was not the undead. He was the Anti-Life. She felt herself trembling once again.

Lydia got another shock when she looked over at Trudy. Her daughter had been sopping up the juices from her almost-raw steak with a biscuit, and was shoveling it into her mouth as fast as she could.

Pat's eyes followed his mother's stare. It was his turn to look shocked, and disgusted as well.

"Trudy! What are you doing?" he asked. "You little weirdo! When did you start doing that little trick?" He stared in horror at his sister. "Yeck! I don't get you! Usually you want your steaks tough as leather. What's up with this? Here I thought you'd turn it down, and you're...ugh! Cut it out!"

Trudy looked up, the sides of her mouth red. It froze Lydia's insides, and started the questions in her mind again that she had been trying to avoid.

To her credit, however, Trudy looked confused. She dropped her bloody biscuit and sat back quickly, staring at her plate.

"I...I don't know. All of a sudden it just tasted so good this way. Must be the cafeteria food, or my tastes are changing."

"Whatever." Pat gave her a disgusted look. "Next time I'll just bring you a live cow to chew on."

Trudy stuck her tongue out at him in jest. There was still some blood and meat on it.

Lydia almost threw up right on the spot. "Trudy! That's disgusting!"

Vlad was laughing. "Don't worry about me. I'm used to my girl doing silly things." He and Trudy exchanged a look.

Lydia almost shouted, "She's not your girl!" but gritted her teeth to keep from allowing it out. Instead, she quickly stood up and started clearing away her own dishes. She tried to sound normal, a trick that was getting harder as the night wore on. "Okay, who wants dessert?"

"I'd love it," replied Vlad, in a low tone that made Lydia cringe. She looked over at him, one of the few times she'd allowed her gaze to fall on his face that evening. He was giving her that "cat-with-a-mouse" look that she knew so well. She felt herself tense up, nerves on edge. Would he go for her right then and there, in front of the kids?

Then, to her horror, Vlad leaned over toward Trudy and pushed her shoulder-length hair away from the back of her neck. Lydia almost screamed when he put his mouth on her daughter's nape.

Trudy pushed him away, giggling. "Don't do that! You know that tickles!"

Lydia had to leave the room, hoping that Pat would stay there to keep an eye on things. To her dismay, however, he was right behind her as she went into the kitchen, his dirty dishes in his hands. Lydia paced nervously as he put his dishes in the sink. She vaguely heard him talking to her.

"Those two 'lovebirds' are just over the top! Was I that crazy with Sara?" he asked, referring to his first girlfriend.

Lydia was too distracted to give him an answer. She could feel her nerves shattering as she imagined what might be going on in the other room. She pushed past Pat and headed back to the dining room. On her way, she picked up the glass ice cream bowls, giving her an excuse to go back to whatever was going on in there.

"Mom?" Pat looked at her retreating back in confusion. Then he shrugged his shoulders and went to clean up the grill.

What Lydia saw when she opened the door froze her, terror-stricken, to the spot.

Trudy, obviously in Vlad's hypnotic thrall, was slumped backwards over her chair, her throat exposed.

Vlad had struck! His fangs were in Trudy's throat, for how long Lydia had no way of knowing.

Lydia shrieked and dropped the bowls, which shattered as they hit the wood floor. A shard grazed her shin as it flew by, causing a trickle of blood to start seeping down her leg and into her sock.

She didn't notice, as all of her attention was focused on her baby. Vlad had turned towards her when she screamed, his mouth bloodied with her daughter's life fluids.

The scream had awakened Trudy also. She sat up and rubbed her eyes, oblivious to the tiny amount of blood trickling down her neck. Lydia's hope sprang up anew; maybe Vlad hadn't gotten too far after all.

"What...what happened?" she asked sleepily, as if just waking up from a nap.

Lydia glanced at Vlad, who fixed her with a warning look, showing just the point of one fang. While Trudy was still sleepily looking over at her mom, he surreptitiously wiped his mouth on a linen cloth and stuffed the once-white fabric square into his pocket.

"I...I thought I saw a...a....rat..." *Lame, but hopefully effective.*

"A rat? In here?" Trudy jumped up, but, dizzy from the loss of blood, fell back down in her seat.

Lydia was surprised, then deeply dismayed. Apparently, Vlad had taken more blood in less time than Lydia thought possible. She shook with fear and loathing as she glanced at him and rushed to her daughter.

"No, not inside. Out there on the porch rail."

"Oh. That's..." Trudy swayed in her seat. "Hey, I don't feel so well. Think I'll go lie down. Sorry, Victor, but..."

Suddenly she stopped in mid-sentence. "Mom!" The crimson line dripping down her mother's shin had caught Trudy's attention. "You're bleeding! What happ...?"

Here she stopped, confused. "Um, Mom? I'm feeling a little...weird..." Trudy's eyes were glazing over as she stared at the wound.

Lydia knew that look. It was the same as the one on Vlad's face, right next to her. The one difference was, Trudy was scared and confused as to what she was feeling; Vlad's look was sheer blood lust. How long would it be until Trudy crossed over from confusion to blood lust herself? Her own daughter, hunting her like an animal! Hunting others!

Lydia backed away, horrified. She stared at Vlad, who was grinning from ear to ear. "Trudy," she said in a low voice, not taking her eyes off him, "go lie down. We can have dessert later. I'm going to go fetch something to...um...clean up...um, this..."

Trudy's eyes re-focused at the sound of her mother's voice. She nodded shakily and left the room. Lydia waited and watched as Trudy wobbled upstairs. She heard the door close.

Then she fled. Out the door, through the kitchen, and, avoiding the patio where Pat was scrubbing the grill, out the side door and onto the lawn. There, she threw herself prostrate onto the grass, sobbing and praying.

"Dear Jesus! God and Savior! This is too much! My children are threatened and my own daughter has been," —oh, how she hated to admit it, but the signs were all there!—,"cursed! Changed into a vampire!" She shook as she lay there, trying not to make any noise that would attract Pat's attention.

As if on cue, Pat turned on his radio, kicking the volume up a notch, as he always did when he was working outside.

A voice behind Lydia, low and mocking, made her jump.

"What an alluring position!" Vlad chuckled low in his throat, observing Lydia lying face-down on the lawn. "I'm just so sorry that I no longer find you so physically appealing."

Lydia jumped up, casting all fear and panic aside. The instinct to protect her children overwhelmed her instincts for self-preservation. She was the mother bear, putting herself between the hunter and her cubs.

"How dare you!" she spat at Vlad. "How dare you do this to my daughter!"

Vlad smiled, disdain in his eyes and voice. "Jealous?" He laughed sardonically. "Well, don't be, my dear. You're still one of my favorite flavors.

"After I...lost you, shall we say?...I decided that the closest I could come to your blood would be your lovely Trudy. Therefore I hunted her down, pardon the term, and got 'acquainted' with her. Her blood is nowhere near the quality of yours, but she will do as my eternal companion."

Lydia couldn't breathe. The world was spinning out of control. "No! Not Trudy!"

Vlad's features twisted into a snarl. "Well, certainly not you! You're nothing but trouble! I'll just keep you around for...entertainment. I'm sure Trudy would enjoy your 'company' as well. Especially at feeding time."

Lydia's eyes widened in shock. "Oh dear Lord, no!" She backed away from him.

Vlad was on her in a flash, encompassing her in an iron grip. She squirmed, trying with all of her now-mortal strength to get away.

"Now, now, dear Lydia. Or should I say, 'mother-in-law'? No?" he asked as he saw Lydia turn pale at his words. He gripped her chin in his hand as he forced her to look at him. In words edged in ice, he continued, "I will do what I wish, when I wish, and no one on earth can stop me. Is that clear?"

Lydia just squirmed harder, trying to wrest her chin from his hold. She spat in his face. "You...Satan! Get away from me! In Jesus' Name, be gone!"

She saw him flinch at that, but he stayed where he was. "That's another thing about you that annoys me," he went on almost conversationally, as if they had just been discussing the local news. "When will you give up this notion? Obviously, you have placed your trust in someone who doesn't care, or I'd be gone. So, Lydia," he whispered, moving towards her throat, pushing her chin up and to the side, "before I have 'dessert', I must ask: where is your God now?"

Lydia gasped and swallowed, her throat dry. Then through her fear, without her willing it or being conscious of its movement, something welled up from the core of her very being. It swelled through her, then burst out, unable to be stopped even if Lydia had been aware of it. Her voice rang true and confident. It seemed to echo around the yard, ringing from the trees and the very rocks.

"He is where you can never hope to go. You lost that chance and that privilege when you rejected His love and fell from grace. You can destroy this body, but you cannot and will not ever touch my soul!"

At this, Vlad let out a loud howl of rage, and plunged his fangs into Lydia's throat. She knew it was his intent to destroy her bodily, and she offered up her soul to her Savior in a silent prayer. As she felt herself failing, she asked a special protection for her family.

Suddenly he pulled away, listening and looking around with what looked to Lydia like anxiety and...could it be fear?...on his features.

He let go of her, and she dropped to the ground. He looked down at her, and with a voice full of venom, he hissed, "This is not finished." Then he turned on his heel, walked toward the gate, and disappeared.

CHAPTER 25

Lydia lay on the grass, trying to catch her breath. She knew she had to get back inside, but all strength had left her.

Movement at a window made her look over; she caught a glimpse of Trudy, silhouetted by the light in her bedroom. With that, Lydia knew what Trudy had seen...and what had to be revealed that night.

She got up slowly and made her way back into the kitchen. Sitting down at the table, a napkin held to her bleeding throat, she waited.

She didn't have to wait long. Trudy ran down the stairs and into the kitchen, fists clenched, to confront her mother. She was in a full-blown rage. Her eyes were wide with anger and disbelief at what she thought she had seen.

"Mother!" she screamed. "How dare you? How could you?"

Lydia looked up. She knew now without a doubt that tonight everything that had happened to her would be revealed, but she wasn't looking forward to it.

"How could I what?" She put her head in her free hand, weariness descending on her like a shroud.

Trudy thumped her fist on the table, making Lydia jump. "Don't mess with me! I saw you with Victor in the yard! How long have you known him? What is he to you? And Dad...*how could you do this to Dad???*"

She was screaming at Lydia. When her mother just sat there resignedly, it caused Trudy to stop her tirade. She stood there, panting and shaking, ready to blow her top again. In a low, barely-controlled voice, she asked her mother, "Well? What of it?"

Then, in a louder voice, *"Why won't you answer me???"*

Lydia sighed and finally looked up again at her daughter.

Something in her gaze shocked Trudy. She sat down worriedly, all anger gone. Instinctively she knew that there was something seriously wrong. "Mom? What is it? What aren't you telling me?"

A sudden, horrible thought hit her. She was now frightened. "Mom? Is this about when you were missing?"

"Trudy, this will be hard for you, but please listen to what I have to tell you." Lydia reached over and covered her daughter's hand with her own.

Then, beginning with that last fateful evening at work, Lydia began talking—and did not stop until she'd told Trudy of her entire ordeal. Trudy's look went from aghast, to bewildered, to shock at what her mother was telling her.

Suddenly Trudy put a hand up to the back of her neck. Lydia could see her reaction mirroring her own when the truth dawned about those "love bites" Victor had been giving her. Slowly, she felt the side of her throat, and recoiled in horror at the punctures down at the base, near her collarbone. Turning practically green, Trudy ran into the bathroom.

She was still getting sick when Pat came back into the kitchen. He dropped the grill brush into the sink and turned towards Lydia.

"Eew, what's with Sis? I knew that rare steak was a bad idea." He looked around. "Where's Victor?"

Then he had a good look at his mother's face. He sat down in the seat Trudy had just vacated. "Mom? Are you okay?" He peered at her, worried.

Lydia rubbed her face with her free hand. She looked up into Pat's questioning eyes. "I have to tell you something; I just told Trudy, and that is why she is in there." She pointed toward the bathroom.

Drawing a deep breath, Lydia decided to go straight to the point, and tell Pat the whole story later. "Victor," she began, "is a vampire. More than that, he is a demon."

"What?" Pat tried to laugh it off, but one look at his mom's face told him she was only too serious.

He stood up, disbelieving. "You can't mean that, Mom. Vampires don't exist. They're imaginary characters!"

Lydia took the napkin off her neck, and the two puncture marks from her bruised flesh started bleeding again. "I don't think I'm imagining this. And neither is Trudy—she has the same marks on her neck."

Pat gasped at the sight. He stumbled backwards, knocking over the chair and fetching up on the kitchen counter. Anger quickly replaced fear, and without waiting for further explanation, he started running towards the front door.

"Pat! Where are you going?" Lydia stood as well, alarm overtaking her.

"Gonna find the bastard and kill him!" Pat flung over his shoulder.

"Pat! He's far too strong for you! Stay here!" Lydia raced toward the door, but he was gone.

Lydia was torn. She wanted to go after Pat and somehow persuade him not to try and find Vlad. She was also very worried that Vlad would find Pat and try to destroy him. At the same time, she felt she couldn't leave Trudy home by herself. She paced, holding a fresh napkin to her neck.

Trudy staggered back into the kitchen, still looking very pale. She looked so shattered emotionally that Lydia forgot her own worries and flew to her side to hold her.

"Oh, my poor baby. I'm so sorry this happened."

"It's not your fault, Mom," came Trudy's muffled voice, buried in her mother's shoulder. "But...why? Why you? And us?"

"I don't know, baby. I wish..."

Lydia cut off as she felt her daughter's body stiffen against her.

"Trudy?" She pulled back to look at her...

Oh, no! Lydia thought, panic-stricken.

Trudy's eyes had misted red. They were glazed over once again, and focused on Lydia's throat.

"Trudy?" Lydia tried to bring her daughter back from wherever the blood lust had taken her. "Trudy, baby, it's Mom!!"

As if from another dimension, Trudy murmured, "Mom? Oh, Mom, what's happening? I...your blood...I...Mommy?"

That last worded ended on a high-pitched crescendo, as if Trudy was once again a small child, afraid of the dark.

However, it was no child that suddenly gripped Lydia in an iron hold. Lydia watched, horrified, as Trudy's canine teeth sharpened and elongated. She was poised to strike, but her eyes still showed that she was greatly confused.

Suddenly she let go of Lydia. With a scream torn out of her deepest being, she turned and ran for the front door.

CHAPTER 26

Lydia tore out after her. She started praying, and fast.

"Lord, don't let her hurt anyone, and don't let her catch up with her brother. I don't even want to think about what might happen. She's more vampire than human now!"

Outside, she looked up and down the street. "Please let the street be empty...OH, NO!"

Lydia stopped mid-stride on the front lawn, horrified at the sight before her. A few houses down, Trudy had a death grip on someone, and was about to thrust her fangs deep into his throat!

Lydia screamed and rushed towards the two, who were locked in a fatal embrace.

"Trudy, stop! For the love of God, stop!"

The creature that had been her loving Trudy turned towards her now, fangs bared. She advanced towards her mother, snarling, intent on a bloody feast.

Her previous intended victim, a young man dressed simply in a T-shirt and jeans, caught hold of one of Trudy's shoulders to stop her. She tried to shrug him off, but he pulled her around so that she was facing him. Even in her panic, Lydia was surprised that he had more strength than Trudy did.

She stood, dumbfounded, and watched as he did something remarkable. He put his hands on either side of Trudy's head and forced her to stare into his eyes. Trudy thrashed and screamed, but was unable to escape the young man's grasp.

He muttered something, still staring into Trudy's eyes. Suddenly, Lydia saw the area just below his wrists start to glow, and then a soft light enveloped both him and Trudy.

Then Lydia knew without a doubt Who was here with them. That electricity that she always felt when her Lord was near now coursed through her, pushing her to her knees. She bowed low to the ground.

Trudy gave one last convulsive gasp and fainted. A black mist rose from her body with a demonic scream, radiating fury and helplessness. Two orbs of light surrounded the mist and seemed to consume it. Soon the night was dark and quiet again.

The young man laid Trudy down gently on the grass, passed His hand lovingly over her throat, and healed all of the bite marks that had accumulated since Trudy had met "Victor".

Then he came to Lydia, who was still bowed low. He touched her shoulder and helped her up. She fell into His arms, and He held her close. A warm, peaceful feeling enveloped her as He healed her throat also. She felt as if she could stay in His embrace until time ended.

He gently pushed her back, gazing into her eyes.

The peace was shattered by Pat, who came roaring back down the street, winded from running, but still in a fierce rage. When he saw his mother in a stranger's embrace and his sister lying unconscious on the ground, he immediately thought the worst. He advanced on this newcomer with a cry of anger.

"What's going on here?" he bellowed, shaking with rage. "What...who is this?" He pulled his mother out of the young man's arms, and looked down at his sister before turning his attention back to this seeming threat to his family. "Man, if you've hurt her, you son-of-a..."

"Pat!" yelled Lydia. She took hold of her son, turning him so that he faced her. "Pat, calm down! It's okay. Trudy will be okay."

"But...who is this?" Pat stuck his thumb at the stranger. He turned and eyed him again, protection of his sister and mother foremost in his mind. He looked again at Trudy's inert figure and tensed up, ready for a fight.

Jesus held up His hand, and light streamed once again from the nail mark in His wrist.

"Be at peace, Pat." He smiled gently at the confused young man before Him. Pat was still too rattled about his sister's stillness on the lawn to pay close attention to the Miracle in their midst. He finally looked up at Jesus, but still didn't recognize Him.

"So who are you? What's wrong with Trudy?"

"Your sister is healed. Please allow your heart to be healed as well."

"Fine. Good. So you say. I'll believe it when I see her sit up. Now for the fourth time, who are you?"

Lydia interrupted, exasperated. "Can't you see, Pat?" She couldn't believe that he was unable to recognize his Lord.

Jesus looked at her and smiled. "He doesn't see because he has rejected Me. He has let the world and its allures take My place in his heart."

Pat was about to say something else, but was distracted by a movement at his feet.

Trudy was slowly sitting up, rubbing her neck. She looked around, confused, then up at the young man she had attacked. A look of panic crossed her face as she remembered what she had done.

As she looked closer at Him, panic was replaced by embarrassment, then quickly replaced by awe and reverence.

She knew, and, like her mother, she got on her knees and paid Him homage.

Pat just stood there, agape at his sister's reaction. "Trudy, what are you doing?"

Trudy sat back on her heels, surprised at his question. Then she lit into her brother. "Pat! Get on your knees! I don't know how, and I don't know why, but it's the Lord here before us!"

Pat looked at his mom, at Trudy on the sidewalk, and at the young man standing quietly before him. He couldn't believe it. "No way! Are you nuts? How could he be...?"

Jesus put His hand on Pat's shoulder. His eyes were sad as He gazed at this wayward son.

"Pat, you would know Me better if you came to My house more often."

Pat had felt the power in Jesus' touch, but he didn't acknowledge it. His scientific mind refused to relinquish itself to the possibility.

He peered at Jesus. "Okay, answer me this. How come people believe that only Christians can be saved? What of those people who have never heard of the Christian God? That's what's bothered me for a long time. Some of my best friends are from countries that don't recognize Christianity."

Jesus answered him, "My Father has created every person in the history of humanity. Every one of His creatures is dear to Him, and so He reveals Himself to every one of His children in a way they can best understand.

"It's those who turn from Him, in whatever name He is known by, who hurt Us the most. We cannot help them, because they have rejected Us. We will not interfere with their decision, except through the intercession of others. We do not want Our children to obey us out of fear or because of a sense of responsibility. We want their hearts and minds, their whole-hearted love, because it's what they have chosen to do."

Pat was still unconvinced, so rattled was he by the events of the evening. He crossed his arms and asked another question. "Okay, what about what's been happening with Mom and Sis?"

Jesus helped Trudy to her feet and held her tenderly. Lydia moved forward and put her hand on her daughter's back, rubbing it gently.

"These events have also been hard on Me and My Father. The Spirit shares our sorrow. This world has heedlessly let in the forces of evil, and We unfortunately find it necessary to step in and purge Our creation of this darkness. Humans have lost the ability to pull back from the abyss, and so it is up to Us to set them right again.

"Your mother, and many like her, has put herself in the palm of the Father's Hand, and He is using them as very willing instruments in His plan. I assure you, none of these souls are in danger. Since they have put their mortal bodies on the line for the salvation of others, they will not perish, but will have a place in My Kingdom. Your sister's torment was another way that the Father of Lies was using to try to destroy your mother. Neither of them is in danger of losing their places in the Kingdom of God.

"I have said it before, and I will say it again. I am with you always until the end of the world." Jesus then stretched His hand towards Pat, placing it on his head. Pat, overwhelmed by all he had gone through and feeling the power of His mercy, fell on his knees, sobbing.

The Lord then turned to Lydia, Trudy still clinging to Him. "Your children must go away. They cannot tell you where they are going. No phones, no technological ties to you. They will not only be spiritually safe, as I have set My angels to guard them, but they will also be physically safe."

As Pat got up off his knees to ask why, Jesus disappeared, leaving the three of them standing in awe of what they had experienced. There wasn't a sound anywhere up or down the street; obviously the Lord had caused this incident to go unnoticed by the neighbors.

Together, they walked back down the street and into their house.

CHAPTER 27

The three of them talked into the early hours of the morning. Pat listened as Lydia told him all that happened to her, as she had earlier with Trudy. The kids were having a hard time digesting all of this, she knew, but she had to tell them now. She had to face the possibility that, very soon, she might not see them again this side of eternity. Together they prayed for guidance and safety, and finally went off to a restless night's sleep.

Pat was up early the next day, dressed in his running gear. He made the morning coffee and fetched in the newspaper. Then, with steaming mug in hand, he went out to the back porch with the sports section.

The yard was a peaceful retreat, with the birds twittering in the trees, the gentle brush of a spring zephyr, and the warmth of the sun. He opened the paper to an article about his school baseball team's victory the previous day and settled in to read the story. This was his favorite time of day, in perfect spring weather, reading about his favorite pastime.

However, he just couldn't concentrate. After a couple of attempts to read, he tossed the paper aside and got up to pace. The events of the night before kept playing repeatedly through his mind. No matter how he approached it, none of it made sense.

He figured that a good sprint or two might help him clear his mind, so he went through his pre-run stretches in preparation for a couple of miles of running.

After finishing his coffee, he took his cup and the paper back inside, where he met up with Trudy. She had just come downstairs, still in her robe, hair tousled from sleep.

"Hey, Trude, want to go running with me?"

She looked at him through half-closed eyelids. "Mmph."

"I thought so. Well, had to ask. See you in a bit. Let you get some caffeine in your system."

"Hmph."

Pat left through the front door. He knew better than to try to engage his sister in any deep conversation before she'd had her coffee, and, quite seriously, they had some things to discuss. He headed off in the opposite direction from where he had encountered...whoever that had been. In broad daylight, it was difficult to believe that he had met...Jesus?

What had actually happened to Trudy? He couldn't negate the bite wounds he had seen on his mother...but...when he had run home after a fruitless search for Victor, those wounds had been gone. How had that happened, unless...?

He shook his head.

Just...run.

Trudy poured herself a cup of coffee and took a small sip. At the taste, she made a face, quickly put the cup down, and went to the refrigerator to fetch the milk. She could tell Pat had made the coffee; it was strong enough to walk out of the carafe on its own!

Better too strong than not strong enough, though, she thought. She could always cut the bitter taste with milk, but there wasn't much that could be done when the coffee was too weak.

After making herself some toast, Trudy sat at the kitchen table to peruse the rest of the paper; but, like Pat, she just couldn't concentrate. She found herself staring out the window; a few times she had to remind herself to chew the toast she had taken a bite of.

Biting...fangs...OH! She shuddered with disgust. *How could such a thing happen? How could such a creature exist? And how did he do what he did, to both Mom and me?*

She felt violated, far beyond merely the physical aspect. Her mind, her soul, her thoughts, her emotions, all held prisoner by that demon that had wormed his way into her heart!

Then she thought of last night, when she had been enveloped in the warm, loving embrace of her Lord and King.

She had viciously attacked Him in her blood lust, and all He did in return was to show her His mercy! He still loved her. Not only had He removed the curse, He had set guardians on her and Pat to keep them safe!

She hadn't even thanked Him. He had disappeared before either Pat or she could say anything. What, then, was going to happen next? There were so many questions.

Her thoughts were interrupted by the sound of her mother's footsteps on the stairs. Lydia shuffled sleepily into the kitchen.

"Hi, Mom. Sleep well?"

Lydia looked pale. "No, not really. How about you?"

"Spotty." Trudy yawned.

Lydia couldn't help but take a quick glance into her daughter's yawning mouth. Happily, she saw that Trudy's teeth were quite normal now. Not that she distrusted the healing powers that had brought them both back to normal. It was just such a relief to see the physical results. She could also relate better to Steve's reactions to herself the first couple of days she had been back from her imprisonment.

"What?" Trudy had caught her mother's look.

"Nothing." Lydia tried to look innocent.

Trudy smiled. "I know, Mom. I looked also." She pointed to her mouth.

Lydia smiled back and went to get the last of the coffee. She brought it back to the table and sat down facing Trudy. They sat in silence, just enjoying each other's company.

Presently, the quiet was broken by Pat's return. He stood outside, catching his breath, then tried to turn the doorknob. It was locked.

Lydia and Trudy were surprised by the sharp rap on the door. Trudy got up and went to open it.

"Why'd you lock yourself out?" she asked her brother as she let him in. "You've never done that before."

"Considering what's gone on around here, I thought it would be best. Keep the vermin out." He bent over to remove his shoes.

Trudy looked at him, shaking her head. "You really think a locked door would keep him out?"

"Why not? He can't go through doors." His voice rose as he perceived the coming argument.

Trudy shook her head in exasperation. "You still don't get it, do you? He's a <u>demon</u>, not a flesh-and-blood human!"

Pat was getting exasperated and agitated by this conversation. He didn't want to accept the fact that the man calling himself Victor was not of human origin. Nothing in Pat's life had ever prepared him for an encounter with myths-turned-reality, and there was no room in his mind to process this possibility.

"Trudy, don't start. Please. We've already been over this." He brushed past her on his way to the stairs.

She caught his arm. "Why can't you just accept what happened? You can't deny what you saw!"

Lydia strode over to them. She could see where this was going, and it wasn't good.

"Guys, hold on a minute." She put her hands out pleadingly. "Let's just agree to disagree and move forward, okay?"

"Forward to what?" Pat snapped. Then, to Lydia's astonishment, he grabbed her hand, pulling it up to inspect it. After a short scrutiny, he let go.

Lydia, stunned by his behavior, stepped back a pace and pulled her arms to her chest. She rubbed the wrist of the hand he had grabbed so roughly. "What was that for?" she asked him, dumbfounded.

Pat pinched the bridge of his nose, eyes squeezed shut. Then he made an impatient gesture with his hand and started pacing. He sighed and said, "I don't know what to believe! All night long I ran this whole thing through my head, and it still makes no sense. Just now I'd thought I'd check to see if there were signs of this 'stigmata' you told us about, and there's nothing. Nada! How do I know you're not hallucinating? Or I am? Are we all going nuts by degrees?"

He flopped down on the couch, head in hands. Lydia came to sit next to him, while Trudy went to the kitchen to get him a glass of water. She knew that he was thirsty; he always was when he'd finished his morning run.

Lydia put both of her hands out in front of her, palms up. "They hardly ever show. In fact, I feel them more than see them. Their appearance warns me of danger approaching. For example, when Trudy let 'Victor' in, and I heard his voice, my wrists started absolutely burning in pain."

Lydia turned to Trudy, who had returned with the water. Pat took the glass gratefully.

She continued. "That's how I knew who it was before I even turned around. I've never been so terrified in my life! That...*nightmare*! In our home!"

Trudy thought a moment. "That would explain the 'episode', but why didn't you say something then?"

"Trudy, if I had, think about what might have happened. You probably would have thought I'd lost my mind. Or Victor may have destroyed all three of us on the spot. He is more than capable of doing that." She didn't add, though she thought it: *You, my dear daughter, may have helped him destroy us, with the power he had over you.*

Trudy's eyes filled with tears as she remembered how happily the evening had begun.

"Why me?" she cried. "Why did he come after me? Oh, Mom, I feel so used!!"

Lydia stood to hold her daughter. Over Trudy's shoulder, she noticed that Pat was deep in thought, his glass of water forgotten. He still looked extremely angry. *Just like his dad, never letting something go until he understood it completely...*

At the thought of her absent husband, Lydia felt a stab at her heart. His absence had gone on too long; she had to try to contact him! Someone at his work should know; but of course no one would be at the office until tomorrow, so...

Trudy pulled away from her, in dire need of a tissue, which interrupted her thoughts. Lydia picked up the box from the coffee table and handed it to her. Trudy gratefully took one and blew her nose. She looked at her mom, waiting for some sort of answer to her questions.

Lydia took a deep breath. This part was not going to be easy.

"Honey, I think it's because somehow he knew you were my daughter. He'd already destroyed me, or so he thought, so had gone after you to replace me." Lydia didn't mention Vlad's plans to take Trudy into his undead existence; that information, she felt, was unnecessary for her to know now. Hopefully, that danger had passed.

Pat suddenly jumped up, startling Lydia and Trudy. He ran upstairs and slammed his bedroom door.

Trudy looked at her mom, wide-eyed.

Lydia put a hand on her shoulder and glanced up the stairs.

"He's frustrated and doesn't know what to believe. If it's not there in front of him, he has a hard time accepting it."

"But he was there last night! He saw what happened! That's what I don't get!"

Lydia nodded. "Nothing happened to him. At least not the sort of things that have happened to the two of us. As far as the Lord's presence, and His touch on him, well, Pat has probably explained that away as emotional overreaction."

"So how can we prove it?"

Lydia sighed. "I don't know, honey. His faith is not very strong, and he has gotten into the habit of believing in this present world at the expense of the eternal one."

Just then the phone rang. Lydia, hoping that it was Steve, ran to answer it.

However, it wasn't Steve. The number on the telephone's screen indicated that it was a somewhat familiar local call; who it was though, she didn't know. Heart sinking, she picked up the receiver.

"Lydia?" It was Fr. Sam.

Lydia brightened somewhat. Here was, hopefully, the answer to Trudy's question. "Hello, Father! It's good to hear your voice!"

"It has been far too long. I wanted to check up on you, to see how things were going."

"Um, could be better." She related what had happened since their last meeting, including what Trudy had experienced. When she had finished, there was silence on the other end.

"Father? Are you still there?"

"Oh! Sorry. Yes, I'm still here. I'm just trying to absorb what you've just told me."

"As are we. Pat's having the most trouble. Nothing...out of the ordinary...has happened to him, except for his encounter with the Lord, which he doesn't believe actually happened. End result is, he doesn't know what to make of all this."

"I have an idea, Lydia. Why don't you bring Pat and Trudy here, and we can talk about it. Perhaps another witness, someone he doesn't know, will help convince him. We have to at least get him to understand the severity of the situation."

"'Severity?' What do you mean?" Lydia wasn't at all sure that she wanted to know. Could this possibly get worse?

Fr. Sam hesitated. Lydia could feel an entire universe of trouble in that small silence.

"Father?"

"Um, well, last night," he said hastily. "You did say that Vlad just 'disappeared', right? No orbs of light taking him away? That means he's still out there."

That wasn't what was behind your hesitation, Lydia thought to herself, *but I'll take it as it is. For now. I really can't deal with any more awfulness at this point.*

Aloud she said, "Right. Yes, of course."

In fact, I will most likely see him tomorrow, in the guise of my boss. So far, she had not revealed this to anyone. It was just another secret she didn't think anyone could handle; if she told Pat, he would probably try to stop her from going back to work.

"Well, then, can you come by, say, about 3 p.m. today? That way we'll have an hour before I am besieged by my house staff once again. Dinner preparations seem to always take three or more people to accomplish. Why, I don't know. It's only me here. And, of course, there's 5 p.m. Mass to get ready for."

Lydia laughed. "It's just because they love you."

"I'm getting wide at the waistline from all their 'love'!" He laughed too. "See you at three then?"

"Certainly."

They hung up. Trudy looked at her mom, eyebrows raised in question.

"Fr. Sam. You know, the priest who helped me when I was found? We're going to go see him this afternoon."

Trudy gave her a wan smile. "Might as well. I was going to go to the mall, but it seems kind of pointless now."

Lydia squared her shoulders and started resolutely up the stairs. "Now for the hard part; getting Pat to go with us."

CHAPTER 28

Surprisingly, Pat agreed to go to Fr. Sam's with his mother and sister. Lydia was expecting an argument, and indeed had braced herself for a lengthy, and possibly volatile, conversation with her eldest as she climbed the stairs.

Pat surprised her, however. Being an open-minded person, and very thorough before he made any final decisions, he was eager to meet someone who had experienced what he himself had only heard through one person, even though that one person was his own mother. He reasoned that perhaps this would all make some sort of sense if told from another person's view.

There wasn't much said on the trip down to Fr. Sam's parish. The three family members were all deep in their own thoughts.

Lydia was in a quandary; she had received a brief text just before they'd left:

Hi dear. Just letting you know I'm OK. Just busy. Steve

Instead of giving her any relief, the missive made the situation even more peculiar. A text again! Why couldn't he call? And just "Steve" at the end? No "I miss you", or even "Love"?

She drove on, worried about why Steve wasn't being more communicative. This was highly unusual. She resolved that she would call his secretary on Monday and put her worries to rest once and for all.

Hopefully.

Trudy sat beside her mother, staring out of the window at the passing scenery; but she wasn't really seeing the new spring growth on the trees or the flowers budding in almost every yard. Her mind was on the beginnings of her relationship with Victor.

She shuddered as she thought of their first meeting, and how she had ended up in front of the library that first night without knowing how she had gotten there. He must have started taking over her mind that very evening!

Her eyes were opened now to the changes that had come over her while in his company. Those little "love bites"—she felt nauseous as she recalled them—the gradual sensitivity to light, the craving for rare meat...Oh, dear God, how could she not have seen this before?

Right then and there, she decided that she would transfer to a school closer to home. She couldn't bear to go back to where this nightmare had started. She would miss her friends, of course, but she knew that, if she returned, the memory of Victor would haunt her everywhere she went. It made her cringe just to think about it.

Pat sprawled in the back seat, head back and eyes closed. He looked like he was asleep, but actually he was deeply engrossed in his own thoughts.

As much as he wanted to believe his own eyes and put this whole episode to rest, he just couldn't get past what his practical mind refused to process. He knew that his dad had been told; after all, Dad had gone to get his mom when she'd been found.

How did Dad finally resolve the seemingly impossible tale that Mom had told? Did he actually even know *the whole story? Perhaps he had seen something that Fr. Sam had also seen.* He wished his dad were here to talk to. He was looking forward to meeting this Fr. Sam; he had a lot of questions for the priest.

They reached the parish house just before 3 p.m. As Lydia turned off the engine and got out of the car, she looked around uneasily. Memories of that terrifying night rushed into her mind, and she shuddered, hugging her body in the attempt to protect herself from the onslaught.

Pat and Trudy were too busy checking out their surroundings to notice Lydia's distress. They were very curious about this place where their mother had been found, and where all of their lives had suddenly and forever changed.

Fr. Sam, however, had noticed. He had heard the car come into the lot and had come out to meet them.

Seeing Lydia's pained expression and how she clutched herself in a desperate embrace, he rushed to her and enfolded her wordlessly in his arms. She burst into tears and held him desperately. All of the worries and troubles of the past few days that she had kept to herself finally burst out of her, and there was no holding back.

The kids came rushing over to them, worried. Fr. Sam looked at them reassuringly and continued to hold Lydia as she sobbed into his shoulder. However, they were far from reassured; they exchanged worried glances with each other, not knowing what to say or do. They had rarely seen their mom like this, and their dad was usually the one to comfort her.

"Mom?" Trudy put a hand on her mother's back. "Mom, calm down..."

Her sobs gradually quieting, Lydia pulled way and smiled shakily at Pat and Trudy. Fr. Sam offered her a clean handkerchief, which she gladly took. She wiped her eyes and said apologetically, "Sorry, I didn't mean to fall apart like that."

The priest gave her a sympathetic look. "Considering what you've been through, who can blame you? Please, come in. I've got some tea ready."

He led the way into the parish house, the kids flanking their mother, their arms around her. The inside was cool and welcoming, with a pot of tea and a plate of cookies waiting for them in the living room.

"Please, sit down." Fr. Sam gestured at the seats around the table.

They seated themselves, and Lydia introduced Pat and Trudy to her friend. She found the need to use the handkerchief again, and then she put it away in her purse. At Fr. Sam's inquiring look, she said, "Don't worry, I'll wash it and bring it back."

"Not necessary. My staff can take care of it."

Lydia shook her head. She wanted to have a reason to return here sometime in the future; she missed Fr. Sam and enjoyed their conversations, but didn't feel she had the right to just show up for no reason. "I'll take care of it."

Fr. Sam shrugged and turned to the kids. He heaved a sigh.

Here we go, he thought. *Father, give me the right words.*

"And what do you two think of all this?"

Pat and Trudy looked at each other. Where to start?

There was a short, uncomfortable silence. Then Pat leaned forward.

"I'd be really interested in knowing what you yourself experienced. Mom told us what happened, but I'd like to get another...I don't know...witness? Is that the word I want?"

"Probably. Sounds about right to me. I can certainly understand why you'd ask. This is difficult even for those of us who lived through it to process."

He took a long gulp of his tea. Lydia could see in his demeanor, and in the tired, haunted look of his eyes, that he had probably not grown less uneasy since that night. She wondered again if he knew more than what he let on.

After putting his cup down, Fr. Sam began to relate what he had seen and what had happened to both him and Lydia. As his tale progressed, Lydia stared into space, a knuckle between her teeth, reliving the whole scenario. Her free hand clenched and unclenched spasmodically, and she couldn't stop shivering.

Fr. Sam broke off when he saw her agitation. "Are you okay, Lydia? Perhaps your children and I should take this into another room?"

Lydia shook her head quickly. "No, I'm all right. Sorry, please go on. It's just a little hard to hear this all over again."

Fr. Sam nodded. "Hopefully, though, it's somewhat therapeutic."

Lydia shrugged, blinking back fresh tears. "Don't know yet."

She caught Pat looking at her. He had an odd expression on his face that she couldn't read.

Fr. Sam cleared his throat and continued on. When he had finished, he sat back and looked at the youngsters.

Pat stared at the floor, chin between his index finger and thumb. The finger rapidly slid back and forth over his bristly skin. Lydia knew that gesture; she'd seen it used many times by Steve. It meant that he was coming to a conclusion about an issue he had been grinding away at. For good or not, she couldn't know.

"Okay, now it's your turn." Fr. Sam turned to Trudy, sensing that Pat needed some time to turn things over in his mind. "Trudy? Your mom told me about your ordeal, but I'd like to hear it from you, if you don't mind. Do you feel like telling me in your own words?"

Trudy looked away, absent-mindedly picking at a loose thread on the worn fabric over her knee. Her eyes filled with tears, and she hiccupped.

Fr. Sam said sympathetically, "You don't have to. It's hard, I know."

Trudy shook her head vehemently. "No, I'll tell you. Like you said, maybe it'll be therapeutic."

Lydia reached over and held her hand. Trudy smiled at her gratefully. Then she swallowed and plunged into her story. She told it rather hastily, not wanting to stop in case the memories overwhelmed her. Nevertheless, she came close to freezing in sheer panic at times.

Pat stared at his sister as she related her tale. He had had some general knowledge about her relationship with Victor, but hadn't heard about how they'd met at Trudy's school, or the way Victor had taken over her heart and mind, slowly but surely turning her into a being like himself.

By the time she had finished, Pat was frightened and, once again, angry. Angry at the way his family had been violated. Angry at the fact that he had been so impotent to stop the events of last night. And, lastly, angry at God for allowing such things to happen in the first place.

He could now understand how his mother and sister could have been taken over; the evidence was incontrovertible, considering that it was coming from three different viewpoints and experiences. Somewhere in the discussion this afternoon, he had come to accept what had occurred as events beyond mortal abilities. Still...

"Father?" Pat leaned forward once again. "I do have some questions."

Lydia could see the muscles in Pat's jaw tense and his hands curling into fists. *Uh-oh, what is going through his mind?*

Fr. Sam noticed too, but he merely said gently, "Yes, Pat? I'll answer them if I can." He picked up a couple of cookies and refilled his tea, shooting Lydia a look that said, *Don't worry. I can handle it.* He sipped the brew and looked at Pat over the rim of his cup, eyebrows raised and interest in his eyes.

CHAPTER 29

Pat surprised everyone by turning sharply and addressing Lydia, anger mounting in his voice.

"First of all, there's been something that's been bugging me since we started the trip over here. What...how much, that is, of this does Dad know? Has he heard all you've told us? What did he see?"

Lydia tried to answer, but Pat's words gushed from him in a seemingly unstoppable flow. As he talked, his eyes grew brighter and his face more flushed. His questions became more of a rant: against what had happened, how much he didn't understand, and at Heaven itself. By the time he was finished, his anger and frustration were back at full throttle; so much so that Trudy inched away from him, closer to her mother. Fear was plain on her face.

Pat noticed the movement, and, realizing he was almost out of control, closed his eyes and sucked in air in an effort to calm himself.

Fr. Sam sat unperturbed. It was obvious that he had dealt with angry people a lot during the course of his priesthood.

Lydia watched her son anxiously. He finally opened his eyes and looked at his sister apologetically. "Sorry, Trude. It just got away from me."

Trudy nodded, wide-eyed, but stayed at a distance from him.

Pat looked confused and hurt. "What? I got mad. Who wouldn't?"

"It's just...I've never seen or heard you like that. Have you, Mom?"

Lydia shook her head slowly, staring at Pat. "No, this is a first..."

There was an awkward silence, while Pat fidgeted under his family's gaze.

Fr. Sam cleared his throat. He addressed Pat, his voice quiet and gentle. "Pat, I can assure you that your father knows everything you do. Well, up to last night, anyway. Your mother can tell you that he had the same questions."

"And he just...accepted it? No questions asked?" Pat looked disbelievingly at the priest and his mother.

It was Lydia's turn to answer. "No, he didn't. What reasonable person would? It's insane, taken on face value. But when he saw the stigmata appear on me, and after we'd gone to the bishop, he had no trouble believing."

Pat addressed Fr. Sam. "And what happened there? Mom says she has no recollection, only that she had a 'message' for the bishop, but she doesn't remember delivering it. Yet everyone but Mom seems to have had some sort of closure on that moment in time." He looked at the priest accusingly.

Fr. Sam was looking increasingly uncomfortable as Pat posed this last question. Now, under Pat's scrutiny, he looked away, not able to meet anyone's eyes.

Ah-ha! thought Lydia, *he* does *know more than he's telling!* Aloud she said, "Okay, Father, I can tell there's more. We need to know. Pat needs to know. Nothing's happened to him; he hasn't seen anything extraordinary. Well, except for my last attack, but he has explained that away, I'm sure."

Pat looked surprised, but Lydia patted his knee and said, "I know how your mind works, dear."

She turned back to Fr. Sam. "And so he doubts. Without concrete evidence, this is all very hard to believe. So, I have to ask: What haven't I been told? What happened that day? It may be the part of the puzzle he needs to have to put it all together."

Trudy sat forward, waiting for his reply. She, too, had been curious about this missing information.

Fr. Sam sighed and looked at his hands, which he was twisting nervously in his lap. Finally, he looked up at them.

"I thought it might come to this, so I called the bishop earlier today to get his permission to tell you. I was under the strictest instructions from him not to repeat what had happened in his office that day...and so was Steve."

Before anyone could voice their questions over this revelation, he held up his hand for silence. Then he looked pointedly at Pat. "But first I do have to tell you that you were indeed touched by the evil that attacked your mother and sister. You are under its power even now."

His audience was even more perturbed. Lydia opened her mouth to say something in protest, but no words came out. Pat sat back with a derisive snort, and looked away towards a curio cabinet filled with knick-knacks. Trudy looked from one to another, shocked at the words she'd just heard.

The priest continued, "Pat, it's true. Hear me out." His gaze encompassed all three of them, drawing them into the words he was about to say.

The young man darted his eyes toward the priest, then away again. He slumped in his chair and crossed his arms. Lydia and Trudy were all ears as they waited for Fr. Sam to continue. They ignored Pat's attitude, except to pray quietly that the priest's words would take hold of Pat's heart and mind.

At least he hasn't walked out; that's a good sign, thought Lydia.

First, Fr. Sam offered the teapot around again, then ate another cookie before he started talking. The anxiety in the air was palpable; he felt it the most himself, as he was praying mightily for the right words.

"Pat," he started, looking over at the sullen young man, who continued to study the curio cabinet, "let me start by reminding you that the devil works on our fears and emotions. Your anger fuels his fire, and he takes advantage of that to pull you further away from God. It doesn't help that you have strayed from your faith."

At Pat's startled look, the priest smiled ruefully. "Yes, your mother has confided this to me, but it's because she is worried about your spiritual future.

"I could tell by the way you were acting earlier that there was something worse than just your own emotions acting up. That anger just now. Tell me the truth--does that happen often?"

Pat thought a moment. "No, actually. That was really out of the ordinary." He shook his head, wondering now at that strange outburst. "Usually I'm pretty even-tempered."

He was suddenly irritated again. "But it's just all this stress we've been under..."

Fr. Sam shook his head. "No, Pat, don't look for blame. Look for your faith. It will keep you buoyed when you are on the darkest seas of your life."

His eyes went to Lydia. They held a deep sadness. "Especially now."

Lydia gasped. What did this mean?

Pat, his irritation forgotten, also tensed. He automatically reached over and grabbed for his mom's hand. Trudy held tight to Lydia's arm, frightened at the ominous-sounding words.

The priest then went on to relate to them, in a trembling, hesitant voice, of all that had occurred that day at the cathedral. By the time he had finished, he was looking at three ashen faces.

Trudy looked at Lydia, her eyes brimming with tears. "Mom?" Then, sobbing, she fell into her mother's arms.

Pat jumped up with a cry and strode to the front door. He left the house, slamming the door behind him. Fr. Sam watched him go, his fingers steepled in front of his mouth, his body trembling with his own emotions.

Once he left the parish house, Pat wasn't sure where he was going. He only knew of the pain that the priest's words had inflicted on his heart.

His own mother! How could she do that to her family?

Then, suddenly it dawned on him that he had already heard all the answers to any questions he had had concerning what was going on in and around his family. He realized that he had just refused to listen to them. It was all making horrifying sense now.

He found himself inside the church, and was jolted at the realization that he had entered the very site where his mother had been found, and where her mission had been given to her. Slowly, he made his way up the center aisle, taking in the tabernacle with its red candle glowing steadily, and the altar where his mother had taken refuge from the evil that had hunted her.

As he proceeded forward, a column of light at the foot of the altar caught his gaze. He stood, awestruck, as the light transformed into the shape of a young man.

Not just any man...it was the same one who had been on their street the night before!

As Pat watched, speechless, the young Man wordlessly opened His hands at His sides. Light emanated from the nail marks in the palms. He pulled up the shirt He was wearing, all the time watching Pat with kindness, and exposed a lance wound in His side.

On impulse, Pat looked down at the Man's feet. He was barefoot, and the nail marks in His ankles glowed with the same light that came from His hands.

Finally, Pat knew, and accepted. He fell on his face, sprawled on the carpet, and sobbed uncontrollably. Soon, he felt a soft touch on his shoulder, and raised his tear-streaked face.

Seeing Jesus' face, he broke into sobs again. How could he have ever doubted?

Jesus helped him to his feet, and held him close while Pat finally quieted his tears. "Oh, Lord, I've been so blind! I'm so sorry!"

Jesus took Pat's face between His hands and looked into his eyes. Pat knew then and there that he had been forgiven. Peace filled his being, along with a strength and resolve that he had not known before.

Jesus' voice was kind and gentle, a balm to Pat's soul. "Know that you are forgiven. Be strong, keep from fear, and renew your faith daily. I will always be with you."

With that, Jesus disappeared once again.

After a moment, Pat brushed his hand over his eyes, turned to walk back to the door, and stopped.

There at the back were his mom and sister, with Fr. Sam behind them.

Lydia ran to her son, Trudy close behind. They hugged each other silently, except for a few muffled sobs. Then they walked together towards the exit, Fr. Sam waiting at the door.

Out in the parking lot, they bid him good-bye, thanking him for all he had done.

Then they rode home in silence.

CHAPTER 30

The next morning, Lydia woke to an empty house. It seemed sad and hollow to her because, not only were the kids gone, but she still had not heard from Steve. There had been that last text message, but nothing since then. She decided to call his office once she'd gotten to work to see if they'd heard from him.

Work! Oh no! How can I go in and face that...that thing that called himself Vlad! Or Victor...Or...what was he calling himself now? She didn't recall hearing what his name was in the guise of an executive businessman. None of the admins had been in the office long enough that last afternoon for her to ask.

Lydia shuddered, and her stomach knotted. Just the thought of what she would be going through in that office made her ill. Her hand was on the phone, her intention being to call in sick, or in the Bahamas, or some excuse, when that Voice spoke gently in her heart.

Where is your faith, Lydia?

Lydia paced, frustrated, her fingers raking through her hair. "Probably hiding under the bed with my courage!"

Please, trust Me.

"I do! I just keep seeing fangs and blood and feeling my heart slowing 'til I'm almost dead, and..."

Don't fear. Remember, the physical part of you is less important than your soul. Keep your eternal soul against the Evil One, and know that those who do live forever with Me.

Lydia put a trembling hand to her mouth, trying to quell the fear rising up in her. She closed her eyes, took a huge breath, and swallowed. Taking deep breaths, she opened her eyes, and felt calmer.

"Right, sorry. It's just..." her voice quavered again, and desperation shook her. "It's so awful! I just want to scream and run whenever I see him, but I don't want to jeopardize anyone's lives there."

Do you regard their lives as important as your own?

"More so. Aren't we commanded to treat all others as more important than ourselves? I've tried to do that, but it's hard to remember when in the presence of someone trying to steal your life!"

As I well know, my dear Lydia. But your co-workers would be in more danger if you don't go.

"What do you mean? Oh!"

Realization hit her. Her presence in that office, in that building, kept Vlad from feeding on anyone else! With God's seal on her, she couldn't be destroyed. At least not spiritually.

With that thought fresh in her mind, she gathered her things and headed for the garage. "Okay, I'll go, but I'm not looking forward to it."

A pause, then: *Imagine how I felt in the Garden of Gethsemane.*

That was something Lydia could not argue with.

CHAPTER 31

Earlier that morning, Pat had tiptoed to his sister's room. Touching her shoulder, he indicated to a sleepy-eyed Trudy that they should be on their way before their mom woke up.

After gathering a few belongings, they left the house, leaving their cell phones on the kitchen counter. They had donned old, unmarked sweatshirts, and had pulled the hoods way down over their faces; even so, they looked around to make sure no one was watching them, so nervous were they about the possibility of being spotted.

"Where should we go, Pat?" whispered Trudy.

"I'm not sure, but I feel as if we should leave our cars here and walk. No one said we had to go far. Besides, someone could trace us if we drove off, and we don't want that."

They walked silently down their street and onto the main road. Once there, they stopped and looked up and down, trying to decide which way to go. The sun was just coming up, and there were only a few cars on the road.

"Phew, it's warm!" Pat said, wiping his forehead. "Feels like August instead of March!"

"Gonna be one of those years, I guess." Trudy said, and heaved a sigh. "Come on, maybe we can get a coffee before we head out."

"Best not," Pat warned. "We can't allow ourselves to be recognized. If that...that *thing* comes looking for us, especially you, anyone who knows where we went would be in big trouble. He'd stop at nothing to get what he wants."

Trudy shuddered, and looked nervously behind them.

"Don't be too worried, Trude. After what happened Saturday night, I actually don't think he would dare. We still have to be cautious, though."

Trudy touched the side of her neck, feeling suddenly nauseous with the memory of her "boyfriend."

"I hope you're right."

They turned and walked toward the center of town as the sun rose higher. It seemed that, as time passed, the sky was becoming paler and paler. It seemed as if a strange brilliance was causing it to become almost white.

Trudy stopped suddenly and tilted her head as if listening to something Pat couldn't hear. To him, she looked as if she was in that same glassy-eyed state that she had been in on Saturday night. Alarmed, he took her arm and shook it.

"What? What is it, Trudy? Are you okay?"

Trudy blinked and looked at her brother. Seeing the fear in his face, she smiled at him reassuringly. "I'm okay, Pat. It's just...listen! No bird song!"

It was true. There didn't seem to be any warbling or chirping, and they were standing under a thick overhang of tree limbs. Usually, a person couldn't think for all the birds calling to each other.

"Hmmm. Weird. Must be the heat."

Trudy shrugged. "Yeah, maybe."

They started on again. Presently they saw the roofline of their church, standing like a beacon against the backdrop of trees on the property.

The idea seemed to hit them both at the same time. The church! What better place to find sanctuary? It sounded like the perfect answer. However, would they be able to get in?

Trudy looked at her watch; it was just after 6:30 a.m. "It's a little early, but maybe Father Taylor will be up and about. Can't hurt to go and see."

"Right," Pat looked doubtful, "but what can we tell him as our reason for needing to stay at the church? After all, we have a perfectly good house of our own not far from here. He's sure to ask questions."

"Well, let's worry about that when we have to."

They started walking towards the church entry, and noticed several other people headed in the same direction. Pat glanced at them, puzzled. "There isn't a weekday Mass this early, is there?"

Trudy was just as perplexed. "I don't think so. No one would hold a meeting this early either, would they?"

Curious, they kept walking, and as they got closer, an unexplainable urge to be inside those walls came over both of them.

They ran the last few yards, feeling a need to escape the outdoors. The pastor had just opened the door for another couple of people, so he waited for Pat and Trudy also. He beckoned them in and shut the door.

The church was dark except for the red sanctuary lamp, its candle recently replaced. Its glow provided a small guiding light. Trudy and Pat looked at each other, mystified. Why weren't the lights on, especially if all of these people were congregating?

Pat turned to the priest. "What's going on, Father?"

Father Taylor shook his head tiredly. It seemed to Trudy and Pat that he had aged tremendously since last they'd seen him. When was that? Two days ago? It seemed so much longer.

"I'm not sure, Pat, but, as you saw outside, you aren't the first ones here today, and you probably won't be the last."

He opened the door to the basement, which also served as the parish social hall. It was dark, except for several candles throwing dim illumination.

"Electricity has gone out. I'm having someone in this afternoon to check on the wiring."

Leading the way with a flashlight, he brought them down to a room already occupied by several people. They all seemed as puzzled as Pat and Trudy as to why they were there; it was as if, after they had left their homes and reached the church, they really couldn't say why they had felt the urge to come in the first place.

"Something's up," said the priest. "I don't know what it is, but I was awakened very early this morning with the feeling that I had to put this place in order and gather plenty of candles and supplies."

There was a knock at the front door of the church, audible even down in the basement hall. Father Taylor sighed and headed back up the stairs.

Pat went after him. "Please, Father, let me get it. You shouldn't have to..."

The tired priest turned and held his hand up, stopping Pat in mid-sentence. "No, you stay here. This is something I think only I should do." He shrugged. "Guardian of the fortress, and all that."

Everyone watched him trudge up the stairs and into the church. They muttered among themselves, puzzled as to what he could have meant. One by one, they settled down in chairs and along the wall to wait.

For what, none of them knew.

CHAPTER 32

Lydia also noted the heat as she drove to work. It was a strange sensation, not like a summer heat that surrounded her due to the air being warmed by the sun. The area around her feet was almost hot, but the air around the vicinity of her shoulders wasn't nearly as warm. It reminded her of when she was walking on a volcano in Hawaii--as if there was a giant caldera just under the surface of the earth.

She parked closer to the office building than usual, thinking she might need a quick escape. Although she had said "Yes" to her Lord's request, she was still nervous, jumping at any quick movements or rustling of leaves. She was still human, after all.

It had occurred to her on the way into work that she hadn't cleaned out her old cubicle. She clung to the thought of doing that task as a welcome diversion from what was inevitable, which was her inescapable next encounter with Vlad.

Lydia almost cried as she walked down the familiar hallway, passing all that she had known since her first day at work here. She could hear someone cursing and banging on the copier. Oh, how she would welcome a messed-up copier over her present circumstances! If she could just return to what had been, she would never complain about that old broken-down piece of machinery ever again!

Kim caught sight of her as she approached her old cube. Lydia suddenly found herself caught up in a tight embrace.

Kim was almost squealing with happiness and surprise. "Oh, Lydia! You've come back to me!" she cried ecstatically.

Lydia laughed and pulled herself out of her friend's arms. "I wish! No, I've come to get my..."

Lydia stared into her cube. It was empty!

"...stuff..." she trailed off.

"Oh! Right. A couple of people came and boxed your things up for you. They need to re-do the electrical in this area, so they took your things up to your new office." Kim looked apologetic. "Sorry I wasn't able to tell you before this. I just found out about it a few minutes ago myself."

Lydia fumed as she stood in the middle of what had been her office. How dare they? No one had the right to move her things without her permission!

"Who was it, Kim, do you know?"

"No, just a couple of maintenance guys. Blue uniforms, not very talkative. Liz on the other side of the wall told me."

Lydia opened the drawers and cabinets. They were completely empty.

She smiled wryly. "Good thing I hadn't left any dirty dishes behind. They'd probably be packed up too!"

Her smile disappeared as she caught sight of something in the trash can. With a cry, she dashed toward it, pulling the items out.

Her Scripture verses! They'd thrown them all away! Not only that, but, oddly, some of the papers looked a little singed around the edges.

Lydia sniffed at them, mystified. "Kim, did they...did you smell smoke when you got here?"

Kim stared at Lydia. "What? You know no one can light anything in here without the alarms going off! Remember the birthday candle fiasco shortly after the new system was installed?"

How could she forget? One little candle, and suddenly everyone in the building had had to go on an impromptu fire drill!

So how did these get burnt?

Then it hit her. Vlad! He must have sent some of his fellow sulfur-and-brimstone minions to do this!

Keeping this revelation to herself so as not to scare Kim, Lydia tried to make light of her last comment. She quickly put the papers in her purse as she said, "Probably one of the workers had been smoking before the job. Guess I just smelled it on the paper."

The two friends chatted for a short time, but then Kim sighed. "Well, I guess I'd better get back to work. Time and tide wait for no one, you know."

"Oh, do you have to?" Lydia noticed the desperation in her voice, and said in a more nonchalant tone, "I thought we could go to the cafeteria and grab a coffee."

"Lydia, it's at least two hours until break time!" Kim chided. "Go on up to that new office and your hunky boss. I'll call you later."

"What? 'Hunky'?" It surprised Lydia to hear that description of Vlad.

Kim smirked. "Oh, please, Lydia! You must realize how drop-dead gorgeous he is! I've seen him...are you blind?"

Kim was right about the "dead" part, Lydia thought to herself. *"Undead" was more like it.*

"Um..." Lydia didn't know what to say.

"Oh, go, you happily-married person!" Kim playfully shoved Lydia towards the door.

Lydia waved and headed off, heart getting heavier with each trudging step.

CHAPTER 33

Lydia considered her options as she made her way through the confusing labyrinth towards her new office. She was not in any hurry to report for work; her throat hurt at the thought of what sort of "tasks" were in store for her.

It occurred to her that, since his office was on her way, she should go in and see how Ned was getting on. She was still very concerned about his state of mind, and was worried that he would inadvertently leak some information about her. Their shared nightmare of that night would be detrimental--not only to her, but to him, and to the rest of the people in these buildings.

Vlad had ways of destroying people inwardly without actually doing them physical harm. She had seen that starting to happen in her own son during this ordeal. The destruction would be spiritual, not physical. And no one would be the wiser.

It wasn't too hard to imagine that that was happening even now, slowly but surely. She determined that she would not trust anyone who had had any contact with Vlad. That would probably comprise everyone in this company.

She was completely and utterly alone, at least physically.

Determined to make sure Ned was getting over his fright, Lydia walked up to the security office door and knocked.

No answer.

Well, he could be out on a call, or just a routine walkabout.

She turned to walk away, deciding she would come back later. To her surprise, the door opened on silent hinges.

After waiting a few seconds for Ned to poke his head around the door with that silly grin on his face, Lydia became puzzled when he didn't appear. The doorway stayed empty.

She pushed at the door, which swung easily inward.

"Hello?" she called as she entered.

She blinked in the dim light. The ceiling lights were off, and the only light came from the glowing screens of the security monitors behind Ned's desk. His chair was turned towards them; Lydia wondered if he'd fallen asleep.

She came around the desk, which she noted with some surprise was clear of soda cups and cafeteria trays. It occurred to her that she had never seen his office without food debris scattered everywhere.

"Ned? You awake?"

He was sitting in his chair, eyes on the screens. There was something odd, however, about the way he was staring ahead without moving, and the fact that he hadn't responded to her alarmed Lydia.

Had he had a stroke? Was he dead?

Her heart in her throat, she shook his shoulder. "Ned!"

He didn't move a muscle, but after a moment, he blinked slowly. Then he looked up at her.

"Hello, Lydia. I thought maybe you'd come and visit me."

There was something about his demeanor that instantly put her on guard. There was no emotion on his face or in his voice; he was usually very joyful at seeing her, or anyone, for that matter.

"Ned? Are you okay?" Lydia looked closer into his face.

Another pause. "Oh yes, I'm terrific. No problem. Can I help you with something?"

Lydia's mouth opened and closed. She stuttered, "Um...I...did you send someone to clean out my cube? Because Kim told me some maintenance guys she'd never seen before put all my stuff in a box and..."

"Oh, yes. I did that. They were new." He went back to staring at the monitors.

After a few moments, Lydia said, "Oh. Um. Okay. Just wondered."

No response.

"I'll...uh...see you later then."

She backed toward the door, her eyes still on Ned. She didn't know what to make of his behavior, and was thinking of calling the medical personnel, when he spoke again, still in a monotone.

"You really don't have anything to worry about, Lydia. Everything's okay. I was scared, but I'm okay now. Silly of me. It was all explained away by some good friends."

Now Lydia was really frightened. She raced toward the door, but suddenly he was right beside her. He grabbed her arm and spun her around.

Lydia gasped. He had never laid a hand on her before!

"Would you like them to explain it all to you, too?"

He smiled then, and Lydia felt the floor go out from under her. His eyes went scarlet, and she could see the pointed tips of fangs in the dim light.

Before he could make the next move, Lydia had the door open and was attempting to get away. He held her in an iron grip, pulling her towards him, back into the office. She could feel a scream welling up from deep within, as she pulled with all of her might to break his grasp.

"Ned!" The sudden call came from a couple of doors down. "The men's room needs more toilet paper!"

Ned shook his head, returning to a normal visage. He glared at the man who had called him.

Breathing a silent prayer of thanks, Lydia used that distraction to get away. It took all her will not to run as fast as she could, screaming in terror the entire way. She looked back, thoroughly frightened, as she turned the corner; he was still watching her, a smirk on his lips.

Not unlike her first encounter with Vlad...

CHAPTER 34

Lydia didn't stop running until she was outside of the fourth-floor office. She waited there until she had caught her breath, keeping a watchful eye out for anyone who might have followed her. She was to the point of panicking and running home, but somewhere inside her she found some remaining reserve of strength. She drew on that, and prayed for more.

Lord, what gives? How could this happen to Ned? Who else has been affected? Who can I trust?

Just then, she heard a noise at the far end of the hall. She braced herself for flight, only to see that it was Teresa with her housekeeping cart. Relieved, she sagged against the wall.

Teresa walked over to her and touched her face.

"Trust in the Lord, and in His emissaries."

Then she returned to her cart and pushed it back around the corner.

"Okay, one question answered," Lydia muttered to herself. "I'm guessing I'll get the others answered as time goes on."

She crept into the office as quietly as she could. The first thing she noticed was the box with her office things on the desk closest to Vlad's door. Feeling nauseous, she walked over to the desk and put her purse down.

Her attempt at entering quietly so as not to draw Vlad's attention was wasted, as the two women in the office greeted her in louder voices than necessary. Then they looked towards the door to see if their "hunky" boss would poke his head out to see what was going on. Lydia could hear their giggles, and she knew they were already head-over-heels crazy about him. She felt so sorry for them.

One of the women, a tall, leggy, twenty-something, walked over to her, smiling. She held out a hand.

"Hi! Lydia, is it? I'm Debbie. That's Brandi over there." The other admin, a curly-haired brunette, smiled and waved from her desk.

"Nice to have you here with us," Debbie continued. "Has anyone showed you around?"

Lydia smiled back and shook her head. "No, I had to leave quickly last week," *no lie there*, "and didn't have time."

"Okay. Well, we're a little short on work right now, so, come on. I'll give you a quick tour."

As they walked through the suite, with Debbie pointing out the break room and the location of various office equipment, she suddenly leaned in close to Lydia's ear to whisper, "How did you manage to get a job as his personal secretary?"

Lydia instinctively pulled back from Debbie's mouth. *You're probably okay, but I can't afford to trust you,* she thought.

At Debbie's surprised look, Lydia apologized. "Sorry. I'm, um, not feeling well, and you shouldn't get too close. Hate to have you get sick!"

"Ah." That satisfied her. "But...how did you land a job with him? Do you know him from somewhere?"

Oh boy. What to say?

Lydia shrugged and attempted a smile. *You might say I know him from somewhere...*

Aloud, she said, "No, just lucky, I guess."

"For sure! Brandi and I would give our eyeteeth to be able to be in that room alone with him!"

Lydia shuddered. *Interesting choice of words,* she thought. She once again felt sick as she had a brief, horrible memory of her own temporary sharp teeth.

To change the subject, in a way, Lydia asked Debbie the question that had plagued her earlier. "What is his name, anyway?"

Debbie blinked, then laughed a little incredulously. "Didn't he tell you? Or was there not much talking going on during that 'interview'?" Debbie waggled her eyebrows at Lydia.

"Oh no! No, no, no! No way!" Lydia felt horrid at the intimation. Too many memories of time alone with him. The attacks, the loss of blood...

She tried to cover the revulsion she felt as those memories almost swept her away. "That is, I'm very happily married. Not interested." She attempted a laugh. "I'm too old for that sort of messing around anyway. I have kids in college, for heaven's sake!"

Debbie cocked an eyebrow. "Uh-huh..."

It was clear from the expression on her face that she didn't believe her.

Debbie took Lydia back to her desk, then returned to her own, across from Brandi, who had heard the entire conversation. They giggled and whispered to each other.

Lydia rolled her eyes. What-*ever*, as Trudy would say.

A pang of sadness assaulted her heart. Trudy! Pat! Would she see them again? She prayed for their safety, and that they would be strong, whatever might happen.

Oh...Steve! She was going to call his office to find out where he was. She'd almost forgotten.

She pulled out her cell phone, and was just about to punch in the number, when Vlad's door opened. Debbie and Brandi peered eagerly for a glimpse of him, their amorous sighs barely concealed.

Lydia stiffened. She could feel the hairs on her neck stand on end. Her throat went dry, and she backed away towards the main entrance.

Vlad stared at her, and after what seemed an eternity, crooked a finger at her.

Lydia stood, petrified under his gaze, unable to move. She found herself unable to breathe, and was starting to become dizzy. The room floated in front of her, with Vlad all too clearly in the center of her vision.

He gave her a one-sided, smug smile, then, his face still out of view of the other women, flicked his glance in their direction. To Lydia's horror, he gave a full-fanged smile while he licked his lips.

His meaning was all too clear. That gesture unfroze Lydia's legs, but she was still so repulsed that her steps were slow and wobbly. Reluctantly, she approached his door, her breath now coming in short gasps. She trembled all over as she got closer to him.

He held the door open for her to enter, then looked out at Debbie and Brandi. He winked at them, which got them flustered and giggly. Lydia could hear them whispering to each other again as he shut the door.

She stood just inside the doorway, refusing to go any further. As she braced for the worst, she was somewhat relieved to see him walk around to the other side of his desk. Lydia noticed once again that there was nothing on its surface. The wood was polished, and shone beautifully in the dim light.

He ran his hand along its surface, seemingly engrossed in the activity of admiring its elegant workmanship.

Finally, he spoke.

"Where is your daughter, Lydia?" His voice was controlled and conversational, but Lydia could see that his jaw was white with tension.

The question took her by surprise. How did he know she was gone?

Of course. He probably tried to get into her mind, which was now closed to him, thanks to the grace of God. This knowledge made her feel a little more confident. "I don't know. She just left."

Lydia was so grateful now that she did not know the whereabouts of her children. He could do what he wanted to her, but she could not tell him! They were safe...for now.

Vlad walked slowly around his desk until he was in front of it again. Lydia inched closer to the door. "Her car is still in front of your house. So, where is my girl, Lydia?"

His voice rose in anger. "Where is Trudy?"

Lydia's mother instinct overrode her fear, and she became the she-bear protecting her cub. "She's not yours! She's *mine*, and God's...and she is out of your power!"

As quick as thought, Vlad was across the room and had Lydia up against the wall, his hands around her neck. She struggled, trying to breathe, fighting against his hold on her throat. He lifted her so that her feet were no longer on the ground, and hissed menacingly in her face.

"Oh, and I suppose there is another question I should ask." He growled at her, his next words turning her veins to ice.

"Where is your husband, Lydia?"

Lydia's eyes widened in horror. She tried to scream, but his grip tightened so that she could only make a choking noise.

He knew! Not only that, he had probably orchestrated Steve's "business trip"!

"A mere couple of text messages? He hasn't called you, has he? No, I suppose he hasn't. Haven't you even wondered why?"

Lydia could only mouth the words as she shook her head disbelievingly. She was seeing black spots in front of her eyes, and knew it was only seconds before she would pass out.

Vlad smiled humorlessly, and his fangs gleamed horribly in the half-light.

Her heart plummeting, Lydia knew it to be true. Vlad had taken Steve! Despair overtook her, and any fight she had had faded out to nothing. She could feel herself crumpling; only his grip on her throat kept her vertical.

Vlad looked triumphant. He finally released her, and she fell in a heap in front of him, drawing in huge lungfuls of air.

Then she started sobbing.

Oh, Steve!

The memories of their lives together rushed in, and painful cries wracked her body.

Vlad bent down and pulled her head roughly up by her hair so that she was staring straight at him, tears streaking down her face. She closed her eyes to keep from having to look at him.

Once again, he breathed in her ear, his breath smelling of decay and death. "There is a way to save him. He's not beyond my power to bring him back to you."

"As if you care!" Lydia spat back at him.

"Ah, ah! Careful! You don't want to jeopardize his life, do you?"

Lydia went quiet, praying for the strength to face whatever beastly suggestion he might make. Then, her body tensing, she asked, "What way are you suggesting?"

Vlad yanked her up off the floor by her arm, causing her to gasp in pain, and held her close to him. He forced her chin up so that his eyes bored into hers.

"It's simple. Obey me! Worship me! Forsake this God of yours, and you can have your husband back!" His eyes flamed.

Lydia looked away, horrified. What was she supposed to do? She would never leave God, but...her husband? Dead? Or...worse?

The Voice whispered in her heart, loving and warm.

Lydia, your husband is safe. Trust Me.

With this news, Lydia's heart leaped with joy. She fought to keep the happiness from showing; she knew she had to feign ignorance so that Vlad wouldn't suspect what had just been revealed to her. She stared at him, trying to look as if she was undecided.

Then she almost shouted at him.

"No!"

"What?" Vlad stepped back in disbelief.

"No, I won't!" Lydia's own eyes flashed now. "I've told you time and time again that my heart belongs to Jesus, and so does my family. You and your kind may be able to destroy our flesh, but that only means that the important parts of us, our souls, go to the Lord that much faster!"

With a howl, Vlad launched himself at Lydia, and would have killed her on the spot...

There was a sudden rap on the door.

"Housekeeping!" called a cheerful voice. Teresa stepped into the room, pushing her cart and humming to herself.

Once again, Lydia was able to take the advantage of surprise to flee from Vlad and certain death. She thanked Teresa in a whisper as she flew past her.

Snatching up her box of belongings, Lydia ran out the main door, and didn't stop until she found herself in her own car.

CHAPTER 35

The sharp, dusty smell of hay and horses woke Steve from a sleep he didn't remember falling into. He lay still, eyes closed, trying to figure out what new hell that monster had in store for him.

This was not the smell of that dank, musty basement where he'd been held for the past...how many days? He'd lost track. Not wanting to be fooled, he kept his eyes closed until he had had a chance to think this new experience through.

He didn't even remember how he'd gotten locked in that hellhole. He had driven to the airport in accordance with his secretary's text, and recalled getting out of his car in the parking lot. From that point until the time he woke up on a bloodstained couch in that basement, rats nipping at his skin, everything was a blank spot in his memory. The events afterward, however, were all too clear.

At first sight of the demon, Steve knew it to be the creature that had terrorized his wife. He had fought with it, but it had far superior strength. The one time he'd tried to overpower Vlad, the vampire had caught him around the throat and had held him up off the ground with one arm. The look in Vlad's eyes...the red mist, the flames Steve could see in them...these were enough to scare Steve into submission.

It also threatened to destroy his family if he didn't cooperate, and so he submitted, teeth clenched, to the veins in his arm being opened and his blood drained into a bowl. Then that fiend would drink it right in front of him as Steve held his wounded arm to his side! Night after relentless night went on like this, until Steve felt he had no life-sustaining fluids left. He did in fact faint a few times, waking to the sensation of rats swarming on him, taking advantage of his inert body to feast on his torn flesh.

Steve had gotten no rest during his imprisonment, not only because of the rat danger, but also because the surface of every piece of furniture seemed to be covered in bloodstains. This he discovered with a small flashlight he had hidden in an inside pocket. It sickened and enraged him to think that these were left over from his wife's time here.

All of his other belongings had been taken away. His captor had used Steve's cell phone to send a couple of texts to Lydia, and then had crushed the device in one hand.

Steve felt so helpless, but his captive condition had also pushed him to prayer like never before. It was strange; he had believed Lydia, especially after the incident in the bishop's office, but had still been the same. There had been no change in him, as nothing had happened to him personally. He hadn't made the connection between these evil occurrences and the need to strengthen himself against them by constant prayer. Now, here he was a prisoner, locked in the same basement room in which his wife had been imprisoned, in the power of an evil entity that threatened everything Steve had ever held dear.

At the verge of despair, he was finally feeling the need to pray. Especially when he was finally alone and the vampire was...where? Not wanting to try and guess, he prayed fervently for his family's safety along with his own.

His arms burned from the pain of being constantly cut open, and the smell of his blood brought the rats even when he wasn't sleeping. When the pain lessened, he would work on the single, boarded-up window, trying to make his escape, even though he knew it was a lost cause. His loss of blood and lack of sleep made him too weak to really do any damage, even though the glass was broken out of it. He found himself praying for death, so as to escape this horrid darkness.

Now, as he lay in...what? Straw?...and heard birds chirping, he realized he had somehow gotten away. How? Or was this all a figment of his overtired imagination? He cautiously opened one eye, fully expecting to see the dark surroundings of the basement and Vlad's mocking face, fangs bared.

To his surprise, he was, indeed, free!

He opened his other eye and sat up, taking in this incredible scene. Late afternoon sunlight came through spaces in the walls of a barn, dust floating lazily through the rays like fine gold powder. A couple of horses stared at him from their stalls. One tossed its head and nickered.

Steve stood up, brushing the straw off his clothes, and considered what he should do next. He wasn't even sure where he was. Lydia had said she had been transported to what she was sure was a huge house in Europe somewhere. If that was true, was he still oceans away from home?

The opening of the barn door startled him. Before he could hide, a young man entered the room, the light from outside surrounding him like a halo.

Steve was ready for a fight if this intruder made any kind of move to stop him from leaving, but the young man only smiled at him, seemingly not surprised by his presence there. He held out a loaf of bread and a glass of some sort of liquid.

Steve hadn't eaten since he left home, and with a nod of thanks to the stranger, took the offered food and wolfed it down.

"Sorry," Steve apologized sheepishly between bites, "I'm pretty hungry."

The young man smiled gently, then turned without a word to feed the horses in turn. Steve assumed from his benefactor's silence that he didn't speak English; therefore, he must still be in another country. Which got him to pacing and worrying.

How to get home? He had to think. First, he should call Lydia. She was probably worried out of her mind. Maybe she could...

Wait. First, find out somehow from the young man where he was. Then, get to a phone and call home...

"None of that will be needed," his new friend said, interrupting his thoughts. "But you must get home. Your wife and children need you to be with them."

Steve stood awestruck. Not only did this young man speak English, he could read Steve's thoughts! Then, alarm bells went off in his head.

What did he say about Lydia and the kids?

He felt close to panic. "What do you mean? Who are you? Where am I?" He grabbed the stranger's sleeve.

Wordlessly, the young man led Steve to the door of the barn and then outside, where his own car awaited him! Once again, all he could do was stare.

How did it get there? Also, how was he supposed to drive it? His keys had been confiscated along with everything else.

The young man cleared his throat, and Steve turned to look at him.

He was holding out Steve's keys to him!

Steve took them, totally baffled.

"How did you get these? Wait..." A tingle of fear crept down his spine, and he stepped back, away from whoever this person was. Friend or foe?

"Okay, who are you, and where am I? Are you in alliance with that demon that calls himself Vlad?" Steve hugged his arms to himself with the memories of those nightly lacerations.

Then he realized something else shocking; his arms were no longer in pain! He looked at them for the first time since he had woken up in the straw. They were clean and clear of any wounds! They now looked as if they had never been scored and cut open!

The light around the young man pulsed and glowed brighter and brighter, until Steve had to shield his eyes. He dropped to the ground.

A Voice of gentleness and love came to him, warming his heart and giving him peace.

My son, you are safe. I have had My angels bring you to this place, and now you must hurry to Lydia's side. The Father's plan is unfolding rapidly, and she will need you to help her.

Steve dared to look up. The young man had not said a word; the Voice had been within his own soul, but his eyes bore that same gentleness that Steve had just experienced.

The Voice continued. *You are only a few miles from home. Once you leave this place, you will know where you are. My angels will protect you on your way.*

"Yes, Lord," Steve whispered, for he had no doubt Who was talking to him.

The angel, who had been his benefactor, helped Steve to stand. He ran to the car and got in. He turned to thank the angel, but he was gone.

As Steve turned the key in the ignition, he suddenly noticed how hot it was in the car. Looking out through the windshield, he saw that the sky was almost white.

That was trivial right now, though. He would consider that later. Right now, he had to get home.

As the car bumped down the country road towards the main highway, wisps of black smoke rose from the ground around the vehicle. It seemed as if they were trying to surround the car.

A column of light stayed over the vehicle during the entire journey, engulfing and snuffing out the wisps as they arose.

CHAPTER 36

Lydia sat in the car, her eyes squeezed shut and her teeth gritted. She gripped the wheel hard, rocking silently back and forth in fear and shock.

A hand softly touched her shoulder, and she shrieked, grabbing for her door handle.

"Lydia, it's me!"

Lydia's fear dissolved instantly into relief. Teresa was sitting in the passenger seat beside her.

She covered Lydia's other trembling hand with her own warm, comforting one.

"Teresa! Oh, you scared me!"

"Why are you afraid?" Teresa asked with tender concern.

"'Why'? Are you kidding? You saw what he was doing! In fact, I think your coming in was a deliberate act, in order to save me!"

Teresa smiled softly. "Yes, it was."

"That was brave of you. Thank you!"

Teresa shook her head gently. "Lydia, please remember, I am beyond his power. There is nothing he can do to me."

Oh, that's right...

Lydia was curious. "Bud did he even try?"

"No. His memory was temporarily disrupted, and he left the room."

"You can do that?"

"No, God can. I only do His will."

"Can you ask God to get rid of him? I'd really like to get back to my normal life..." Lydia laughed weakly.

Teresa shook her head, then leaned toward Lydia, a serious look on her face.

"Lydia, realize this. Much more will be asked of you, in order for your participation in the Father's plan to be completed. Still, it is your decision, and yours alone."

Lydia leaned her head on the steering wheel and closed her eyes. After a moment, she sighed, sat up, and turned to Teresa. "Tell me something."

Teresa nodded and waited for Lydia to go on.

"Why?" Lydia asked.

Teresa sat quietly, waiting for Lydia to continue.

"Why me? Why all this? Why does God need me here, in this mess, getting tortured, my heart broken, my spirit crushed?"

"The same reason He has needed all others throughout history to work His will." Teresa stared intently into Lydia's eyes. "You do know, and believe, don't you, that God is a God of love, right?"

Lydia nodded.

Teresa continued, "Because of this, God will not force His will on anyone. Even now, you and all of the others assisting in His plan can say 'no more', and God would understand. He is not a Lord of fear. He wants us to serve Him out of love, not because we think we risk death or alienation if we don't serve Him.

"Humanity must be involved in its own salvation. Without that, if it was just God repairing whatever goes wrong, salvation would be merely a mechanical thing. The bond of love must be two-way; humanity must love God enough that His plans will work through us. How can people love an objective, automatic life-fix? You are an example, you and the others, of your answer to God's love."

"But the horrors we've gone through..."

"Echo the suffering of Our Lord in His Passion. Remember, He was not just suffering physical pain. He was suffering the torture of all the sins and degradations humanity has issued forth since its creation, and those that will be forthcoming until the end of its time—physical, mental, spiritual. All of it, and He never turned back.

"'Crushed spirit'? Oh, yes, He knows of crushed spirit. All of His children's sins from all time rested within that cross on His shoulders and were pounded into His hands and feet."

Lydia stifled a sob, her eyes welling with tears. Quietly, she said, almost to herself, "Yes. He tried to show me that in a dream not too long ago."

Teresa nodded sadly. "I know."

Lydia sat up straighter, closed her eyes in prayer, and then asked, "Okay, what am I supposed to do next?"

"Now you must go back inside. A warning, though: you must be stronger now than ever before. Your spirit and faith will be tested more severely than at any other time."

Her words shook Lydia, so much so that she instinctively reached for her car keys.

Then she stopped herself, and with a half-smile on her lips, said wryly, "Some pep talk..."

Teresa gave a sad kind of smile in return, and disappeared.

CHAPTER 37

As Lydia slowly walked back through the building, she silently prayed for God's protection for the people in the offices she passed. Because she had seen what had happened to Ned, she felt a need to beg God's divine watchfulness over her co-workers, friend or stranger.

She could hear them as she entered her office suite and made her way to her desk: two male voices behind Vlad's door.

Brandi looked up from her keyboard. "Oh, there you are! What happened to you? We saw you race out of here so fast!"

"I...had to get to the bathroom. Not feeling well..."

"Oh. Hope you're better now."

Brandi flounced over to Lydia and lowered her voice. "We finally found out his name!" she whispered, glancing toward the closed door. She announced it as if it was a huge triumph.

Well, good, thought Lydia sarcastically. *Now when we get a memo from him, we'll at least know who it is...*

Brandi copped a surprised look when Lydia didn't answer. "Well, don't you want to know?"

Lydia feigned interest, but in her head she was thinking, *I already know. It's Death. Sin. Corruption. Lies. Darkness. Evil. Pick one. They all work.*

Aloud, she said, "Well, certainly. Of course. And it is...?"

Brandi whispered dreamily, "It's Mr. Valentino." She sighed. "Can you believe it?"

Valentino....sheesh...

Debbie laughed from across the room. "He can creep into my tent any time he likes!"

Both women giggled, darting love-struck glances at the closed door.

Brandi started back to her desk, and stopped.

"Oh, yeah!" She turned back to Lydia. "I was supposed to tell you. Mr..." she sighed again, "Valentino...wanted you in his office as soon as you got back. Oh! And," here she tiptoed back to Lydia and leaned toward her again, "he's got a babe of a friend in there with him!"

"Save at least one of them for us!" Debbie giggled.

Lydia sighed and shook her head. She wished her co-workers knew what she knew, but there again, if they did, who knows where they would be? Either destroyed, or part of the cursed undead, like poor Ned. Personally, she would have preferred the former, given the choice...and the sooner the better.

However, that was cowardice, and she would not let God down by taking the easy way out. She understood now why she had to do this.

She prayed especially for Debbie and Brandi as she made her way once again to "Death's Door", as she was beginning to think of it. What evil was waiting for her this time? She hoped that the other man in the office was just a normal, everyday guy with financial reports or the latest stock options. With all of her heart, she prayed that this was the case.

Lydia knocked tentatively on the door.

"Enter," came the command from within.

Lydia's heart knocked unevenly in her chest at the sound of his voice. She opened the door, and came just inside, standing in the same place as the last time she had been in there. No sense in taking chances if she didn't have to.

Vlad was at his desk, with another man of exceedingly good looks sitting across from him. Both were relaxed and drinking glasses of wine. Lydia could see why the girls in the front office were dazzled by this newcomer. Quite the...

Wait...what? Since when did Vlad take up alcohol? Well, Lydia reasoned, *if he could 'eat' a dinner at my house, I suppose it's possible.*

"Oh, Lydia, do come in." Vlad got up, as did the stranger. Lydia was disgusted with Vlad for playing the gentleman, but she forgot about that as she took in the visitor's sharp, expensive-looking clothes and the smooth, graceful way he rose from his chair.

Suddenly she noticed that, like Vlad, he did not cast a reflection on the glossy surface of the desk! She glanced at the desktop, then raised her eyes to the stranger's face...

He was smiling at her, and she could just make out the fangs peeping from between his lips!

Her heart thudded in her throat, and she froze. Her eyes darted from one to the other of the vampires, her skin crawling and her pulse pounding.

Vlad smiled knowingly. It was not a friendly smile.

"Lydia, I would like you to meet a colleague of mine. He will be taking my place while I am on an extended trip to my ancestral home."

"Do you mean that nasty huge house where you imprisoned me, or is Satan calling you home?" Lydia knew that that crack would probably land her in a lot of trouble, but by now she didn't care. She was going to be going Home soon anyway.

Vlad growled at her, but didn't say anything in response.

Instead, he leveled a cool gaze at her and then looked at the wine glass in his hand. He held it up to the half-light in the room, looking through the fluid and giving it a little swish, as if at a wine tasting. Slowly, he smiled and brought it up to his lips. After taking a drink, he set the glass down on the desk. The red fluid sparkled in the light.

"Ah, very nice, for its type. An average taste, I think."

The other vampire took a taste in turn and nodded his agreement.

Vlad's next remark shook Lydia to the core. "Your husband's blood isn't nearly as good as yours, Lydia, my dear."

Lydia put a hand to her mouth, eyes wide with terror. A strangled scream escaped her lips. Slowly, she stepped backward towards the door.

Vlad went on. "But I have never really developed a taste for male blood." He turned to his colleague. "What say we try Ned's again? I'm sure he would be more than glad to part with some of his."

Lydia whirled and ran from the room. The shocked secretaries in the front office watched her rush out of the office and down the hall. They turned and looked questioningly at each other.

"What gives? Twice in one day?" Debbie asked her friend.

They shrugged and went back to work.

Lydia splashed cold water on her face and rinsed out her mouth. Her nausea remained, but there was nothing left to bring up. She looked at her white, shocked face in the bathroom mirror. When Teresa had said things were about to get worse, she had been telling the absolute, horrifying truth!

As if on cue, Teresa appeared in her housekeeping uniform, spray bottle and rag in hand, just in case someone came in.

Lydia whirled on her, panic-stricken.

"You told me Steve was safe! Those two fiends are in there drinking his...his...oh, Teresa! My husband!" she wailed.

Teresa held Lydia close as she fell into her arms, and put her hand on Lydia's head.

As if in a dream, Lydia saw once again the horrid basement...but it was empty. Then she saw the window. The board lay on the basement floor, broken into several pieces. The rocks that had been pushing the board up against the window hole were lying scattered, inside and out.

She drew back from Teresa's hand, puzzled. "What...?"

Teresa held Lydia's hands and gazed into her eyes. "He *is* safe, Lydia. God sent His angels to take him out of there. This time, however, they made it look as if Steve had escaped through the window. It gives him a little more time before they start looking for him here."

"Then, what...those glasses..."

"Cow's blood. Lydia, you must never believe anything the Father of Lies or his minions tell you."

Relief flooded Lydia's body and soul. She sagged against Teresa, her strength about spent. "Thank God!"

Suddenly Teresa stiffened, staring unseeingly into space. Alarm in her voice, she tugged on Lydia's elbow. "You must return! The girls in the office! Their lives are in peril! And more importantly, their souls!"

"What?"

"Come! *Now!*"

CHAPTER 38

Lydia left the bathroom and sprinted down the hall. Friendly or not, as silly and gossipy as they may be, these young ladies were still God's precious children! They did not deserve the danger that Lydia had left them with.

She opened the office door on a grisly sight, one which almost sent her retching back to the bathroom.

The vampires were in the midst of feeding on Debbie and Brandi. The women were trying to fend off their attackers, but were growing more and more feeble by the moment. Signs of their great struggle were everywhere. Papers, blood-spattered, covered the floor between the girls' desks. Chairs were toppled, and there were sprays of crimson on the walls and floor.

Lydia's scream came from the very depth of her being. She had been too late! Those young ladies, so infatuated with what they thought were good-looking men, had left themselves open to destruction.

The vampires turned towards her. Lydia was sickened at the sight of their gore-smeared faces. Then, fear gripped her as Vlad smiled open-mouthed at her, his fangs stained with Debbie's blood. "You left," he said, sounding like a boy caught with his hand in the cookie jar. "We came out of my office looking for you, and here were these two young ladies, fairly swooning over us and ripe for the taking. So, you see, it's really your fault."

The stranger was gazing intently at Lydia. Without taking his eyes off her, he spoke for the first time. His voice was deep and somewhat hypnotic.

"Is this the one you told me about?"

"Yes, my liege."

"The one you were going to take into our world."

"Yes."

Lydia gulped. A demon higher in the ranks than Vlad! Why was he here?

A cold realization gripped her. These demons were determined that she would not spend another day on Earth. Was she that dangerous to them? No, it was her determination to do God's will, no matter the cost, that was sparking them to destroy her.

They continued, watching her closely.

"Why did this not happen?" the newcomer asked. "Why is she still alive?"

Vlad looked uncomfortable. "This is something I'm still trying to understand."

The other vampire started toward Lydia. "Well, let's find out together then."

As they approached, Lydia whispered, "Into Your hands, Lord Jesus, I commend my spirit. Please, before that, I beg you to help Debbie and Brandi!"

His Voice: gentle, reassuring; His hand in hers.

I assure you, Lydia, I will take care of My daughters. Do you put their needs before yours?

"All before me, Lord. Let no one escape Your tender Mercy!"

Well said, Lydia.

With that, a calm, gentle peace engulfed Lydia. She could see that further terrors were imminent, as the two demons came toward her, fangs at the ready. Just for now, though, she felt nothing but that peacefulness...

As the vampires got closer, Lydia could see two columns of pure light appear beside the still forms of their victims. The light enveloped them, and they were taken up.

The glow faded from the room. Lydia sent up a silent prayer of thanks, then turned her attention back to the menace before her.

It couldn't be helped...the human need for survival took over, and Lydia whirled and ran for the door, all courage evaporating.

The door slammed shut on its own, and Lydia could hear the locking mechanism click into place. She screamed again as she pulled on the doorknob. Her nails tore at the crack between the door and the jamb, bloodying her fingers.

Just in time, she bolted to one side as Vlad leapt at her.

The reprieve was momentary; he was much faster, and grabbed her as she tried to escape. He laughed as he held her close, his breath reeking of blood. He turned his head toward his companion.

Then his smile faded as he realized that the bodies of the two secretaries were gone.

The other vampire caught his expression and turned to see what Vlad was staring at. Then he, too, stared.

For a time he just stood facing the empty desks. Slowly, comprehension came to his face. He turned, eyes narrowed, and slowly approached Lydia.

Vlad's superior commanded, "Turn her around." It came out as a low, unearthly growl. Vlad turned her and pinned her arms behind her back, facing toward the other monster. She struggled harder as he got nearer.

His voice froze her soul. "Who are you?" he demanded. "Furthermore, *what* are you?"

Lydia struggled against Vlad's pinioning hold. She tried not to look at her interrogator. "What do you mean?" she gasped, out of breath from fear and from the fight she was putting up.

"You. Your escape. Your mended skin. Our inability to read your mind, although it was easy enough months ago, and now...this!" He indicated the empty room behind him.

Lydia called forth the last reserve of her courage, drawing on her faith in her Savior. She stopped fighting for a moment and turned towards the other vampire.

"I had nothing to do with any of this, except in my obedience to the One who loves me. None of this is accomplished by me. God's love for His children keeps them safe! I do not fear you!"

The vampire cocked an eyebrow. "And us? Are we not also His children?"

Lydia answered him, "You threw that away when you disowned Him! When you decided that you were better than Him! This is why you are lost!"

Then she spat fury at him: "And why you will ultimately lose!"

Vlad growled and tightened his grip, making her cry out in pain. At a signal from his superior, he shifted his hold so that he held Lydia's arms behind her with one of his, while his other hand reached around front. He grabbed Lydia's chin, twisting her head up and to the side. He held it tightly against his chest, exposing the expanse of her throat.

Lydia could no longer move at all. Any time she tried, pain would shoot dizzyingly up her arms, almost making her black out. She would have gladly welcomed the darkness of unconsciousness, as opposed to the evil that was now upon her. Her eyes rolled in terror as he stood before her, eyes red, inches from her unprotected neck.

"We'll see who loses..." he growled.

He grabbed her shoulders, and, with one quick thrust, buried his fangs in her neck. The blood spurted forth, her heart slowed...

...and suddenly she found herself in a peaceful daze, floating blissfully free...

Lydia, fight him!

The command puzzled her. She couldn't work out why she should fight. The months of fear, the pain...all gone. She was...okay...How could she fight when it was...all gone now...

Suddenly, blinding white pain shot through her, tearing her out of her trance, forcing her back to reality. She could feel the nail marks again on her wrists, and, along with them, the thorn marks on her head as well—their first appearance since her visit to the bishop. They pulsed with pain, and droplets of blood appeared, which ran down her face and arms.

Both vampires fell back with a cry, and Lydia crumpled to the floor. Vlad's cohort grabbed Lydia's wrists, and the contact made her scream in agony.

"What is this?" he roared. As full comprehension dawned on him, he pulled Lydia from the floor and shook her like a rag doll. He threw her onto the surface of a nearby desk, and raised a fist toward Heaven, screaming his fury.

Then, he brought the fist down through Lydia's chest, creating a massive hole through her ribcage and tearing into her heart. Vlad clawed through her side, exposing and ripping her vital organs.

Lydia, in unbelievable pain, passed out into blessed unconsciousness. Right before fading into darkness, the last thing she saw was a bright light pulsating over the three of them, descending from somewhere beyond the ceiling.

The two vampire demons were so intent on their destruction of one of God's chosen ones that they knew nothing of the light descending upon them. The light parted into three columns, then transformed into towering angels. They wore military-looking garb; one held a sword almost as long as he was tall.

The two others looked to him and waited.

Raising the sword, the leader pointed it toward the dark destroyers, still intent on their victim. Too late, the vampires finally noticed that they were not alone.

The two angels fell on them. With a cry of mingled surprise and anger, Vlad and his cohort fought their captors, to no avail. They were vanquished almost immediately. Their bodies transformed into dark, oily smoke, which the angels surrounded and bore away.

The remaining angel sheathed his sword and stood sadly over Lydia's bloodied body. After a moment, he picked her up. Then they also disappeared.

CHAPTER 39

The bishop watched through the window of his study, waiting. The day, although early, was once again shaping up to be rather warm for spring. A breeze blew through the screen of the open window, fluttering papers on his desk and cooling his perspiring face. No birds twittered outside; his many bird-feeding stations were quiet and vacant. He would have thought it strange, but for the events of the past few days. Now, it made perfect sense.

About a week earlier, he'd been awakened in the early morning by the sudden need to call his good friend and confidant, Archbishop Cecil LeJeune, who presided over a diocese on the other side of the state. It was time to tell him about Lydia and the message; he was sure of it in his heart. After fidgeting and waiting impatiently for the start of the business day, he had leapt at the phone and called right as the clock struck 8:00 a.m.

"Yes, Frank, what can I do for you?" The archbishop himself answered; although he had a very competent secretary, he didn't stand on procedure or protocol, and often answered the phone first.

Bishop Frank could hear said secretary harrumphing in the background. He smiled; she was known to be a stickler on whose job was whose, often reminding her boss, "I don't go trying to run the church, so don't try to run my office!" Still, they were close friends and could not imagine things any other way.

He said to the archbishop, "Sorry to bother you so early, Cecil, but there's something I have to tell you. It won't let me rest until I do."

"What is it, Frank? What's wrong?" Archbishop Cecil was used to the playful banter the two of them had had since their days in the seminary. To hear Frank speak so urgently worried him.

The bishop squeezed the bridge of his nose while he thought of how he should phrase what he needed to say. *Well, in for a penny, in for a pound. Nothing to do but say it plain...*

He quickly related his meeting with Fr. Sam, Steve, and Lydia. To his credit, the archbishop kept quiet until Bishop Frank was finished.

A pause on his end, then, "I have to admit, it's a hard thing to believe. Coming from anyone else, I would think that psychiatric help might be in order. I know you, though. In thirty years, you've never been one to be swayed by fantastic stories. What I'd like to know, though, is why you are telling me this now?"

"I was told in the 'message' not to say anything to anyone until the time was right. This morning I woke up with the most urgent need to call and tell you. I have to say, strange things are happening here, and I am getting increasingly anxious."

"Such as?"

"Well, I don't know about how the weather is where you are, but here it is unbelievably warm. It feels like August! No birds out, I haven't seen a single squirrel or chipmunk for days, and even my feral cats haven't been around. The sky is almost white, and...I occasionally see wisps of what look like black smoke rising out of the ground, as if the landscape is smoldering."

Another pause, then the archbishop spoke again. "Frank, it's time to get the ecumenical councils together. There isn't much time. We have to find out from the other faiths what they are experiencing. Everyone must be told, at least the religious leaders, worldwide."

Bishop Frank was amazed at his friend's words, spoken with such sudden urgency. He hadn't expected Cecil to believe him so quickly and with so few questions.

"Cecil, I'm glad that you believe me. It's a huge relief. I have to admit, this sort of thing is hard to fathom. Out of curiosity, though, I must ask: what convinced you? It almost seems as if you'd been expecting something like this."

Archbishop Cecil sighed. "Yes, in a way. I've been having strange dreams myself lately. Bolts and columns of light from the sky, and plumes of oily black mist rising from the earth. Between them, stars floating everywhere; and, yes, the weather here has been very strange, too. However, have you noticed? The heat comes from the ground and not from the air."

The bishop thought about this for a moment. "Hmm...yes, you're right! I hadn't noticed."

"Call a meeting with your local ecumenical council for tonight. I will send out...oops, I'll have Doris send out...a massive e-mail to every bishop in the country, and one to the Vatican as well. We have no time to lose!"

After he hung up, Bishop Frank turned to his computer and called up a letter he kept on file for the convocation of the ecumenical council. He checked to make sure the e-mails were current, added the correct date and the meeting time, and hit SEND.

That evening, the bishop pulled up to the meeting hall and was astounded by how many people had come. He walked into the room and gazed out at the ministers, rabbis, priests, and other local religious leaders who were milling around, talking in small groups or trying to find seats. He hoped there was enough room; usually when he called a meeting like this, the number of attendees was so small that they would end up going to a nearby restaurant to convene instead.

There had to be at least a hundred souls here, if not more, and they all looked worried. The bishop headed for the front of the room where a podium with a microphone was set up.

"Frank! Long time no see!"

He turned to see Rev. Tony Longwirth, the Episcopalian priest from down the road. He was sitting with his wife, Danielle, who co-pastored the church with her husband. She was deeply absorbed in a conversation with a Methodist minister on her left.

"Hi, Tony. How are things at your end of the street?"

Rev. Tony's eyes grew serious. "Not so good. We've been getting calls for days now from people having nightmares. Ghosts, and vampires, things that go bump in the night. I've even found some of my congregation huddled in the church basement; they'd broken through the old coal delivery door and had gotten in that way. They're scared to leave, with absolutely no idea why. I have to tell you, if you hadn't called this convocation, I would have."

An old rabbi, who had been listening in on the conversation leaned over from the row he was seated in. "I've had people come to me, scared to death, certain they'd seen the Lilith or one of her offspring in their children's rooms!"

Bishop Frank and Tony exchanged puzzled looks; they'd heard of the Lilith myth, but didn't know anything about her.

"Could you please explain this 'Lilith'?" Tony asked. "I'm afraid we don't know that much about her."

The rabbi looked grim as he explained, "In Jewish mythology, Lilith was Adam's first wife. Yes, yes, I know," seeing the looks on his listeners' faces, "that's why it's called 'mythology'. Not supposed to have happened. Yet..."

"Same with vampires," muttered the bishop.

"And chimera," added Tony. It was the rabbi's turn to look puzzled. "Sorry. I'll explain later. Please continue."

"Lilith left Adam because they were constantly quarreling. God dispatched three angels to find her. They caught up to her at the Red Sea, where she was giving birth to demons by the hundreds. She refused to go back, and God punished her by killing a hundred of her 'children' a day. She retaliated by killing off human newborns, and some people even today believe she is real."

There was a silence as the two other clerics absorbed the tale.

"Wow," Tony finally said, "I've never heard of this."

"Me either," said Frank. "I'd heard of feminist organizations using the name; wonder if they know its roots?"

"I don't know. All I know is, in my years, I have seen an increasingly strong indifference to the possibility of demonic influence. Séances, Ouija boards, tattoos of pentagrams and demons; don't people know these are not mere symbols and parlor games? They call into this world powers that they cannot control!"

"The problem being," Tony said, "is that the people who do this are often so far away from their spiritual roots. Either that, or they are searching for God, and are being whispered onto the easy path by Satan and his destroyers. They are convinced that this path is the right one, because they get instant gratification. The Bible, however, is strewn with proof that the way to God is on the difficult road and in the arduous climb. Spirituality, when connected with the True God, whatever name we call Him, is not a walk in the park!"

"So true," said the bishop. "Well, I must get up to the podium. Time to start."

The convocation started with an opening prayer, said in several languages, and then Fr. Sam stood up in the front row. The bishop had asked him to be present and to give his witness as to the reason they were all there.

Adjusting his Roman collar, the priest nervously walked up to the podium.

"My fellow religious leaders, prelates, ministers, priests, and all leaders who look to a loving Higher Power, greetings." His voice started shakily, but he became confident as he continued. "Bishop Frank has asked me to relate to you what I have seen concerning the situation before us, and I would invite comment and witness from others as well."

Then he launched into the telling of his experience with Lydia that fateful afternoon in his office. His audience, Christian and non-Christian alike, were riveted by his words.

No one spoke for several minutes when he finished. Then, a hand in the third row was raised.

Fr. Sam pointed to its owner. "Omar? You would like to add something? Please, come up."

The imam from the only mosque in a 50-mile radius stood up and walked wearily to the front of the room. He adjusted the microphone and looked out at a sea of curious faces.

"My brothers and sisters, this has been very enlightening. I realize that what we all just heard was from a witness in the Christian faith. Please hear from an old man who has tried to keep the laws of Allah for most of his life.

"I have also heard from other non-Christians tonight, and so I can accept and believe what the priest has said, because of the testimony of others.

"My people have told me about dreams, so realistic, so vibrant in color, that when they awake they cannot discern their waking experiences from their dreams. Many have spoken of Iblis, the fallen angel who believes himself superior to humanity because he was made of fire and man from clay. They have seen wraiths of smoke from the ground, and many have seen his image in them."

There was a loud murmur as the attendees spoke among themselves, nodding in agreement. They, too, had noted the strange goings-on between sky and earth.

"I've a brother in Ireland who says the people there are overrun by banshees!" spoke an anonymous voice from the crowd.

"Our missionaries in South America have heard stories of chupacabras in their midst," interjected another.

The voices were getting louder, and tinged with alarm.

The bishop went up to the podium. With hands raised, he spoke into the microphone.

"Please, brothers and sisters, we must stay calm. We have our flocks to look out for. We can't allow them to panic, so we must keep our heads!"

The assembly finally quieted down. They looked to the bishop for his next words.

"I am as much at a loss as you are concerning these events. All I can say is, be ready." He looked out at the good people before him. "I've already heard of people heading towards their particular houses of worship to seek refuge.

"Let them in. Take them to a safe place. And wait. Wait until you are told in your hearts that it is safe to emerge. Be sure to get in all the supplies you may need to feed a large number of people for several days. Water. Food. Candles, in case flashlights don't work." He shrugged at that last remark. "Not sure why I said that last one, but please take it to heart. And, above all...pray!"

With that said, the bishop left the podium. After a few minutes, the group broke up, gathering once again in small groups as they headed for the door.

Bishop Frank walked back to Tony. "Chimera?" he asked, eyebrows raised.

"Head of a lion, body of a goat, tail of a serpent. Greek Mythology. Nasty creature. I told the rabbi of it after you left."

Bishop Frank said, "I don't get the connection. Vampires, Lilith, banshees. All dark spirits. I'm not getting why anyone would be fearful of a chimera."

"I have several Greek congregants. They see it as a terrifying monster. Fire-breather. Destroyer, like any of the others we've heard of tonight."

The bishop nodded. Then he held out a hand to Tony and his wife. "Be safe. Keep me in our prayers, will you?"

"Absolutely!" Tony and Danielle shook the bishop's hand in turn. "Pray for us, too."

"You can rely on it!"

As Bishop Frank turned to go, Danielle put a hand on his arm. He stopped, and looked at her questioningly.

"Frank? I know it seems dark now, but I really do think the Father of Lies has made a huge error in his assumption of us humans."

"Oh? How so?"

"I believe that he is trying to scare people away from trusting their senses, in the many forms he is taking before us. Each conformed to that which frightens us the most. That would keep us from trusting others, and then also God. But look how many people are showing up at our doors! I think we'll come out okay on this, I really do."

Bishop Frank squeezed her hand. "I hope you're right."

Now, as the bishop sat in his study, he could see people approaching the cathedral.

It had begun.

CHAPTER 40

As Steve got closer to home, the sun blood-red on the horizon, he was aware of the increasing heat in the air. It was hard to tell if it was a natural phenomenon, or because of the intense urgency he felt as he drove up the highway. Fear and anxiety held him in an intense grip, so much so that he thought he was starting to see things that weren't there. Faces, objects, indiscernible figures, kept appearing on either side of the car, just out of his line of vision, seeming to chase him. Luckily there wasn't much traffic along his route, because he kept jerking the wheel and weaving in his lane to escape the hallucinations.

They seemed to increase as he got closer to his own street. With them, however, came shafts of light, like sunbeams through clouds, although there were no clouds in the sky. They seemed to be enveloping the visions Steve was seeing and carrying them away. New ones kept appearing, and it was difficult to keep his mind and eyes on the road he was traveling.

"I'm either going to need an eye doctor or a shrink," he muttered. "Or both."

As he turned onto his own road and saw his house, a cold, unexplainable panic gripped him. He studied his surroundings, trying to figure out what had caught his mind. Nothing was different. Everything looked the same, but the urgency he'd felt on the road was now overpowering. He broke into a cold sweat, and put his foot down on the accelerator. Praying no one would step into the street, he gunned the engine and sped the rest of the way.

Peeling rubber, he screeched into his own driveway, grazing the mailbox and coming within inches of hitting the garage door. Heedless of this, Steve jumped out of the car, leaving the engine running, and bolted towards his front door.

Unlocked and wide open! Not good! Lydia always locked the door when she was home alone. He looked up and down the street, wondering if she'd gone for a walk. Even so...

Then, down the street a little further, he noticed his children's cars. Of course! The kids were home, and they weren't very attentive to keeping the door secure. He breathed a little easier, mentally readying his stock lecture.

When he turned back to go into the house, Steve was surprised and shocked to see the young man/angel from the barn standing just inside the door. This time, however, the angel was no longer in simple farmers' clothes. He was wearing what looked like a military uniform of sorts. His expression was grim.

Panic gripped Steve once again.

"Why are you here?' he cried at the angel. "Where's my wife? Where are Pat and Trudy?" He brushed past him, looking around wildly.

"Lydia! Trudy! Pat!"

Suddenly he came to a screeching halt at the horrific sight in front of him.

Lydia lay on the couch, her clothes drenched in blood, her face and throat disfigured so badly that she was unrecognizable. Her eyes were closed, her hair matted with the sticky substance. Gratefully, he could see that she was still breathing, although barely. It looked as if her chest had been caved in, but it was hard to tell due to the cloth swathing her midsection.

Dizzy from the shock, he clutched at the wall to keep himself from falling. The angel was at his side in an instant, supporting him.

"What...what happened?" He could barely get out the words as he stared at the battered figure that was his wife.

"Don't worry. She lives." The angel's voice was deep and melodic. "We must get her to the church."

"'Church'?" Steve was incredulous. "'Don't worry?' What's not to worry about? Look at her!"

All of Steve's emotions from the day, and from his ordeal with Vlad, were coming to a head, and anger wracked his body. He spun on the being beside him.

"No, she is not going to church! She is going directly to the hospital!"

Another voice in the room—soft, feminine. He hadn't seen her sitting in the corner; a young woman with a gentle demeanor and an intense, warm gaze. She spoke again.

"She must be taken to the church. No medicine on this earth will save her. Only the Savior can heal her and make her whole, but He has need of her brokenness now. We must leave immediately."

Steve vehemently shook his head and started to protest, but was interrupted by a small sound from the couch. He looked over, hope a flame in his eyes.

Lydia was twitching slightly, and a small cry escaped her lips. It surprised Steve that she could make any sound at all, so bruised and violated was her throat. He could see the fang holes and the purple marks left by the squeezing of powerful hands in the skin of her neck.

Suddenly her eyes flew open, and she stared blindly for a moment at the ceiling. She cried out and tried to sit up, but fell back just as quickly, pain contorting her features.

Steve rushed to her side, but the young woman got there first. She looked apologetically at him, then turned to her patient. "Lydia? It's Teresa..."

Lydia's eyes focused on her. "I'm..." she gasped. "I'm still...here?"

Teresa nodded her head once. "Yes, you are still of this earth."

Lydia groaned and turned her face toward the window and the darkness outside.

Teresa touched her arm. "Your husband is here," she whispered softly.

Lydia whipped her head back around, wincing at the pain, but with a joyful look on her face. "Steve?"

Teresa silently moved away, while Steve tried to find some way to embrace his wife without causing her further pain. He finally settled on clasping her hand, pulling it up to kiss and caress it.

"Oh, Steve," she rasped, "I didn't think I'd ever see you again!"

"I...oh Lydia, what happened?"

"They know!" Lydia tried to raise her head, grasping Steve's hand desperately in both of hers, eyes wide in sudden panic. "The demons! They know! God's plan is unfolding, the fallen are starting to wake up, and God's angels are arming themselves for war!"

The effort to speak was becoming too difficult. She lay back, coughing, and a spray of blood shot from her nose and mouth. Steve cried out in fright, clutching at her, not knowing what to do in his panic.

"We must go! Now!" Teresa tugged on Steve's arm. "Take her to the church! All are waiting!"

Shaken by the amount of blood he'd seen when Lydia coughed, Steve adamantly refused. "She needs a doctor!"

Lydia's hand covered his. It was cold and clammy, as if Death itself was touching him. He turned to look at her again. She was trying to say something, but had no strength left to do so.

He put his ear down to her mouth. "What is it, love?" he asked gently.

Lydia worked hard at the effort, squeezing her eyes shut and concentrating on speaking. Beads of sweat popped out on her forehead. She finally managed one word: "Church..."

Steve sat back quickly. "No! You'll die!"

Lydia shook her head faintly.

"Die...hospital...church...live...," she gasped, and then she went terribly, terribly quiet.

With an anguished cry, Steve stood up, and, scooping up his wife's body, headed for the front door.

"Where are you going to take her?" asked the angel.

"Church! You heard her! I'll not refuse her wishes!" He looked sadly at Lydia's bruised, ashen face. "Even if she dies because of it."

CHAPTER 41

Ned sat in the dark basement in Building Four, listening for the scurrying of rats. Occasionally he would pounce, cat-like, lifting a furry, squealing rodent and chomping into its body. Within seconds, he would drain the little animal and toss it into a pile of previously-dispatched rodents. He would take them into the forest later and bury them.

He smiled grimly, wiping the blood from his lips. It had been a happy day when he had gotten the notice about possible rodent activity in the building. Now he could do his job and satisfy his blood lust at the same time. It was the perfect set-up.

Lately, though, he couldn't quite shake the feeling that something wasn't right.

His friends, the two men who had set him straight about his fears, hadn't come to visit him recently. He missed the blood they usually brought him. It was so much better than the animals he had to hunt for himself. His self-confidence, the feeling that all was right with his world, was starting to erode. He felt a small glimmer of unease, as if he was missing something important.

A low noise in the darkness under the basement stairs caught his attention. He peered into the black space, apprehensive at possibly being caught and exposed, but couldn't see what was causing it. He got up from his stool, kicking the rat carcasses aside, and walked toward the steps.

"Who's there?" he demanded. There was no fear in his voice, only curiosity. It still struck him as strange that he was so fearless now, but his friends told him that it was one of the benefits of believing in them.

The noise became a growl, and as Ned peered under the steps, a shadow even blacker than the space around it leapt at him.

He staggered back as the shadow enveloped him. It covered him as he fell, shrieking, to the floor. He struggled to breathe, then went limp as the black shadow invaded his body, being breathed into Ned's nose and pouring into his eyes and ears.

Kim woke up at her desk, startled. She looked around at the empty cubes, and then up at the wall clock.

Six o'clock! How did that happen? And how come no one had come by and looked in on her? Didn't anyone notice her light was still on in her cube?

Besides her own, the only illumination came from the security lights in the building. This gave Kim the willies; after what had happened to Lydia, she was afraid to be the last one here at night. Now, from all signs, she sure seemed alone.

She hastily gathered up her things and grabbed her jacket.

As she was heading toward the exit, a sudden urge in her bladder caused her to stop in mid-stride.

Oh bother! I'll never get home in time! She sighed. *Guess I'll just have to hit the bathroom first.*

She went back through the room toward the hallway leading into the rest of the building, laying her gear on a nearby cart.

The hall was dark, illuminated only by the exit signs and the red eyes of the security cameras. Kim gulped, her heart racing, and crept out of the relative light of her own office room.

The bathroom was a few paces down from her door, but it could have been a mile away for all she could see. Looking up and down the hall, which she realized was futile for the lack of light, Kim hurried across to the other wall and turned right. Brushing her hand blindly along its surface, she finally reached the bathroom door. Quickly, she ducked in, fumbling for the light switch, trying not to think of what might be hiding in the stalls.

Hooray for light!

She momentarily thought of maybe spending the night in there. but the smell of disinfectant was already getting to her, and she was beginning to feel ill. She quickly took care of business and sped back to the door, holding her stomach. Even though she was feeling nauseous, the relative safety of the lit bathroom held her back from leaving. She looked longingly up at the fluorescent bulbs, and then reluctantly hit the light switch.

Plunged back into darkness, Kim waited a couple of minutes so that her eyes could adjust to the change. She opened the bathroom door a crack, looking out for...what? She couldn't place the reason why she was so anxious, except for finding herself in a dark, empty building...

Hurrying out, she ran toward her office, where she flew through the door and picked up her belongings. As she started once again toward the exit, she suddenly heard a noise from one of the cubes on the far side of the room.

Whistling!

Someone was here, after all. It wasn't much of a tune, but she wasn't going to be a music critic now. It sounded like heaven to her. She walked quickly over to the source of the sound.

The nameplate on the cube wall read "Stanley Germaine." He was at his computer, peering at a column of numbers on the screen; a young man, glasses hanging down low on a Roman nose, dark brown hair in dire need of a trim.

Kim watched him for a moment, not sure if she should or could trust him. He looked harmless enough, but looks could be misleading.

Well, she had to get to her car! How else, except to try to get there on her own! Tonight, for some reason, she had a strange feeling that that was not a safe option.

Come to think of it, she considered, *I* have *seen this guy around. Usually in the cafeteria by himself, eating lunch and reading a novel of some sort. Not much of a talker.* She looked closer. *Kinda cute, though.*

Suddenly he turned around and smiled at her. Kim felt her face color with embarrassment.

"Yes? Can I help you?" His tone was kind and warm.

"Oh!" Kim blurted, flustered by her gaffe in manners. "I didn't mean to stare! I was just so surprised that anyone else was still here!"

He was gently amused at her discomfort. "Not a problem. Actually, I just got here. I'd gone home and suddenly realized I'd left some loose ends in a project and I thought I'd better finish it."

"Ah. Well..." stammered Kim, not knowing how to ask him to walk her out to her car. She fidgeted uncomfortably. "Well, I...guess I'll be going..."

Idiot! Ask! "Um...bye."

"See you around!" Stanley waved to her cheerfully, and then turned back to the screen, once again absorbed in his project.

Kim marched to the door, mad at her inability to ask his help. She stormed out into the warm night air.

Halfway to her car, she got over her anger, and realized with a start where she was. Fear replaced anger, as, heart thudding, her footsteps ate up the ground between her and the relative safety of her car.

The sound started almost imperceptibly, and then quickly rose to a crescendo of howling noise. It was all around her; terrified, she started running. She'd never heard anything like it.

The first thing she thought of was banshees, like her uncle used to tell her about when she was young, scaring her into hiding beneath her bed at night.

As she sped to her car, she noticed some movement under a large, shadowy oak to her left. Panic-stricken, she let out a scream.

Banshee!

A hand suddenly thrust out from the darkness and took hold of her shoulder. Kim desperately fought back, wresting the hand away from her.

A light suddenly shone in her eyes. "Ma'am?"

Kim blinked. The light was lowered, and she recognized the speaker.

Ned!

"Oh, man, it's you! I am so relieved!" Kim put a hand on her chest, feeling her heart racing like a runaway train. "You really gave me a scare!"

Wait...

Kim listened. No rushing noise now, and no howling. It had stopped!

Ned came closer. "Why were you running?"

Kim took a couple of steps backward, warning bells going off in her head. Now that she had caught her breath and gotten back some of her senses, she noticed that Ned sounded...not quite right, somehow. Even more odd than he had been recently. His eyes seemed somewhat glazed and unfocused.

"I...I was scared. Dark. You know, weird noises and things. I'm not usually here this late. Thanks for your concern, though. I'll just be leaving..."

She turned and started walking away, trying to seem confident. Nervous, she looked over her shoulder to where Ned had been standing.

He was already gone, which suited her fine. His weirdness had risen about fifty percent since the last time she'd seen him. As she approached her vehicle's door, she started pulling her keys out of her pocket. They snagged on a string deep in the pocket's interior.

Cursing, she stopped to work the keys loose, nervously listening for the return of the banshees. Finally, after some unsuccessful pulls, she gave up and yanked the keys as hard as she could. They came free, but she could tell that her pants would need some repairs.

As she hit the "unlock" button on her key fob, she heard movement behind her. She spun around, ready to defend herself.

Ned again!

Kim sighed and rolled her eyes, exasperated. "Ned, I'm fine! Good night!"

She tried to turn back to her car, but found herself paralyzed by his stare. Her keys dropped to the cement, and, as he approached, she felt rooted to the spot. All she could see was his cold dead eyes.

Suddenly they were two red orbs. Before she could move, Ned had his hand around her throat, and had parted his lips to reveal long, sharp fangs.

Kim finally found her voice. She screamed, loud and long, pushing at Ned and trying to work his hand free of her neck. Her legs kicked at him as she squirmed under the forward press of his body. He pushed her back against the car, her head over the roof, and thrust his mouth down, tearing at her throat.

The pain was incredible. Kim could feel the pull of her blood being sucked out and the dull pain in her heart as it was deprived of its necessary life fluid. The world dimmed around her as she fell into near unconsciousness.

A flash of light caused Ned to pull away from his grisly feast. He looked up from his victim and hissed as the light neared.

Kim was awake enough to be cognizant of the light, but not much more than that. She slumped to the ground as Ned let go of her, intent on destroying whatever this thing was that had interrupted his meal.

A column of light stood not ten feet away. Steadily burning, motionless, as if it was waiting. It seemed to stretch up into the heavens. Ned covered his eyes with his arm, snapping and growling at the light, but unable to approach it. He turned back to Kim, grabbing her back into his embrace, and, putting his maw over the fang holes, went to work again.

Kim cried out feebly.

Suddenly a spark shot from the column, hitting Ned square in the back of the head. He dropped Kim once again with a howl, and bolted away into the darkness.

But the light was faster. It caught him, overpowered him, enveloped him as Ned's screams cut the night air.

It was over in seconds.

Kim watched through half-closed eyes, feeling the blood ooze out of her veins, as the light faded to reveal Ned unconscious on the ground. A figure looked down on him. After a moment, it turned and walked toward Kim.

She couldn't believe her eyes. Was she hallucinating? Did this mean she was dying?

He knelt down and put his hand on her shoulder, smiling gently.

"Stanley?" Kim managed to croak.

"Shhh...yes, Kim." He smiled. "Yes, I do know who you are. You're the real reason I'm here tonight."

Kim tried to speak, but he put a finger to her lips. Then he put his hand on her ravaged throat and closed his eyes, turning his face toward the heavens.

Immediately, a ray of blindingly pure light shot from the sky and entered the top of Stanley's head. It didn't seem to faze him; as Kim watched, the glow raced to his shoulder, down his arm and hand, and then into her throat.

Kim braced herself, not knowing what to expect.

The charge hit the skin on her neck, and she could feel it healing immediately. Her heart, which had been slowly foundering, was back to its regular rhythm.

She felt her throat in wonder. Then she sat up with a little help from Stanley, and looked over at Ned.

"What's going to happen to him?" she asked. In spite of his weirdness, she'd always thought he was a good guy. What happened to him had not been his fault.

"Watch," was Stanley's simple reply.

Kim saw an orb of light dancing its way down to the inert form from somewhere above. The light formed into yet another column. This one transformed into an angel with a sword. He lifted it high over his head and jammed it into Ned's chest.

Kim screamed and buried her head in Stanley's shoulder.

"Not to worry, love. Look!"

Kim forced herself to turn back to the scene, and gasped at what she saw.

One, two, then three separate dark forms were being pulled out of Ned's body, screaming and twisting. Ned's body arched as the demons tried to hold on to their refuge. The angel removed the sword, and, transforming back into light, caught up and trapped all three forms as they tried to escape. Then the light faded slowly away.

Kim looked at Stanley, then back at Ned. "Is he...?"

"Dead? No, but we have to get him to safety."

He looked pointedly at Kim. "You, too. And..." he looked down at her belly, "...the baby."

Kim sucked in her breath and moved away from Stanley, her hand instinctively going to where her infant slept in her womb. "How...how do you know about...?" She hadn't told anyone; she'd only found out a couple of days ago herself.

Stanley smiled sadly at her. "Kim, I'm an angel. I was sent to keep an eye on you. There's nothing about you I don't know."

Kim was puzzled. "What about my own guardian angel? Why would I need double-coverage, so to speak?"

Stanley laughed. "'Double' is a good explanation. Your guardian angel resembles you too strongly to make an appearance. That's why they must stay invisible. Imagine looking over your shoulder and seeing yourself standing there!"

Kim thought about this. "Yes. I see your point."

"Good."

Stanley stood up. "Now, which church do you attend? We should get you there."

He caught Kim's uncomfortable look. "Ah, yes. How about your husband? Where is he?"

Kim turned away, eyes tearing up. The angel looked at her with compassion, waiting until she could speak. "There's no...husband," Kim sniffed, wiping her eyes. "The father...I don't know..."

Stanley put a hand on her shoulder and spoke gently. "Is there a church you would be comfortable in? It'll be a few days before it will be safe to go home again."

"What do you mean by 'safe'? Why can't I just go home?" The idea of being in or near a church was making Kim nervous.

"What you just saw is a foretaste of what is to come. Your friend Lydia? There's a lot more to her disappearance than she told you. That's not her fault. Suffice it to say, that period of time started the unfolding of the Master's plan to cleanse the world of the evil it's invited upon itself."

Kim was shocked speechless. She had had no idea!

She looked at Ned, then back to Stanley. The only church she could think of in her bewilderment was Lydia's.

Before she could answer, Stanley nodded. "St. Stanislaus it is. Let's go."

In a flash, Kim found herself standing in the foyer of a church. Ned lay snoring in a heap beside her. She danced nervously away from him and looked around for her angel protector.

Stanley was gone.

CHAPTER 42

Pat and Trudy sat against the wall in the now-crowded church basement, drowsing against each other's shoulders. People were ranged throughout the room, finding space in storage closets and sprawling into the kitchen. Someone, probably the property caretaker, had opened up the classrooms that led off from the main hall, and people had pushed desks and tables aside in order to find a spot to camp out in.

And still they came, throughout the day and into the evening.

Most carried provisions...a basket of fruit here, a grocery bag full of canned food there. All supplies were accepted gratefully, and room was made for the newcomers, whether or not they brought anything to share. No matter how full the place looked, there always seemed to be room for more.

They all had one thing in common; they had no idea why they had come or why they had expected others to be there. Groups of people spoke in low tones while others, like Pat and Trudy, tried to doze on any flat space they could find.

In the evening, as the darkness set in outside, a young lady entered the room. The only reason anyone took note of her among all the others was that she was followed by two men, who grunted under the effort of carrying an unconscious body between them.

Pat blinked, He nudged Trudy, who was still asleep.

"Trudy!" he hissed.

"Whurr...," mumbled his sister. She opened a sleepy eye. "Whu...what?"

Pat pointed discreetly. "Isn't that whatshername, Mom's friend from work?"

Trudy followed her brother's finger, and sat up, surprised. "Wow, yeah. Kim? I think it's Kim. I thought she lived in the country, though. Why would she be here?"

"Maybe she got caught up in whatever's going on out there," Pat jerked a thumb towards the outside wall, "and had to seek refuge close by."

"And...who's that being carried down? Looks drunk." Trudy sniffed. "Some time to be hanging one on."

"Well, not many people are privy to the things we know, sis. Try to be a little compassionate."

Trudy was about to reply when Kim glanced over and saw them. One of the men behind her whispered something in her ear, and she nodded. They took their snoring burden into a classroom and laid him carefully in an unoccupied corner.

Kim, meanwhile, waved at the kids and came towards them, carefully picking her way over backpacks and sleeping bodies.

"Oh, you guys, I'm so happy to see you! I didn't think I'd know anyone, but here you are!" She was genuinely relieved to see a pair of friendly faces. Especially ones that could tell her more about what Lydia had gone through. Maybe then this would all make sense.

"Yeah, hey...Kim, right? Kind of surprised to see you here. Meaning," Pat added hastily, so as not to sound rude, "you're not a townie. You still live out by the dairy farm?"

"Oh, yeah. I was just passing by and felt a need to visit." She tried to sound convincing, but she had always been a lousy liar. At the doubtful looks she was getting from the kids, she smiled ruefully.

"It's that obvious, huh? Guess it's a good thing I don't play poker. Would have lost the ranch by now..." She sighed and looked away, all efforts at joviality gone. "I'm not sure I can explain why I'm here. It's all so...unbelievable."

Pat's chuckle was short and humorless. "Try us. We're past masters at unbelievable."

"For sure. We've been having 'unbelievable' for breakfast, lunch, and dinner for days now." At Kim's puzzled look, Trudy dismissed her comment with a shake of her head. "Never mind."

She looked around. "Let's find a more private spot where we can exchange info. Because from the look on your face, Kim, I can tell we may have a lot in common."

Trudy's comment caused Kim to be even more bemused. "Why do you say that?"

Trudy sighed. "That look on your face, when you came in? I've seen it elsewhere..."

"Where?"

"In the mirror."

Pat stood up, surveying the hall. There! A small door under the basement steps! It was still closed; with any luck, it would be unoccupied.

"Do you have a problem with small, enclosed spaces?" he asked Kim.

She snorted with amusement. "Have you seen the cube where I have to work?" she replied.

"Ah, good then. Follow me."

The girls followed him as he dodged milling bodies and their accompanying paraphernalia. As they passed the classroom where Ned was sleeping, they heard him snort and belch as he started to wake up.

"Who is that, anyway?" Trudy asked. "Is he with you?"

Kim looked nervous, and instinctively put a hand to her throat. Trudy saw this, plus the barely-controlled fear in Kim's face, and reflexively did the same, looking over at Ned.

Never mind. I can guess.

"In a manner of speaking. Can we move on?" Her eyes were pleading.

Pat frowned. "If he is a part of why you're here, shouldn't we wait for him to wake up? He'll probably benefit from our conversation..."

"No!" Kim exclaimed loudly, then lowered her voice when she realized she was attracting attention. "No, I...I can't. Not now." She looked over at Ned, and Trudy could see her break out in a sweat. Her body started trembling.

"Maybe not ever..." she whispered, mostly to herself.

Overriding the objection Pat was about to make, Trudy said, "Never mind then." She put a hand on Kim's arm and looked at her brother. "Pat, let's go."

"But..."

"Later!" Trudy insisted. "It may be best if the two of them don't meet up until we're sure."

"Sure of what?" Pat asked.

At the look in Trudy's eyes, he realized what she meant, even before she whispered the one word that explained it all: "Victor."

He nodded his understanding. The three of them continued to the door under the steps, where Pat tried the knob.

It opened to a dark, musty, but relatively clean storage area. Fortunately, no one was inside, so they took the space for themselves, finding some chairs in the deeper recesses of the room.

Once the door was closed, they were in total darkness. There was a sharp intake of breath from Kim, and she grasped for Trudy's hand. Once she found it, she held on tight, as if she was afraid she would float away from safety.

"Okay, closeness is one thing," she gasped. "Darkness, especially after tonight...not so much."

"We're here, Kim," Trudy spoke softly. "It's okay. We really are safe here."

They could hear Kim gulp. "I'm not so sure."

"Kim," spoke Pat, "trust us. Trust God. This is His house, storage places and all. We wouldn't be here if it wasn't safe."

"I don't know. I want to believe you, but..."

"Why don't you tell us what happened? Go slowly...we seem to have all the time in the world."

Pat's voice was comforting in the darkness. Trudy marveled silently at the change that had come over him in the past few days.

"Um, okay, here goes." Kim took a deep breath, and then told them everything, from when she had awakened at her desk, to finding Stanley, to the attack by Ned...all of it. She had to stop several times to choke back sobs. Trudy squeezed her hand, uttering soft, comforting sounds.

If Kim could have seen the looks on Pat's and Trudy's faces when she told of having been ravaged by Ned, she could have put her fears about being believed to rest. As it was, she thought she sounded like she'd gone crazy. Especially when she finished her story, and no one responded for what seemed an eternity.

Kim broke the silence herself with a nervous laugh. "Guess that sounds pretty insane, doesn't it?" she asked shakily.

Pat's voice was solemn. "No, Kim, not at all."

He then proceeded to tell her what had really happened to his mother. Trudy chimed in with her own experiences. She could feel Kim's fear through the tight grip on her hand.

The events of the past Saturday were especially hard on Kim.

"You guys could have been killed!" she whispered, terror in her voice.

"But, Kim, you see, God was with us. He has some sort of...purpose, He said...for us. We don't know what it is, but we are secure in the safety He guaranteed us."

Just then there was a commotion outside of their secluded den, and Pat heard his name mentioned.

"What the...?" he murmured as he pushed open the little door.

He could hear someone on the steps above him. A little dust rained down on his head, and he swiped it off the back of his neck.

"Yech!" he exclaimed. "What say we get out of here?"

"I second the motion," Kim agreed, beating him to the doorway.

They crawled out, dusting themselves off.

The population seemed to have doubled in the short time they'd been in the closet, and they stared wide-eyed at the crowd. Pat craned his neck to look up the steps, but no one seemed to be interested in his presence. People occupied that area all the way to the door, making it all but impossible to go up or down. He couldn't make out anyone he knew.

"Who could have...ouch!" He yelped as he felt fingernails dig into his skin. Turning, he was about to give his sister a tongue-lashing...until he discovered it was Kim's nails, not Trudy's, that were gripping his forearm.

She was staring, wide-eyed and terror-stricken, at a figure sitting at a nearby table. It was the man who had been brought in asleep.

Kim looked around frantically, ready to bolt. "I have to get out of here! I can't..."

"Miss Long! Is that you?"

Kim stiffened, her back to Ned. He was squinting at her, trying to see if he'd recognized her or not.

Her breath came out in stifled gasps. She clung to Pat and beseeched him, "He knows me! Oh, no! Please help! I can't face him. Don't let him near me!"

Pat gently detached himself from her grip. There was a small, half-amused smile on his face as he looked over at Ned.

"I think Ned's back to normal, if what I'm seeing is real. I don't recall Victor doing that."

Kim looked nervously over her shoulder.

Ned was bolting down a cheeseburger someone had brought from a fast-food restaurant on their way to the church. His eyes were closed in sheer pleasure; a number of people looked on, astounded at how quickly he could put away a burger. There were three other wrappers beside him, and a large soft drink was half gone as well.

Kim turned towards him, astonished. She got up enough nerve to walk over to him, Pat and Trudy close behind her.

Ned's eyes twinkled as he nodded. He spoke through a mouthful of beef and bread. "Thought it was you. What are you...and I, for that matter...doing here?" His meaty hand swept the room. "Where are we, anyway?"

Pat intervened. "You don't remember coming here?"

Ned shook his head and swallowed. "No. Last thing I remember was, I was in the security office watching...well, never mind what I was watching." He giggled.

A couple of little kids looked questioningly at him, and he whispered to them, "'Barney the Badger' cartoons." They giggled along with him, and Ned gave the adults a broad wink.

"Is there anything you remember?" Trudy asked him.

"Um..." He popped the rest of the cheeseburger into his mouth, licked his fingers, and took a slurp of soda. "Yeah. I heard a knock at the door, and turned to see two suits standing there. That's it, until I woke up in that room over there."

"And aren't you curious as to why?"

"Nah, not right now. Maybe after dinner..."

Pat cocked an eyebrow at Kim. "Sound normal to you?"

Kim sighed and shook her head in amusement. "Yep, sounds like good ol' Ned to me."

Just then there was a commotion at the top of the stairs. The pastor waded through the sea of people, hurrying towards them. His face was gray with the strain he'd been under. The crowd parted as he hurried up to Pat.

"Pat! Trudy! Thank heavens I found you! You have to come upstairs with me. Now!"

CHAPTER 43

Steve gripped the steering wheel, his eyes fixed on the road, as he scorched up the main street of town. Occasionally he looked over at Lydia, who lay reclined in the passenger seat. She was barely breathing; Steve broke into a cold sweat as he imagined the worst.

"You mustn't worry. Just get her to the church, and trust in God." That annoyingly calm voice...the woman called Teresa, sitting in the back seat, reading his mind. Again.

As he got to the intersection where he would turn towards the church, Steve glanced in the rear-view mirror.

Read this, sweetheart, he thought, and yanked the steering wheel in the opposite direction. The tires squealed as he gunned the motor, flying up the hill to where the hospital stood.

Reaching the emergency-room parking lot, he jumped out and hurried to the passenger side. Lifting his wife tenderly out of the seat, Steve turned towards the building.

Inexplicably, he found himself in front of the church!

He almost dropped Lydia in utter disbelief.

"What? How? I..."

He turned on Teresa, who was climbing out of the car. His eyes narrowed. "Did you do this?"

"Do what?" She raised her eyebrows innocently and walked past him into the church.

"We had to."

Steve spun around at the voice; the angel had reappeared.

"Lydia wants it this way, and so does the Master. There was nothing you could have done to prevent yourself from bringing her here."

"Then why didn't the two of you bring her here yourselves? Why wait for me?"

The angel shook his head. "Listen to yourself. Is that what you would have really wanted? Think about it. What would you have done if you'd gotten home and she wasn't there? Especially in light of what you had been told before you left the barn."

"I'd be tearing the town apart, looking for her! I'd..."

"Yes, you would, and you would have put yourself in very real danger. Events are unfolding," he continued, looking up at the night sky, "and cannot be called back."

Steve followed the angel's gaze. Lights, like thousands of shooting stars, zipped and spun across the dark heavens. As he watched, he felt something cold waft against his leg.

Startled, he tried to see past Lydia's body to what had touched him. All he could see was a bit of mist. It was black—blacker than anything he'd ever seen—and menacing. It floated and shifted, while Steve held Lydia tight, hoping he could protect her somehow.

In a flash, the angel grasped the wraith and shook it once. It stilled, and then slowly evaporated. Steve could hear a shriek as it disappeared. He turned frightened eyes to the angel.

"You were meant to see this, Steve, to convince you. At the moment, you are still in no imminent danger, but I must advise you to get inside without delay!"

Steve needed no other encouragement. He dashed to the doors, which opened by themselves, and ran down the aisle. The doors closed quietly behind him.

Fr. Taylor was waiting at the altar. The candles were lit; they were the only illumination in the church, aside from the candle above the tabernacle. Out of the corner of his eye, Steve saw motion in the shadows. They turned into two figures he knew and loved, and they rushed toward him.

"Dad!"

"Daddy!"

Their forward progress was halted by the sight of their mother in Steve's arms. Happiness turned to horror as they took in the bloodied, motionless form.

Pat's jaw worked up and down as he tried to speak.

"Dad?" he whispered hoarsely, unable to take his eyes off the grisly sight. "What happened?"

Trudy sat down where she was, shocked, unable to do anything but to stare into space.

Steve was about to answer Pat when Fr. Taylor cleared his throat.

They turned to him.

"Please... put her down here."

Steve looked down at his wife's face, scored by claw marks and spattered with blood. His throat closed, and he shook his head.

"No," he choked out, "She's not heavy. I'd rather..."

"Steve. You must." The angel was beside him again.

Steve squeezed his eyes shut, tears leaking out of the corners. He stood for a moment, head bowed, then nodded, his eyes still closed.

He knelt down and placed Lydia gently in front of the altar, sobbing.

Pat knelt down also, and touched his mom's still face.

Suddenly the quiet was rent by a shrieking wail. Trudy threw herself on her mother, body heaving in sobs.

"No! Mom, no!" she cried, clutching her mother's shoulders, her head to Lydia's chest. She looked up at the angel imploringly. "Please, is she going to be all right? Oh, please say she'll be okay!" She clutched the angel's legs, weeping inconsolably.

Almost reverently, Steve straightened Lydia's legs and arms, lovingly sweeping her stiffened, blood-soaked hair from her face. Pat's tears fell hot on her skin as he looked on the face of the woman who had always been there for him.

One tear landed on her eyelid, and she twitched.

Pat cried out, "She's awake!"

Hope rose in their hearts as they watched her.

Lydia groaned and opened her eyes slightly. With excited cries, the kids and their dad leaned in towards her. She smiled at them, raising a weak hand to touch each of them in turn. Then she stared at the ceiling and lay quietly again. There was a look of expectancy in her eyes.

The priest and the angel, however, were aware of changes taking place outside. They stared uneasily at the roof of the building. Sounds of rushing wind, accompanied by unearthly wails and cries, were becoming increasingly louder.

The angel seized Steve's arm. "Quickly! Down the stairs, all of you! Fr. Taylor, you as well."

"But...Mom!" protested Trudy.

The others looked confused. Weren't they safe where they were?

"This is her time. See, the terrors arise around us!" The angel pointed at the stained-glass windows; there were wisps of oily mist creeping in around their edges.

Steve was incredulous as he stared at them. "In here? They can come in to such a sacred place? Where are we safe, then?"

"Go into the basement. You will not be harmed."

Steve wanted to ask why. However, he did not get a chance.

A bright light attracted everyone's attention. The tabernacle was somehow giving off sparks. Not only that, now-familiar orbs of light were amassing at the apex of the ceiling.

A small sound from Lydia snapped their attention back to her. Amazed, they watched as her body started floating upwards, steadily, towards the roof.

The angel herded them bodily towards the basement. "Go! You will most certainly die if you stay here!"

Steve spoke through choked sobs as he watched his beloved float ever upward, disappearing through the ceiling as the orbs parted for her.

"What difference does it make? If she dies, I'd rather be dead with her." Trudy and Pat nodded agreement.

Once again, the angel took hold of Steve and turned him so he was paying attention to him.

Steve gasped as the angel grew in size and power, and a sword appeared in his grasp. His voice boomed out in a deep, rumbling thunder.

"If you died here, in this room, disobeying God's command through me, your soul will be lost to Him, and to Lydia, for all eternity!"

The door to the basement banged open, and everyone rushed through it, quaking in fear. When the door closed, they all held each other, trying to get their breath back.

As they recovered their senses, they realized something was different.

"What...?" exclaimed Pat, looking down the stairs.

Then they all noticed, in the light of a single candle, that everyone in the basement—hall, rooms, storage pantries—was asleep.

As they found empty space between bodies and settled in, they too became very drowsy. Pat searched the hall with his eyes until he found what he was looking for. Before he nodded off, he mustered a small smile.

Kim and Ned were asleep against the far wall, shoulders together.

CHAPTER 44

Lydia felt her body being lifted off the floor, but was unconcerned as to how it was happening. She had seen her Savior beckoning to her, and that was all that mattered.

It came as little surprise when she floated bodily through the church's ceiling, and it was mildly interesting to see the orbs as she passed through them; she could see the gentle, smiling faces of angelic beings in each one.

What surprised her was when she stopped rising some fifty feet above the building. Her body righted itself, and she suddenly found that she was looking at it instead of being part of it. She watched as her body's arms came up to a ninety-degree angle from her sides. Light from the heavens poured into her, shooting out from her hands and feet, causing her body to glow like a beacon.

Feeling a presence, Lydia turned and saw Thérèse in her saintly glory.

"Come," Thérèse said, "we must go to a safe place."

"Um…" Lydia indicated her body, which was now rotating slowly.

"We will leave it for now. It will attract the demonic entities hiding on the earth, and when they attack, the angels will do away with them."

"Is this Armageddon?" Lydia was puzzled; if she was in spirit form, didn't that mean she was dead? Wouldn't it follow, if she was in glory, that she would know these things without asking? She was confused.

"No. This will only take away the present danger. Please, come."

Lydia followed Thérèse, not knowing what else to do.

Suddenly she found herself in a low-ceilinged, large, comfortable room. Many people from all countries and all walks of life were seated at tables arranged around the vast room or walking in small groups, talking among themselves. Saints and other holy entities accompanied many of them.

The room was created of large timbers and beams. The walls were unadorned, but colored in a pleasing shade of...what? The actual color was one Lydia had never seen before.

What caught her interest above all, however, was the enormous hole in the floor in the center of the room. It was obviously created there on purpose, considering the beams that formed it. Rails surrounded the hole and gave observers a full view of the earth below.

Although the earth seemed round, Lydia could also easily see every continent, every ocean, every island. It was all like a dream, where physics and practicality were turned on their ear.

Thérèse smiled at Lydia, and then moved off into the crowd, intent on another of her charges.

Lydia walked to the edge of the hole and looked down. Millions of small lights rotated slowly above the earth. She could easily make out a near view and a distance view at the same time. It was unbelievable, yet she had no trouble believing it.

Suddenly, the land's surface changed. She could no longer see the ground; the wisps she'd been seeing all day were now becoming plumes, as demons screamed from the earth. They roared towards the bodies suspended above every church, synagogue, temple, and mosque all over the world. As they hurtled with hateful intent towards the lights, they were snatched out of the air by the orbs, which became powerful, frightening stewards of God's vengeance.

Even though most people had gotten to safety, there were still many out in the world that hadn't believed or had ignored the warnings within their own hearts. Now they ran screaming in the streets, chased by hideous creatures from their deepest fears and imaginings. Their hard-headedness finally vanquished, many saw the beacons in the night and ran towards them. As they approached the buildings above which the glowing bodies rotated, they suddenly found themselves in dark refuges among sleeping people. They knew only that before they, too, succumbed to a deep slumber.

Lydia, watching from above, was overwhelmed. Even though she had been warned of these events, she was still dumbfounded by what she was seeing.

"Thank you, Lydia." She turned, knowing that Voice.

Jesus stood by her side, another figure beside Him. They looked astoundingly alike. Lydia knew Who the other One was at first sight.

The Father, the Creator! Abba!

He smiled at her and cradled her chin in His hand. The Hand that had created the universe! That had put all the planets and galaxies in their place! Who guided the course of nature and seasons!

Who had created...her.

She fell down in worship.

He lifted her up. His eyes were older than time, yet younger than an early spring day.

"My Lord and God!" breathed Lydia.

Suddenly, a loud scream erupted from below. Lydia tore her attention away and watched as a cloud of angelic light swallowed up hideous wraiths by the score.

She felt she had to ask.

"Will this mean evil will be forever gone, and we can live in peace, in Your Light?"

The Father shook His head, watching the scene below. "History shows the fallibility of My children. They remember My deeds and mercy through one or two generations, but there the telling of it fades into folklore, and My people forget Me again."

"Can anything be done?" Lydia felt a pang of sorrow for the future of her species.

"Much is done throughout time. People continue to pray and do good deeds. This is what saves humanity. I will not interfere with the events of people, unless it is requested of Me by good people who love Me."

As the earth's surface cleared, and the devils were finally expunged from the world, the angels returned to the heavens.

Lydia watched as the sun rose in the east.

She had one more question. Turning to Jesus, she put her hand through His. She knew she was not fully in either world now, earthly or eternal. Her hopes revolved around His answer.

"Do I get to stay?"

CHAPTER 45

Steve woke up suddenly. For a reason he couldn't understand, he knew that it was now time to leave the basement.

What would he find, though? Heart thudding with apprehension, he got up and started for the door to the upstairs. Trying to work out exactly how he would get up them without waking anyone, he bumped into someone else who was awake.

Two somebodies.

His kids!

They embraced silently, then, without a word, walked toward the stairs together. Picking their way carefully through the slumbering refugees, they made it to the top without disturbing anyone.

Fr. Taylor was at the top, stretched across the entrance, keeping vigil against all comers, even in his sleep. Steve was about to step over him when the door suddenly dissolved in a golden light.

Blinking in the sudden brightness, the trio looked into the church, shading their eyes. What they saw filled them with both joy and trepidation.

There, in the altar area, was their dear Lydia, lying in the same place she had been in before she was raised up through the roof. A shining figure stood at her side.

As the light dimmed, they saw Who it was, and rushed out to meet Him. After kneeling in homage, they turned their attention to the form in front of the altar.

They had hoped upon hope, as they had come out of their refuge, that their dear Lydia would have become healed and whole, but it was not so; she was the same as when she had been lifted up. If possible, she looked even worse.

Sick in their hearts, they looked up inquiringly at the Lord.

He explained, "Our Enemy and his minions were attracted to her, and to the others, angry at having their plans destroyed, especially by mere humans. Once again, their pride caused them to misjudge their capabilities, and My servant angels fought and vanquished them. However, the demons were still able to get at her physical being; that is why it was there above the church. Be assured, though, she is safe; her spirit lives.”

Trudy started crying. Steve held her, looking at Jesus through blurry, tear-filled eyes. “Does this mean,” he gulped, “she’s not coming back to us?”

Jesus put a hand on Steve’s shoulder. He pulled Pat into His embrace as well, holding the three of them.

“She asked Me the same thing, although not in those exact words. I have told her that she can decide. If she chose Eternity, though, could you blame her?”

Even in his grief, Steve could see His point. “No, I really couldn’t. If it were me, I’d choose to be with You. In fact, if someone called me back, I would be very unhappy.”

Trudy looked up. “Dad!”

Steve smiled at his daughter. “Think about it, dear. Eternal happiness, no time constraints, no sadness...”

“No thorns on roses...” Trudy, in spite of herself, had to smile. She remembered having this very conversation with her mom not so long ago. “I remember her saying about the same thing.”

“Pat?” Steve looked at his son inquiringly.

Pat sighed. “A week ago, if you’d asked that, I would have given a far different answer. Now...” He looked at each face in turn, then down sadly at his mother, “I could understand it if she were not to return here. Not saying that it would be easy, but knowing where she was would soften it a bit.”

Jesus nodded. “It’s settled then.”

He bent down and picked Lydia up.

To her family’s surprise and joy, her eyes opened. She looked around at her loved ones, then up into Jesus’ face. He brought her up and kissed her gently on the forehead. Her body was suddenly enveloped in a soft light, and when it faded away, her once-ravaged body was totally healed.

Jesus set her back on her feet. She looked lovingly into His eyes and then turned to Steve.

With a cry of wonder, Steve took her in his arms, kissing her with fervor. Pat and Trudy joined in the embrace, laughing and crying at the same time.

Steve pulled back and looked adoringly into his soulmate's eyes. "Lydia! I...I can't believe you chose here instead of Eternity!"

"Oh, Steve, I couldn't leave now. When I learned of what my dear family will be asked to do in the future, I had to come back. Not to say," she added hastily, glancing over at Jesus, "that it was an easy choice, but I felt I needed to stay here awhile longer."

"'Future'? What is going to happen?" Steve asked anxiously. Here he thought their troubles were over!

They turned back to Jesus, who was watching them with love.

"That will be revealed in time. Don't worry, you aren't in any danger as long as you keep My Word and pass it along to the next generation."

With that, His form shimmered with a golden glow, and as He disappeared, He held out His hands in a blessing.

They watched until the glow dissipated, then they turned back to the basement. There in the doorway was the priest, who had silently observed what had transpired. As they moved toward him, he put a finger to his lips and looked nervously over his shoulder.

"No, don't go back in there. Not now. People are starting to wake up, and there will be a lot of questions. It's best that they all just go home."

"But why would that matter to us if they have questions? They don't know that we were a part of this," Steve protested. "We need to get our things."

Fr. Taylor shook his head. "You'll be mobbed."

"Why?" Steve looked over at Pat and Trudy. They shrugged their shoulders, mystified.

"Those people down there know more than you think," Father went on. "You see, Pat, Trudy, that closet under the stairs is not exactly sound-proof. Someone overheard you; someone who knew you. After you left to go upstairs, that person spread what he had heard throughout the downstairs. When I came down to look for you, I heard you myself, but thought it best to feign ignorance."

Ah, thought Pat, *that's why I heard someone mention my name.*

"I'm afraid," the priest said to Steve, "that your wife and family will be overrun by people wanting to know everything. I want to give you time to get ready and regroup before the storm breaks."

He reached around behind him and retrieved two backpacks. Pat's and Trudy's.

"I don't think you brought anything in with you, Steve."

Steve smiled ruefully. "Oh...yeah. I was a little distracted..." He looked over at Lydia.

Pat snorted. "Ya think?"

Their pastor pushed them towards the exit. "Go. Get home. It might be best not to answer the phone or the door for awhile. Call me if you need anything."

Steve nodded, and led his family out the door and into the early light of a bright spring morning.